INVITATION TO A HANGING

Jakes had the hemp strands slung over the thick branch and the nooses dangled in place. The men loaded the rustlers in their saddles. Somewhere a noisy magpie scolded them. Matt searched up and down the two dusty ruts for sight of anyone or thing. This needed to be over quickly in case some others came along.

He stepped to Stearn's pinto. The noose looked to be set right around the man's throat. The long knot was beside his left ear, so when the horse was driven out from under him, the fall with the weight of his body would snap his neck.

"You have anything you want to say to God or us about your crimes?"

"You boys are making the biggest mistake of your lives," Dikes said. "I just hope God forgives you."

Matt moved back. Each rancher held a coiled up lariat in his hand. At his nod, they busted the horses on the butt. Their mounts charged away. The unmistakable snap of spines cracked like gunshots . . .

RANCHER'S LAW

DUSTY RICHARDS

St. Martin's Paperbacks

This is a work of fiction. All of the characters, organizations, and events portrayed in this novel are either products of the author's imagination or are used fictitiously.

RANCHER'S LAW

Copyright © 2001 by Dusty Richards.

For information address St. Martin's Press, 175 Fifth Avenue, New York, NY 10010.

ISBN: 978-1-250-09356-1

Our books may be purchased in bulk for promotional, educational, or business use. Please contact your local bookseller or the Macmillan Corporate and Premium Sales Department at 1-800-221-7945, ext. 5442, or by e-mail at MacmillanSpecialMarkets@macmillan.com.

Printed in the United States of America

St. Martin's Paperbacks edition / July 2001

St. Martin's Paperbacks are published by St. Martin's Press, 175 Fifth Avenue, New York, NY 10010.

10 9 8 7 6 5 4 3 2

I want to dedicate this book to some great cowboys in my life, folks who opened gates of opportunity. Others were good friends and some plain touched me along the way. They're in that great pasture in the sky because the boss man needed them up there.

The list goes like this: Shorty, who gave me wisdom and some "jobs" I've enjoyed. Ben, who loaned me a great horse when I needed one and lots of good advice. Pete, who always had a smile and a rodeo to announce. Wilford, who showed me the wagon road and made a great pard. Bill, whose rough-sounding ways always held a ring of honesty. Phil, who had a great gift to be an announcer. Loyd, whom you could sure count on for the extra mile.

Then thanks to my writers' group, who gave me some wonderful advice regarding this book, and Lynn Carney, who slaved on it to dot all the i's. Hat's off to my wife, Pat, who delivered food, water, and encouragement to the computer through the entire time this book was being created.

And to all my readers, thanks.
Dusty Richards

PROLOGUE

A low winter sun shone through the grimy windowpanes. She watched the diffused light flood his bare, muscular back as he shaved. Leaning forward over her dresser, he peered into the smoky looking glass. His galluses hung to the knees of his canvas pants. Deliberately, he scraped away the reddish whisker stubble and foamy lather from his suntanned cheeks.

"Have you heard any word about Clell Lyman lately?" He paused in his task and turned to face her with his steel-blue eyes.

"No," she said quickly. Seated on the edge of the bed, wringing her hands in her lap, she looked at the tin ceiling tile for help. This new drift of his conversation made her feel even more rejected, and it kindled an angry, jealous flame inside her that threatened to flare up. Why, he'd been gone for weeks serving warrants in the Indian Territory, and the first time he gets back to Fort Smith and her—all he can talk about some half-breed killer on the loose.

"Do you think he's somewhere around Fort Smith?" he asked, swishing the razor's blade in a pan of steaming water.

"He may be in Texas for all I care," she said.

He raised his eyebrows at her reply, then went back to shaving. The chill in the room forced her to clutch her chenille robe tighter. There wasn't enough heat upstairs in Molly Mather's Cathouse to keep the water in a pitcher from skimming over with ice at night. The past summer, why, her room would have baked bread. She ground her molars. And him . . . he comes back from God-only-knows-where and acts more damned interested in a fugitive than in her body.

"Where did you leave that spotted bulldog today?" she asked, realizing for the first time that that pest wasn't along with him.

"You mean General Ben McCollough?"

"Your dang dog." She smirked in disapproval at his back.

"Ben's out where I stable my horses, buried in a haystack to keep warm."

"Smart dog." What she really meant to say was: "The stack is a good place for that blunt-faced devil." She hated how he leered at her and snorted all the time out of his pug nose. Suited her just fine that that blessed bulldog had been left out there.

"Tillie," he said, and turned back toward the mirror to scrape his chin. "Where does that Indian woman of Lyman's live? Nelda Horsekiller?"

"Shack Town across the Arkansas, I guess," she said, still filled with bitter resentment over his deliberately ignoring her earlier attempts to lure him into her bed.

"Get dressed," he said, using a towel to scrub off the soap remains.

She frowned at his request and did not move. "Where're we going?"

"I've got half a notion that he's hiding out at her place."

Finished shaving, he twisted around with his palms turned up like he was lifting her to make her move. "Come on, I want him behind bars. He killed a close friend of mine and a damn sure good deputy marshal."

"You go. It's too cold outside." She hugged the robe tighter with her clenched fists.

"You need some fresh air," he said, putting on his woolen shirt.

"But—"

"Come on."

"Aw, all right." She couldn't say no to him. The handsome galoot stole her heart the first time she saw him downstairs in the parlor. But the real reason she loved him so much was that he never acted ashamed she was a dove. He was always polite, always treated her like she was some-body special. He took her out to those fancy restaurants on Garrison Avenue to eat, and later, in some saloon, he let her stand at his elbow and watch him gamble like she was a real lady.

She went to the oak wardrobe and drew open the double doors. Her blue dress would look the most respectable. She let the robe slip from her shoulders. The room's cold air quickly enveloped her bare skin above the flimsy camisole and she hurried to put on her clothing. The small buttons proved hard to catch.

When at last she dropped her backside on the bed to pull on her shoes, she looked up at him to see if he'd changed his mind about taking her. The set to his chiseled jaw was unmoved. Obviously, he wanted her to hurry.

She raised up from lacing her footwear. "It's real cold out there."

"You have a long coat." He nodded to the closet.

"It's still awfully cold," she insisted.

"I won't let you freeze." Ready to go, he held open the door to her room while she shrugged the coat on and tied a scarf over her head. Men! She gritted her molars at the thought of heading into the wintry weather outside. Her door locked, she pocketed the key. Then she pulled on the kidskin gloves, her latest, most expensive indulgence.

Outside on the top landing, a gust of sharp wind threatened her. She grasped the wood railing, but his powerful arm encircled her protectively. Going down the outside stairs, her soles crushed pellets of snow. She noted a covered buggy and horse hitched in the alley below. His strong presence beside her quickly swept away any reluctance and even the frigid air.

In the buggy, he covered her with a buffalo robe and put a woolen blanket over her shoulders. She smiled, pleased at his concern for her comfort. Her reaction drew a twinkle in his blue eyes when he took his place beside her and undid the reins.

"Git up, hoss."

The rig rolled down the alley. The iron rims grated on the brick surface. At last, he guided the horse out onto Garrison Avenue. She noted the barkers, already in mid-afternoon, working the sidewalks, extolling the wonders and bargains inside their respective businesses. Texas cowboy hats like his, knit sailor caps from the river boats, even unblocked ones topping blanket-wrapped Indians mixed and mingled about. Through the conjested street filled with farm and freight wagons, bicycles, rigs, and horseback riders, he skillfully drove the three blocks to the ferry.

Somehow, leaned against his hard form all wrapped in her cocoon, she forgot the eye-tearing wind and charge of arctic weather. Sitting beside him on the seat, like any other respectable woman, filled her with a warm pride.

The ferry ride to the west bank was marked with the dingy river water slapping the side of the barge with a hollow sound that made her stomach queasy. Ferries had been known to sink, she reflected. Don't let this one do that. Oh, God, please don't let it go down.

Deep chugging of the steam engine, the stink of hot wood burning in the boiler, and the resulting slash of the small paddle wheel added to the sounds of their crossing. When at last he drove the horse off onto the plank docking, she felt grateful to be on dry land in the Indian Territory.

"Do you know where she lives?" she asked, getting a whiff of sharp smoke coming from the city of shacks lining the riverbank. Some were made of old packing crates with lettering on them, others from rusty sheet iron and sun-faded canvas tents. The sturdier-looking ones appeared to be constructed from small logs with low dirt-covered roofs. She doubted the occupants could even stand up inside them. Blank eyes of mixed breed and Indian children peered at her from open doorways. Why didn't those kids close their doors against the cold?

Looking at the unchinked logs and cracks, she decided the temperature must be the same inside as out. A cold chill went up her spine. Never again would she complain about her room upstairs. Then she realized this was where all the worn out doves spent their final days. Not only did Indians live here, but the rest of society's outcasts as well. Black, white, and red, color had no prejudice in this camp. When all they could do was shuffle around and empty night jars, this was where they moved to. The deranged, demented, diseased, whiskey-sodden drunks, Chinese dope addicts, and the cast aside misfits of Fort Smith's society languished in this hellhole of despair, separated from those better off by the Arkansas's muddy current.

"Where does Nelda Horsekiller live?" he asked, halting the horse beside a humpbacked white woman. She wore several layers of rag clothing and bore a load of sticks for firewood on her back. Her drawn face was shriveled with lines like a prune. Tillie guessed her to be an immigrant from Poland or eastern Europe.

"She lives in dat one," the woman said pointing.

"Thank you, ma'am." He tipped his hat and drove the horse past her with a cluck of his tongue.

The woman said something like "dunk-you" after them. Tillie didn't get it all, but turned her attention to the half–log-walled tent with a stove pipe coming out of the canvas roof through a patch of metal. A better-looking quarters than most. She turned in the seat and watched him open his sheepskin-lined jacket, the butt of his Colt pistol obvious to her. The sight of the revolver made her heart stop. Oh, no, would he be shot making this arrest? The one he sought had already killed another marshal. Her breath caught in her constricted throat when he reined up the horse.

The sudden realization that this might be the last time she ever saw him alive stabbed her chest. She wanted to reach out, grasp him by the arm, hold him, plead with him, beg him not to go—to be so careful. Somehow numbed in place, the words never made it to her lips.

"Stay here," he said, finished wrapping the reins around the butt of the whip. "I'll only be a minute."

Or a lifetime, she added silently, nodding her head. She looked hard after his tall form striding across the frozen ground, watching as a piece of tattered newspaper tumbled along past him to catch on a tree stump. It fluttered there.

She wanted to glance away from his back and the knee-high black boots that were so hard for her to pull off. Why couldn't she turn her attention to the brown river? It roiled past at the foot of the steep slope behind the shacks amongst the towering bare sycamore and pecan trees. But no, she continued to stare after his movements until he stopped before the doorway.

He knocked on the door. In an instant, she saw a hatless figure tear out of the back of the half tent and rush away behind the other structures.

"Tillie!" he shouted to her, with the gun in his fist. "He's getting away!"

She bobbed her head. *I saw him.* Her fingers fumbled with the leather lines. Filled with impatience, she stripped off her gloves and undid the reins. Her man was already running down the street after the killer. Stopping at intervals, he stood on his toes trying to see over the shacks for the escapee. Nothing.

"Heeyah!" she shouted, and the rig lurched ahead, spilling her back onto the seat. She regained her place and swung the buggy in beside him as he ran. Then pressing her heels hard on the dash, with all her strength to draw on the reins, she hauled the excited horse to a stop. He stepped on the rig and hanging half out, told her to go on.

Scooted to the front edge of the seat, she laid the lines to the horse's back and the animal responded. She drove pell-mell through and around objects, wheelbarrows, fleeing people, even a stray pig that ran off squealing in their wake. A dozen barking, snarling dogs charged out to add to the melee.

With his free hand, her man clung to a top brace. This stance left his head and upper torso exposed, while he searched for the elusive fugitive.

"There he goes!" he shouted.

She spotted the hatless figure running away behind the shacks. In reflex, her sharp front teeth sunk into her lower lip; she pulled down the horse. Her man leaped to the ground and rushed off, jumping over a scabby rail fence and disappearing.

Alone in the buggy, she trembled under the blanket. Drained by this wave of helplessness, she wildly searched for any sign of the fugitive. The pop of a pistol made her jump and forced her to hold down the excited horse. Ahead of her, from between two hovels, a dark-faced man burst into the street. For a second, he stopped and looked at her in disbelief. Then like a dogged animal, he fled in the other direction.

He's getting away! Not on her life was he doing that! She slapped the lines and shouted to the horse. He half reared and plunged ahead in pursuit. The rig tipped from side to side in the frozen ruts. Intent on her quarry, she pressed the horse for more speed.

The breed turned to look over his shoulder, but not in time. Horse and shaft struck him to the ground. She stood up and sawed on the animal's bit as they passed over his prone form.

At last she managed to draw the horse to a halt and turn him around. The sight of her man's cowboy hat and him looking unscathed, standing over the downed breed, warmed her charging heart. The lump in her throat proved hard to swallow. Thank God. He was safe. She closed her tearing eyes.

"You'd make a heckuva a deputy marshal," he bragged, grinning at her.

"Don't sign me up yet," she said, tying off the reins and bolting down from the seat to cautiously walk over for a closer look at the prisoner. "He all right?"

"You couldn't kill him, honey, if you cut his head off."

Several of the curious onlookers laughed at the Texan's words. He cuffed Lyman's hands behind his back, then jerked him up. With a lariat from the buggy, he placed a noose around the prisoner's neck and tied the other end to the tailgate.

"If you can't run fast enough to keep up, I'll save Judge

Parker a hanging fee," he said to the breed, who to her looked unsteady on his feet.

"You wouldn't . . . ?" she asked, aghast at the notion of dragging someone to death behind her back.

"Darling, you just never mind," he said, helping her into the seat. "It's all up to him to keep up. Let's get to town."

"I'm ready," she said. Underneath the buffalo robe he carefully arranged over her, the strength drained from her legs. She wouldn't want to do this kind of work. Being a dove could be trying at times, but this law work hurt her heart.

He took up the reins and paused. "You know, Tillie, you would make a great marshal."

She raised her gaze to look into his steel-blue eyes. All the strong resolve and gut-wrenching concern over the chase melted into mush. That handsome devil. . . . At last the words slipped from her lips: "I reckon I'd do anything you asked of me, Luther Haskell."

1

A cloud of thick cigar smoke hung in the back room of the Texas Saloon. From the overhead wagon wheel fixture, the yellowish candlelight flickered through the haze onto the faces of four men. Behind a fan of cards, Matt McKean looked hard at his hand, then raised his gaze to study the other players. It was time, he figured, to learn where he stood with these three. Could he risk the exposure of his plans with the whole group or should he do it individually? Test them one at a time. Undecided about his next move, he made no raise, simply discarded a five of hearts and a seven of spades. Jack, queen, ace, all he could hope to do at best was pair one of them.

Across the table, Dan Charboneau met his look from under his frosty brows. The older man's face was the color of leather from sixty years of being out in the blazing sun, except where his hat protected his bleached forehead. He was short and burly, with steel-blue eyes that never seemed to blink and a snowy mustache that didn't move as he held out the deck. Matt discarded two cards and drew two new ones. He left his draw on the table.

"What'll it be for you?" Charboneau turned and asked the youngest of the four ranchers. In his early thirties, Porter Reed always looked red-faced, his skin never tanned. He and his late father had brought their large herd of Herefords to the Christopher Basin from Kansas. Three years earlier, his father, Yancy, died in a horse wreck. Matt wondered if the son would ever be ready to fill the old man's shoes.

"I'll take one."

"No bet?"

Porter shook his head. Good, Matt decided, he had nothing. Simple enough, the fool was drawing to an impossible inside straight. Matt picked up his draw and slid the new pasteboards in the fan. The sight of two more ladies drew a smile to his thoughts.

Charboneau looked across at Louie Crain for his draw. The tall, thin bachelor in his forties tossed out a fifty-cent's raise and asked for three new ones. Crain had a pair. Matt watched for a flicker of the rancher's eyes when he looked at his new cards. Not a thing—good, he probably had nothing.

Everyone stayed in, though Matt wondered why Porter tossed in his four bits. Perhaps his mind was no longer concentrating on playing cards.

The dealer checked the bet, drew two for himself, and made a scowl, which could mean good or bad in Matt's book. The Frenchman made a sharp hand anytime at poker. Still undecided about his next move, Matt slumped in the captain's chair and pitched in a dollar raise.

Porter folded. Crain saw his bet and Charboneau tossed in his cards. Matt spread out his three ladies on the felt.

"Beats my pair," Crain said in disgust.

Matt rose, reached for the small pot with both hands, stopped, and looked around at the three of them. "Boys, this here is sure penny ante, compared to the cattle we're losing to them rustlers."

"Huh," Charboneau grunted. "What do you suggest we do about it?"

"We know who the three of them are."

"You certain?" Porter asked, obviously taken aback by Matt's words.

"Sure as I am the damn sun will come up." He looked right at Porter.

"That's pretty sure."

"Who you thinking about?" Crain asked, leaning forward. He searched around as if to be certain they were alone.

Matt had no worries about the security of the back room. Lincoln Jeffries made damn sure that they were left alone with only an occasional barkeep coming, knocking first, to take their order for a new bottle of whiskey or more cigars. These chambers strictly belonged to the Christopher Basin's Stockmen's Society on Thursday night or any other night that they wanted it.

"That Texas cowboy Luke Stearn," Matt began. "How did he get that many head? His S Star is all over the place on young cattle."

Charboneau relit his cigar butt, drew deep, held it pinched between his fingers, and leaned back in his chair. "You figuring that Burtle is in on it, too?"

"T. G. Burtle. He's number two of three," Matt said, feeling more at ease. So far the men around the table acted like they were in this with him.

"Three? Who's the third one?" Porter asked.

"Ted Dikes."

"Teddy Dikes!" Porter slumped in his chair, taken aback. "Why, he bought that place—"

"Yeah, I know, he acted like he came in here all legitimate like. Bought the KT from Earnie's widow, but boys, sure as shooting, he's fell in with those other two wolves."

"I ain't so sure he's into this rustling." Porter looked half sick at the notion and dropped his chin. "Them other two, I wouldn't argue about them, but I don't think Teddy's in on that rustling business."

"Ain't no maybe about any of them," Matt said, and slapped the table top with his palm, unable to control the rage inside his chest. "That upstart from New York is in with them others!"

Charboneau held up his hands in surrender. "All right, but what are we going to do about them sons a bitches? The only thing that the law out of Prescott ever does when they send a deputy over here is count our cattle for the tax rolls. If we caught them boys red-handed, they'd probably turn them loose over there."

"Boys, there is only one judge and jury. That's hemp rope." Matt sat back in his chair. His cards were on the table; the men were either with him or not. Made no difference, he'd get it done himself if he had to. Having them on the vigilante committee only added to the respectable appearance that it wasn't a personal vendetta on his part. Folks might start asking lots of questions, since that big spring on the Earnie Matson place joined his range. If that old bitch had sold out to him at his price—no matter, it was that damn Yankee coming in there, giving her twice what it was worth that wrecked his plans to acquire it. All that was a nevermind now, Dikes buddying around with those two lobo wolves had fixed his fate.

"When?" Charboneau asked, taking the stub of the cigar from his colorless lips.

"You all in?" Matt asked, looking around the table hazed with their smoke. The adrenaline surged in his veins. He had to suppress his excitement. Too many things counted on his plan working. He couldn't afford a show of confidence or jubilance over his victories at this point. Fighting back his own excitement, he casually began a man by man search of their faces.

Crain nodded grimly, then ran his fingers through his thin black hair.

Charboneau deliberately ground out the butt in the ashtray, then raised his gaze to meet Matt's. "You can count me in."

Matt turned to Porter. This would be the real test. The man looked deep in thought and rubbed his palms briskly over his pants legs under the table. A visible shudder of his thin shoulder under his galluses; his Adam's apple bobbed as if he had tried to swallow something large.

"Damn, it Matt, I can sure agree them two drifters are probably using a running iron . . . but Teddy Dikes? Hell, Matt, he's ate supper at my house a dozen times."

"He's courting your sister?"

"Sort of. Hell's bells, I can't believe he's rustling. His folks have lots of money. He don't need to steal nothing."

"Porter." Matt looked him square in the eye. "He's after some kind of excitement. Why else would some rich boy buy a damned two-bit ranch and go to wearing cowboy garb? And I say he's running with that pack and doing what they do."

"Porter, that makes an awful lot of sense," Charboneau broke in. "Them three are thicker than mud. Two weeks ago, I seen them together up on the Beaver. They weren't up there looking for no butterflies. Besides, that's miles from their outfits."

"You see them rustling?" Porter's voice had a high-pitched edge.

The older man twisted on his mustache and nodded as if considering the matter again, then made a wry face. "Nope, but I seen two big calves carrying Burtle's fresh mark this week."

"Oh, no." Porter collapsed.

"You want out of this?" Matt asked, sharp enough to get his attention.

Porter wagged his head no. "I just hope to God we're right."

"We are," Charboneau said, as if the whole thing had been settled forever. "Now, what do we do next?"

"Saturday at noon," Matt began. "We'll meet at the Alma Creek crossing. Wear masks. Keep out of sight. They'll be coming through there sometime in the afternoon on their way to the schoolhouse dance."

Their card playing over for the night, they stood up without a word, except the dejected Porter, who remained in his chair. Matt slipped on his suit coat, satisfied his long-awaited plans would unfold in the next two days. Patience. He needed lots of it. And in due time, he would control the entire Christopher Basin. Eliminating two of them homesteaders and that rich kid would be enough sign for the next ones drifting in this country with their long loops to keep on tracking.

"Alma Creek Crossing?" Charboneau asked, and put the weathered Stetson on his head. Matt gave him a nod. Then, like a small bear, he lumbered out the doorway into the hall. Crain followed him with a wave and shut the door behind him.

Porter poured more whiskey into his glass. Still seated, he looked like a man who had lost his best friend. Matt realized Porter was the weakest link. Somehow he needed to resolve the matter before they left this very room.

"I sure hope you know for certain that Teddy's in on this." Porter tossed down half the glass's contents.

"You worried about your sister?"

Porter swiveled his head around and frowned. "Yes. And I'm hoping we're dead right about Teddy being in with them other two."

"If I showed you a calf with his brand on it, sucking one of my cows, would you believe me?"

Porter blinked, and swallowed hard. "You've got one?"

"Yeah. Seen her last week up on the mesa. A brindle cow carrying lots of longhorn blood. That's why I figure we missed her last spring. She hid out. The calf weights four-fifty."

"Why? Why would he do that?"

"Excitement. He's here for a high old time. Live dangerous. Your sister, she might be lots better off without his kind."

"Oh, Matt. It will break Margie's heart."

Determined to convince him of the matter, Matt pulled out a chair and sat on the edge of it. "What would your old daddy do?"

"Hang him." Porter dropped his gaze to the table and warily shook his head in defeat. "I was with him and two other ranchers back in Kansas when they caught this kid red-handed with three of our horses. They strung him over a walnut limb on the spot."

Good enough. Matt nodded as if he understood. That lynching had left a real mark on Porter. Good thing he didn't want him to find that calf, because there wasn't one—yet—that he knew about.

"All right." Porter raised the glass and with another shudder of his thin upper torso beneath the snowy-white shirt, he tossed down the contents. After a great sigh, he said, "I'll do my part. I'll be there at noon."

"It's the right thing," Matt said, and rose wearily. He still had a ten-mile drive back to the ranch. Taking his stiff-brimmed hat from the wall peg, he considered the Brown Hotel across the street, but dismissed the notion. No, he had plenty to do before Saturday. Best get home and make all the arrangements.

He reached his ranch headquarters in the starlight. The buildings and pens set back in the tall ponderosas at the base of Loafer Mountain. At the corrals, he drew the buggy horse up. One of the hired men could put the bay up in the morning, only hours away. He fastened the lead to the hitch rack.

His wife, Taneal, would be asleep upstairs. With his thumb, he rubbed the light bristle on his chin and considered the large log home. She wouldn't want to be disturbed at this hour. That's why they slept in separate bedrooms.

He entered the dark house and the pine floors gave small groans under his soles. His hat and coat hung on the hall rack, he combed back his short brown hair with his fingers, then headed in the shadowy light for the kitchen. A small candle night lamp flickered in the room filled with the rich smells of spices, cooking, and wood smoke. He looked about and noticed a fresh-made loaf on the table. In passing, he tore off a large hunk of it and went to the side door. With a mouthful of the sourdough drawing his saliva, he eased the door open with a thin squeak.

In the faint light, he could see Lana's shapely form under a blanket on the cot. Wallowing the sourdough around with his tongue, he was ready for her. Dessert came next, he mused, and shook her shoulder to awaken her.

"Señor?" she asked in a sleep-filled voice and bolted up. "You are home?"

"Sí," he said, and took another bite of the bread. He stepped in front of where she sat on the edge of the bed in her flowing white gown. His free hand grasped the nape of the neck and roughly he forced her to get to her knees before him. The rest of the bread stuffed in his mouth, he swiftly undid his belt and britches to expose himself.

"My sweet Lana," he said around the mouthful. "I have thought about you the entire ride home." He took the back of her hesitant head and forced her closer. She understood her obligations. Feet set apart and engrossed in his personal pleasure, he slowly chewed on the mouthful of bread. It had been a fruitful evening.

"Where's Randy?" Matt demanded. Seated at the great table with sun spilling through the open windows and the cool early-morning breeze lifting the lace curtains, he fumed over the absence of his son at breakfast. "Get that lazy thing up!"

"I swear, Matthew McKean, you act like some kind of wild bear in the morning," his wife, Taneal, said, coming into the room, wrapping the long white robe around her slender form. Her light brown hair up in a French braid, she took a cup of coffee from her place and went to look out the front door.

"Is he here?"

"I would think so," she said with a shrug, not looking back standing in the open doorway.

"Lana! Go upstairs and get him up!"

"Matthew, you don't send a young woman to wake up a young man in his bedroom."

"I don't care whether it's proper or not. Lana, go get his ass up!"

The Mexican girl of eighteen looked wide-eyed at him, then at his wife, who told her to stay. She wore a simple white blouse that showed her proud breasts and a full skirt that hugged her narrow waist. Her olive fingers fussed with the ties of the apron behind her back as if unsettled about what she must do next. Her dark eyes looked close to panic. At last, he shook his head at her to dismiss his order.

Taneal came stalking back, her glare fixed on him. "What's got you so fuzzed up this morning?"

He bolted to his feet and pointed at the table. "I want that boy's ass down here and right now. You've babied him long enough. He's sixteen. That's old enough, and he needs to pull his weight in this outfit or get the hell out."

"Matthew, he's a boy."

"When I was his age—"

"You were the only male at home. I know, I know. The rest of the men were gone to war. We aren't at war any longer, Matthew."

"He's going to think it's war, if he don't get his lazy ass down here and start doing a day's work on this ranch."

"Someone calling me?" Randy entered, putting his shirt on over his head.

"This is not the place to dress, young man," Taneal said in disapproval and looked around for Lana, who had already exited into the kitchen.

"Hell, I heard all the screaming and thought the gawdamn house was on fire or something."

"Enough of your lip. Did you check that spring yesterday?" Matt demanded, ready to smash his mouthy offspring upside the head.

"It's working."

"It need digging out?" He looked down at his plate of eggs, peppers, and potatoes, which was growing colder by the minute and realized he was still standing astraddle of the chair.

"Needs more water."

"You saying it's slowing down?"

"He told you—"

"Shut up!" He waved Taneal aside with his hand. He wanted that hatchet ass boy to tell him what he found.

"The damn thing is running about half what it was and I couldn't pry open the mountain and get it to run any more," Randall said.

"I won't be talked to like that!" She stood in defiance at the end of the table. "I am not your cowboy nor your laborer."

Matt dropped on the chair and waved for her to take her place.

"I don't bid at your beckon call, Matthew McKean. And

Randall is your own son, not some Mexican peon you own under slavery terms."

"This is his ranch and he better learn how to run it." He pointed the fork at her. The only thing that kept him from going down there and jabbing it through her long face was a tiny thread of containment.

"If I were him, I would tell you to take this place and. . . ." She glanced away without finishing her threat.

"And what?" he demanded, knowing full well what she meant, but he wanted her to say it. To spit it out.

"Put it up your pompous ass!" She glared back at him.

"Well, I keep you up pretty damn well, Miss Priss."

"Not well enough for me to put up with your tyrannical rages every time you come back from Fortune with a hangover. Did you lose money at cards last night?"

"No," he snapped, and resumed feeding his face. She needed a good horsewhipping. Some day he would give it to her.

"Don't plan anything for Saturday," he said to the boy between mouthfuls of food.

Randy shrugged, then raised his gaze and blinked in question at him.

"Don't ask, I'll explain later."

"What's so damn secret about Saturday?" Taneal demanded.

"None of your gawdamn business!" He threw down his fork and napkin on his plate and stood up. "You're asking for it."

"Hump," she snorted out her long slender nose. "You lay a hand on me and you'll wake up the next morning a gelding."

"We'll see about that. You heard what I said about tomorrow, boy?"

"Yeah."

"What?"

"Yes, sir."

"Today I want you to start riding them colts. It's your job to break them."

"You're going to get him busted up trying to ride them. Those aren't colts. They're all outlaws from hell. You sold the good ones."

Matt paused in the doorway of the kitchen and turned around to face her. "That's how I can afford my highfalutin wife, selling the good ones. They bring more money. I want them all rode at least two hours apiece today," he said directly to the boy. Then he started and turned back. "And don't plan on anything for Saturday. You understand?"

The boy nodded.

"What's so gawdawful important about Saturday?" He heard her asking as he went through the kitchen. "Some folks need a day off. . . ."

He needed a day off from her sharp tongue. What happened to that sweet girl from Ohio whom he married when the bluebonnets flooded Palo Pinto County? The one who so cheerfully cooked for him and his trail hands coming on that long cattle drive to Arizona from Texas? Maybe if some of their other children had lived, and she hadn't had all those miscarriages . . . Hell, he built her the biggest house in Christopher Basin, ordered the finest furniture from St. Louis, hauled it all in from the railhead at Flag.

She couldn't still be mad about finding him with that Mormon gal. That had been years ago at a dance. Lucille was her name. Hardly out of her teens and good-looking. Her dark brown eyes alone would have fully aroused an eighty-year-old man on his deathbed. He'd danced a waltz with Lucille, when she, kind of sly, suggested they meet at his wagon after two more sets.

He'd glanced down at her ripe form in the calico dress and agreed to the whole thing without thinking. Afterward, he rejoined his wife, who made some snide comment about his last partner.

"Her? Nice young lady," he said, and went after some lemonade for both of them.

He danced with Taneal and the next tune with Sam Haygood's widow, Mae, a gray-headed woman twice his age. That was to take Taneal's mind off Lucille. His wasn't, and the longer the dance went on, the more he felt a growing need for the shapely one. He showed Mae to her place and strode across to where Taneal sat on the wall benches.

"I'll be back," he said to his wife like he was on his way to relieve his bladder or to take a snort of some moonshine, the ordinary things he did every Saturday night during the dance.

Moments later at his wagon, that out-of-breath Mormon gal rushed over and said that she couldn't be out there with him for long. Only a few minutes, or her husband would surely miss her. So they had to be fast. Quicker than a fox, she crawled under the wagon ahead of him, lay on her back across the bedroll, and drew up the dress above her waist.

He looked around, but saw nothing out of place in the darkness. Filled with a huge urge for her, he jerked open his pants, dropped to his knees, and joined her under the rig.

Right in the middle of everything, Taneal, screaming like a panther, began kicking his feet and legs. He raised up, mad as hell at her interruption. Lucille, with a look of fright, slithered out the far side, shrieking loud enough for all to hear, fighting down her dress and running off as fast as she could across the school yard in the starlight.

Wearily, he backed out while trying to dodge his wife's flying fists and shoes. He finished pulling up his pants and buttoned them under her barrage.

"I knew you were out here with her." Like a buzz saw, Taneal's fists pummeled him on the shoulders. "You no-account horny devil!"

He finally took hold of her flailing wrists and got her calmed down.

"Ain't nothing happened here," he said to the gathered crowd of onlookers. "Just a little family misunderstanding."

But he could have killed her for the snickering that went on as the curious moved away. He held her in place by the forearms and they stood glaring at each other in the starlight. Not a word was spoken until the others were out of earshot.

"You can sleep by yourself from now on," she hissed. "And screw every little hussy in this basin that you want to. But you won't ever touch me again, Matthew McKean."

Outside the ranch house in the fresh morning air, he shook his head and closed his eyes to the distasteful memories of that fateful night. She had damn sure kept her word all those years. He looked across the open yard, anxious to set the entire matter aside, and noticed the cowboys had put away his buggy horse. Good enough. He headed for the blacksmith shop, where the activity centered on shoeing horses. The ring of hammers on steel pealed off in the fresh, pine-scented air.

Sid Jakes stood, rolling his own, and overseeing the three ranch hands. They each shod a different horse. The lanky, older foreman nodded morning to him. Jakes came from Texas with Matt. Tough as cured mesquite and despite his age, still the best man on the place with a riata.

Henry Davis gave his usual morning grin looking up from shoeing. Another of Matt's veteran hands, Henry came from back in the Tennessee hills. Lacking two teeth in front, the wiry little man was dependable, though a bit dense. Beside Henry, and nailing shoes on the bald face horse, labored Sweeney O'Brien, a drifter who never had much to say. He nodded at the boss, spat tobacco to the side, then businesslike he resumed his nailing.

Lefty Mounds was the youngest crew member. Sweat streaked his face, and he gave a sudden look that said, "Oh, hi," then he fought with the horse's kicking hind hoof grasped in both hands.

The action of the horse drew some cursing from Lefty as he moved about on the end of his hind leg. Finally out of patience at the fuss going on, O'Brien grunted and went over beside the jittery animal. He caught the lead, shouted a command at the upset horse, then slapped him hard on the ribs with the side of his hammer. His actions settled the bronc for Lefty.

Matt went over to the side of the shop to join Jakes. He and his foreman squatted on their heels to observe the hands at their work. There was plenty on Matt's mind about how they would handle the rustlers at the crossing. No place for errors once they were committed. He fretted about all the details left.

"Henry and O'Brien are getting ready to pack some salt up on the rim," Jakes said. "Soon as we get these here shod."

"Good. Then have Lefty help Randall saddle them colts today. I told him to ride them some."

Jakes raised his thin eyebrows as if skeptical of the plan, then shifted his weight to the other leg. "Those two may be all day saddling one of them."

"Good. Come dark, they'll have it figured out how." He gave a head toss toward the side of the shed and rose. What he had to tell Jakes needed to be said in private. Less folks knew about it, the better for all concerned.

When they were out of earshot of the crew, Matt kept his voice low. "Give them boys the day off tomorrow. Send them into Fortune. Give the three of them each ten bucks to blow." He dug the money out of his pants and handed it to Jakes. "I don't want them rooting around up here."

"Whatever you say, boss."

"I want you to stick around. And without them noticing, gather us up three good long new ropes. We're going to need them tomorrow."

Jakes nodded. "I'll get it done."

"Fine. Have 'em saddle up that chestnut for me. I'm going to do a little checking around."

"Be careful riding out there by yourself. You might ride up on one of them brand blotters."

"I do, he won't ride away."

In deep thought, Jakes stared off into the distance like he was considering it. "You know, I've lost some good friends that a way."

"Yeah." He wanted to tell the man that in twenty-four hours, this basin would be rid of its three biggest trouble-makers. He looked up in time to see his son dragging his way from the house, scuffing his boot heels along in the dust. Must have plenty of lead in both his boots and his ass, the way he was coming. To ignore him and not lose his temper twice in the same morning, he went inside the blacksmith shop.

The smell of acrid coal smoke from the forge filled his nose. He heard Jakes send Lefty off with the boy to help capture the colts. Matt would have liked to have been a mouse sitting on the corral the rest of the day. No. Best he went scouting. How could he be certain that those three rustlers were coming to the dance? They were a part of the usual crowd there every Saturday night. A regular ritual for them to be there. Only it would be his bad luck if for some reason they changed their routine. He hoped not. If they only caught one or two of them, those left would certainly be on their guard.

"Blocky's saddled," Jakes said from the doorway.

"Good, see you later."

He went out in the bright sunshine, took the reins from Henry, tested the cinch, then satisfied, he swung up. The big gelding built a bow in his back. Matt checked him up close, hoping to walk it out of him. In the far corral, he could see the two boys had the initial front-feet-flailing colt snubbed to a post; a deep red bay, he sure was fighting them. Both of the boys were taking turns at their courage, and making false starts for his head to ear him down.

Anxious to be on his way, Matt used his spurs to nudge the horse beneath him. Blocky gave two short crow hops before Matt pulled his head up, then set him into lope.

"You bucker, you. I'll take that starch out of you before dark," he promised the pony. Then he looked off to the pine-timbered knoll to the south, across the wide-open grassland. This high country still beat Texas. He swung Blocky east on the road and let him run.

Close to midday, he spooked some cows and their calves out of the trees. Easing Blocky downhill, he wanted to take a good look at the brands. Most of them wore his ear notch, but that meant little. Rustlers would notch the calf to match the cow and then scorch their own brand on its hide. When a working cowboy saw an owner's ear notch, he figured the calf had been worked and let it go, never checking the match.

Matt had seen at least one S Star brand like that on a big calf. His notch was in the left ear on the half-grown critter, the S Star burned in the hide. That threesome was getting a lot bolder at it. After tomorrow, there would be no more of that, and allowing a respectable period, he would have his lawyer contact the Dikes family and buy the place. Them being back east, not knowing the value and by then anxious to part with their sad memories of the real estate, he should take it off their hands well worth the money.

Absently he rose in the stirrups, and sent Blocky into a trot to keep up with the bunch of cattle that moved away suspiciously at his approach. He wondered if either of those other two cowboys had proven up on their homesteads. In that case, he would need to claim or buy them both before more squatters moved in. Kinda like rats, they always settled in some abandoned nest and saved themselves the work of building a new one. Both places had some water, too. A commodity that came scarce up there.

Then he noticed a two-year-old brindle bull break out of the brush. He sure never left one a stud carrying that much longhorn blood. Must have missed the wiry devil at roundup. A real maverick. No. The stag wore Ted Dikes's ear mark. Matt pushed the big horse to go faster. He wanted to see the other side of the animal. What brand was on him? The boughs of the junipers scraped his legs as the horse scrambled over rocks and jumped downed trees.

The critter cut to the right to try and beat him to the timber, and Matt could read the fresh TK brand. He reined up the horse on the hillside and nodded. Not missing the other signs either, he could see the dried black blood on the insides of the steer's legs as he fled into the trees. The sumbitch had cut him, too. That steer didn't belong to Ted Dikes or those other two. Sure he understood the brand laws in the territory, but that two-year-old had to come from one of his older Texas cows to carry that much long-horn blood. It was stealing, by damn, in his book. With all that he had invested, all the cattle he owned, some upstart with only a long loop shouldn't be able to come in here and take his living away from him and his family. Something had to be done about it.

By noon tomorrow, something would.

Overhead, the sun produced a blinding glare. Nothing stirred the air. No one spoke. Except for the occasional snort of one of their horses on the picket line stretched between two saplings, there were no voices. The ring of a spur rowel pealed like a schoolhouse bell when someone moved a foot. A crow called and another answered. The men sat around with their backs to pine tree trunks or squatted on their boot heels. Some whittled, others just whiled away the time.

Matt decided there wasn't a hell of a lot to talk about. When he glanced uphill, he could see Randy seated on his butt, dozing part of the time. Matt had told the boy coming over what they intended to do and why. Told him straight out that his very livelihood and future depended on ending these rustlers' reign. This was a real man's work and you never told anyone, your maw or anyone, by God.

"Someone's coming," Charboneau whispered, and stood up. He brushed the dirt and pine needles off the seat of his pants. "Could be them."

"Nope, it's a wagon," Porter said, and looked relieved as he settled back down to the ground. "Probably one of them Mormon families from Goose Creek."

Matt agreed. A string of them had small farms along that waterway. Clannish, they ran a few cows and kept kinda of to themselves. They were no great threat to his ambitions for the basin. In time they'd probably all move on. They were more farmers than ranchers, and it was damn sure a hardscrabble way of life at this elevation to miss the late frosts with their spindly little apple orchards and food plots.

It took a long time for the wagon to pass through on the road just over the rise from where they waited out of sight. Matt could hear the children screaming and playing. They must have stopped at the ford to let the team drink and to wade in the cold water. He fretted, hoping that they soon moved on, in case the three rode up while they were there.

At last, to his relief, the wagon left. He had food in his saddlebags that Lana had packed for him, but no real appetite. So close to having his plans completed, he worried the three might not show. It would be hard to get everyone together again. Some of them, like Porter, might change their minds. Word could get out to those three rustlers. No, it had to work this time.

"They're coming," Jakes said, ambling down the hillside on his high boot heels, collapsing his telescope. "I recognized that purple silk scarf that Dikes wears."

The time had come. Men began getting to their feet, pulling up their masks, and checking their rifle chambers. No one said much, only a few short words were exchanged.

"Come on, let's get this over with."

A nod, and everyone spread out. Matt motioned for Randy to stay with him. They slipped through the junipers. This made the best place to ambush them. Plenty of cover. Jakes carried the ropes, all made up. The nooses on the ends looked official enough.

Matt shifted the Winchester to his left hand and dried his right palm on the butt of his pants. He regretted still wearing his bat wing chaps, but they planned to head for the rim afterward. That meant some tough country to cross and to circle through coming back. He would need them to protect his legs. Still, the leggings stifled his movements.

The cedar aroma filled his nose. When he glanced back, Randy's face looked flushed. The boy swallowed hard, then nodded he was coming.

"Hold it right there!" Charboneau said. "Get them hands high!"

"What the hell—"

Matt charged out of the brush in front of them with his

Winchester ready. His tightened chest only let him use half of it for air. A lack of oxygen made him feel light-headed. The threesome had their hands high.

"Boys, we ain't got much money," Dikes said through his handsome grin. His frisky sorrel pony danced around under him.

"Get his horse." Matt motioned to Randall, who wore a bandanna over his face.

"We don't want your money," Matt said, taking charge as the others held their rifles on them. "Get their guns."

Crain, wearing a flour sack mask with holes, cautiously jerked the rifle out of Burtle's scabbard and sent it to the ground. Then he stepped in and took the man's handgun from its holster.

The whole time, the Texan Burtle wore a cross look on his face, like he planned to bolt out of there. Matt read it. "Git a hold of that other bridle, too," he said to Randy.

"What're you boys fixing to do here?" Luke Stearn asked, frowning in disbelief as they relieved him of his Colt. "Hell, boys, we're just on our way to the schoolhouse dance. We ain't—"

"Shut up and get off those horses," Matt ordered.

"You can wear them damn masks," Burtle said, obeying and stepping off his pony. "I know who the hell all of you are."

"So you do," Matt said. "We represent justice, and you better be making peace with your God. Get their hands tied."

"Whatever for?" Dikes screamed, holding the men back with his outstretched hands.

"You three have done your last rustling in this basin," Matt informed him.

"Rustling! I never took any cattle that wasn't legal mavericks," Dikes protested as they forcefully tied each man's hands behind his back. "This ain't a court of law! You can't do this!"

"When the law isn't enforced by the authorities out here, then Judge Hemp takes over," Matt said, seeing that their hands were bound. He set his Winchester down. "Get those nooses on that limb. You boys be thinking what you want to say to your maker."

"This isn't justice!"

"Ain't going to do no good, Teddy" Burtle said. "These rotten bastards done got their minds made up."

"Why did you have to throw in with 'em?" Porter asked.

"Throw in with them?" Dikes asked, nearly hysterical. "That you, Reed? Gawdamn, I never took nothing that wasn't fair. You tell Margie that I love her."

"Well, I've got proof says different," Matt said quickly. He couldn't afford a breakdown with Porter and have all of them thinking Dikes might not be guilty. His plan was too damned close to fulfillment. "Get them over under that tree and bring their horses."

When he turned back, he frowned, seeing Randy on his knees puking up his heels. Matt scowled. *That damn chicken.* He went and jerked away the reins from the boy and with disgust, gave him a swift kick. "Next time I'll bring a damn man."

On all fours, the boy moaned in protest and lurched forward to vomit some more. The sour stench ran up Matt's nostrils as he dragged the three ponies up to where the rustlers stood.

Jakes had the hemp strands slung over the thick branch and the nooses dangled in place. The men quickly loaded the rustlers in their saddles. The ropes placed around their necks were drawn tight and the ends tied off. Somewhere, a noisy magpie scolded them. Matt searched up and down the two dusty ruts for sight of anyone or anything. This needed to be over quickly in case some others came along.

Time to wind this down. He stepped over to Stearn's pinto. The noose looked to be set right around the man's throat. The long knot was beside his left ear, so when the horse was driven out from under him, the fall with the weight of his body would snap his neck. The main thing was to get this done with, and fast.

He spoke to Stearn with his hand on the pony's rump.

"You have anything to say to God or us about your crimes?"

"Innocent. God's damn sure going to punish all of you for this."

Next, Matt went to Burtle's horse, examined the hangman's knot, and satisfied it was proper, asked him the same.

"I'll see every one of you fuckers in hell for this," the Texan snarled.

Ignoring the tough man's comments, he stepped over and stopped beside Dikes, dreading the words that the kid might spout.

"Want mine? You boys are making the biggest mistake of your lives. I just hope that God forgives you."

Matt moved back. Each rancher held a coiled lariat in his hand. At his nod, they busted the horses on their butts. The mounts charged away. The unmistakable snap of spines cracked like gun shots. Two of them. Burtle's noose failed, and he danced in midair gurgling and strangling. The rustler fouled his pants and the stench filled the air.

Porter's eyes flew open. "Do something!" He fought off the mask. "Don't let him suffer like that."

Matt shook his head. "He won't for long."

The ring of the rustler's spurs sounded like school bells as his dying body fought to stay alive. With a flat hand to Porter's shoulder, Matt forced the distraught man toward their horses. They still had to cover their tracks. He had no sympathy for that tough bastard and his talk about seeing them in hell. Let him strangle forever.

They trudged over the hill, with Porter still glancing back and looking white-face scared. Matt forced him to go on. He wasn't having anyone breaking their ranks, not even the weak-kneed Porter. At their horses, the men tightened their cinches and took down the picket rope.

"God, Matt. Can I go back and do something for him?" Porter pleaded. "One of us should have shot him. Put him out of his misery."

Filled with impatience, Matt motioned for his foreman to go check. Jakes rode to the top of the hill, looked over at the three rustlers, and turned his pony around. He nodded that it was over. His actions gave Matt some breathing room. Next, he must disperse them so they didn't draw any attention.

"We need to spread out after we ride up the creek. Everyone needs to go their separate ways. Act normal. Not a word about this can ever leak out. Our lives and our families depend on it. Don't tell a soul." Matt looked for each man's solemn nod, then swung up in the saddle. "See you all at the dance tonight."

He looked with bitter disgust at the ashen-faced Randall seated on his dun. Nothing he could do about that for the time being. He spurred his horse for the stream.

The fiddle music carried in the evening air. The usual Saturday night crowd of ranchers and settlers was gathered at the Lone Pine Schoolhouse. Matt stood beside the buggy; Taneal on the other side was busy gossiping with Lucy Burns. Nothing out of place in the twilight that spread purple shadows across the grounds. He went and unhooked the horse. Needed to feed him some grain and tie him to a tree. Unlike the old days when they came in a farm wagon or buckboard like most folks, they had a nice buggy with a leather seat and a top to drive to the dance.

"No, Randall was sick tonight. Couldn't keep anything down." He heard Taneal tell Lucy as he hitched the horse's lead to a tree and went back for the feed bucket.

"What's wrong with him?" Lucy asked.

"I think it's those bronc horses that Matt has him riding. I believe he's all busted up inside."

"No such thing," Matt said, returning to join them. "He ate something on the ride today that didn't settle. He just got sick to his stomach. He was perfectly fine till we had some work to do."

"You aren't a doctor either, Matthew McKean." Taneal glared at him.

"If he ain't better in the morning, you can take him to Fortune and have him checked out by Doc."

The three of them looked up as a racing horse and rider burst into the yard. The intruder came charging through without any regards for the safety of all the playing children. You didn't do that on the school grounds. A few angry voices were raised to complain about his disrespectful invasion. Mothers rushed to protect their little ones. The rider dove off his mount and ran into the hitch rack. It was Jacky. Out of breath, he collapsed on the rail.

"Oh, my God!" he gasped. "There's been a triple hanging!"

"Who?" someone shouted at the cowboy. People rushed outside the school building and came on the run from across the grounds to hear the news.

"Stearn, Burtle," Jacky managed to say between gasps. "And Teddy Dikes."

"Oh, no! Not my Teddy!" Margie Porter's shrill voice carried over the school yard. "Tell me, Jacky, it ain't so?"

Skirt in her hand, the attractive girl of nineteen rushed down the schoolhouse stairs. She made her way through the crowd to confront the visibly shaken messenger.

"Sorry, ma'am." The cowboy's hat in his hands, he nodded it was so and dropped his head.

"Do something, Matthew," Taneal said, sounding annoyed at his lack of action.

"Boys, boys," Matt said, holding up his hands and starting across the yard. "Get a wagon and some blankets. Several of you menfolks come help me get them down." Then, fatherly, he laid his hand on the young messenger's shoulder. "Do you have any idea who did this, Jacky?"

"No, sir. I just saw them up there. Hanging—" He shook his head, unable to say any more for the tears streaming down his cheeks.

"Where are they at?" Matt asked, to his own relief that at the last minute he recalled that he wasn't supposed to know their location.

"At the Alma Creek Ford," Jacky managed to say, and whipped off his kerchief to mop his wet eyes and face. "You can't miss them."

"I've got a rig still hitched that we can use," one of the Mormon men said.

"Good, I'll ride with you," Matt said, turning to Taneal. "I'll go help them take the bodies down." He shook his head in disapproval. "Then we can have them properly buried."

"Yes, you should go. People look to you for leadership. But, Matthew, shouldn't we send word to the sheriff?"

"Good idea," Matt said, then with hint of sarcasm added, "He'll send some deputy over here in a week or two."

"He's the law, and he needs to know about this crime," she insisted.

"We'll send him word in the morning. I have to go with the wagon now," Matt said. "I'll be back." The man was there with his team and rig ready to leave.

"Be careful," she said, sounding concerned. "No telling who did this."

He agreed and climbed up on the spring seat beside the Mormon man. Matt believed no telling was right, and it needed to stay that way.

2

Under a cloudless sky, Luther jogged his team of bays down
the rutted Texas Road toward the settlement. Any wagon
tracks that ran southerly in the Nation carried the same title,
because if you went far enough down it, you arrived in the
Lone Star State. The ruts were still mud-filled from the past
hard rain. They called this community Oats. The small
crossroads contained a store with a smattering of raw cabins
clustered around it. A few straggly pines that barely escaped the axe and crosscut saw stood above new corn
patches.

Since early morning he had hurried, hoping to find Choc
Bleau at home. The breed, who spoke three dialects, made
a good posse man to help him serve warrants and make
arrests where he was headed in the Kiamish District.

Framed in thick braids, a brown face popped up in the
waving green blades. Armed with a hoe, she blinked at him
in the distance, then she spoke sharply to her force of small
faces who were equally equipped. Skirt in hand, she began
to run across the rows through the knee-high stalks toward
the cabin, looking back as if to check if he was still driving
his bays up the road.

Nancy Bleau was her name, a full blood. The smaller
ones were her and Choc's brood of half a dozen field hands
up to the age of perhaps twelve; she obviously planned to
leave them to hoe weeds in her absence. At her current rate
of travel, her long legs taking such great strides, she would
be at the cabin door before he came up to their place.
Choc's hounds began to bark in excitement. They ran out
to the road as if to guard it so he couldn't go past them.

A low growl from under the seat drew from Luther.

"Shut up, Ben. We ain't having fights with Choc's hounds today."

Still looking unconvinced of the matter of calling off any altercations, the thick-set English bulldog licked his face with his wide red tongue. He gave Luther a sardonic pose, "How come?" then he dropped back to the floor of the bed.

Ignoring the spotted hounds' chorus, Luther took the lane toward the cabin. Their incisive throaty racket reached a level where he could no longer hear the worn wagon hub knock. Nancy disappeared through the open front door. He reined up and she reappeared, smiled, and armed with a broom, dispersed the noisy pack to the rear of the house from where they spied distrustfully around the corner at the newly arrived rig.

The brake set and reins wrapped around the handle, Luther looked up in time to see Choc's frame fill the opening. Good. He wasn't gone somewhere. The tall breed ran the webs of his hands under the yellow suspenders as if testing their elasticity and nodded a hello. Luther returned his welcome and climbed down, anxious to stretch his stiff legs and back.

The half Osage's black hair stuck straight up. It gave him a look of being much taller than six three. He leaned back inside and found the unblocked gray hat with the greasy eagle feather adornment to complete his dress.

Luther reached in the wagon, took Ben by the plump midsection, and put him on the ground. Without hesitation, but still a wary look out for the pot-lickers, Ben went around and lifted his leg to all four wheels. The ceremony completed, Luther ordered him to stay under the rig. He checked on the dun saddle horse, whose lead rope was tied to the tailgate; he was fine. That accomplished, he turned to see Nancy returning around the cabin's corner.

"Damn hounds," she said, out of breath. A warm smile spread over her face as she stuck out her long brown hand to him. "Good to see you, Luther."

"Good morning." Funny thing, Luther decided, how her

hand could be so callused from work, yet still feel definitely feminine to his touch. Straight-backed with her raven-black hair parted in the middle and bound in thick braids, she filled out the wash-worn calico dress with an appealing firmness.

"Nice to see you again, Nancy. You sure have a great-looking corn crop this year."

She glanced over as if to check on it. Hard put to suppress her obvious pride, she beamed at his approval. "Doing good now. If it don't get too dry this summer."

Luther agreed.

"You must have got up pretty early," Choc said with a slow grin, and stepped off onto the log stoop. "You usually never get here till lunchtime." He shaded his eyes with his hand and looked for the sun to tell the time.

"I did. I've got a wad of warrants to serve in this district."

"We better eat lunch before we go," Choc said.

"He's worried you won't stop and eat." Nancy laughed out loud at her husband's expense.

Choc gave her small frown of disapproval.

"He's probably right," Luther agreed.

"Come on," she said, with a wave for him to follow her inside. "It won't take long. I already have stew on the stove. And some corn bread left from breakfast."

"Who you looking for this time?" Choc asked with his full brown lips pursed.

"First, can I hire you?" Luther asked, at the base of the stoop.

"How long?"

"Couple of weeks. You got other work to do?"

Luther could see that Nancy had stopped to stare at her husband. His reply affected her, too. A noisy crow went by overhead. The pine floor of the cabin creaked as if in protest.

Choc shook his head. "There's a stomp dance coming up, but I can always go to a dance."

Satisfied, Nancy agreed with a hard nod of approval to

his words and headed across the room to the stove.

"It pays the same," Luther added. "Buck a day."

"Good," Choc said, and motioned for him to take a seat opposite him at the wooden table.

"I'll wash my hands first," Luther said. After holding the lines all morning and messing with harnessing the team earlier, they needed to be cleaned. He searched around for the washbowl.

"There is a basin." She pointed to the dry sink and tossed him a flour sack towel. With hot water from a cast-iron kettle off the range, she filled it for him.

"What's been happening up here?" Luther asked, busy cleaning his hands.

"They say they will pay our allotments in August this year," she said over her shoulder.

Choc shook his head. "They never do them on the time they say."

Luther agreed and dried his hands. Then he came over and sat on the straight-back chair reserved for company and no doubt Choc when there weren't guests. He scooted it up to the table as Nancy delivered them each a blue and white china bowl of stew. Obviously, this must be her best serving ware. Then she added the half skillet of corn bread to the table.

"Should we have coffee and celebrate?" she asked her husband who agreed with a grunt between spoons of stew.

From the top shelf of her open cupboards, she took down a small cloth sack. Soon she had the beans in a grinder tucked under her arm and swirled the handle with no effort.

"Good thing you came," she said, and laughed. "He's pretty stingy with his coffee."

To suppress his amusement at her words, Luther nodded he heard her. No doubt she used his presence to gouge her husband a little about his thriftiness over the coffee beans. Choc was no big spender, and little doubt the dollar-a-day posse man's wages that the U.S. Marshal's office paid him helped them out financially. Few other employment opportunities existed in the district besides logging in the hills.

Lumbering only paid fifty cents a day, and that was after and if the sawmill sold the wood.

Luther set the warrants on the table, picked up the first one, and recalled previously arresting the same one-eyed breed.

"Curly Meantoe," he said, reading the first name.

"He may be up near the Clam Shell Schoolhouse," Choc said, and stopped eating. His great brown eyes blinked as if in deep thought, then he nodded in certainty. "He has a sister up there."

"She's married to a Fox," Nancy put in, busy stoking the range's firebox and adding wood.

"Their name is Clothesrod." Satisfied with knowing the man's identity, Choc went back to eating. "He won't be hard to find. What he do?"

"Says robbery." Luther turned to the next warrant on the tabletop, took another bite of the rich stew, and read the next name. "Buddy Hart."

Nancy swiftly turned and looked hard at her husband.

"He killed a white man, huh?" Choc asked without looking up from his food.

"That's the warrant. Murder. You don't have to go with me after him," Luther said.

Choc shrugged as if to dismiss his concern.

"He is your half brother." Luther wanted to see Choc's response, though he counted on some lack of it being the nature of the man.

"He broke the law. He is another criminal. I will help you find him."

"First or last?"

"First," Choc said, his attention still focused on the stew in his bowl. "He hears we are after him, I bet he will run. We better get him first."

Luther agreed. He glanced over and saw Nancy turn back to the stove. Hard to tell if she looked relieved or had simply accepted it. All the way from Fort. Smith, the past two days on the road, he had wondered how Choc would take this warrant for Buddy Hart. There were other trackers available, but the Osage was Luther's favorite one to hire. In a tight place, he always felt that he could count on him.

Luther felt good that the matter was settled. When he looked up, she delivered them cups of steaming coffee.

"Good coffee," Luther said in approval, after his first sip of the searing hot brew.

"You know," Choc began, holding up his stained mug. "If you don't have coffee all the time, it makes a bigger treat."

She gave her husband a peevish look of disapproval behind his back for Luther's sake. Then she went off to sit on edge of the iron bed and drink her own.

Sunlight shone on the forest floor through a filter of thick leaves. The musty sour smell of the rotted mulch permeated the early-morning air. Choc rode a short coupled roan pony ahead of him up the steep trail. A couple of saucy jays screamed at the mounted intruders. Luther's Texas dun horse's shoes clanked on the rock outcropping. He knew his posse man did not approve of the bell-like sounds they made at times, but unshod, the gelding would have been footsore and crippled by this time.

Beneath Luther's horse's belly or behind him trotted the spotted bulldog, named for Luther's father's favorite commander in the war. General Ben McCollough, the former Texas ranger, hero of the Wilson Creek Battle in southern Missouri, who was killed by cannon fire at the Elkhorn Tavern fight called Pea Ridge. Luther's daddy spoke so highly of the man, thus the name for his forty-five-pound tagalong. Somehow, Ben knew the ways to avoid the gelding's hooves. Aside from a sneeze or two, his presence remained close to invisible.

With his hand resting on his gun butt, Luther shifted the harness around his waist to relieve some of the pressure of it on his leg. Choc pushed aside a low oak branch and looked back to warn him. He acknowledged the branch and ducked it.

They reached a bench on the mountain and reined up as

a soft breeze swept Luther's face. From under the towering hardwood canopy, he could see across the deep chasm to the next green range. Somewhere in these mountains, Choc had said earlier that Buddy Hart made his hideout. No one had seen him since the murder. Luther knew no one admitted seeing him for fear his guilt might be shared by anyone who claimed to have been in touch with the twenty-year-old.

"You been to this place before?" he asked.

Choc shook his head. "Not in a few years."

The exact location of Reed's lair was irrelevant; Choc's knowledge of the general area would let him find it. Luther looked down their back trail and saw nothing, but it wasn't good to take any unnecessary chances.

Choc gave him a head toss and they set out again. Words were a short commodity between them, unless the half Osage hit a streak where he talked for hours. Otherwise, he used hand motions and faces to explain his next moves.

Fox squirrels chattered in the overhead ceiling. Bottom limbs of the great red oaks, ash, and hickory reached far above them in this forest of ancient growth. A faint smell of smoke rode on the air. Only a whiff, but Choc indicated they should stop. Luther searched around. It would be hard to find a place in this glen to tether their horses, the trunks of the giant trees were so vast around.

"You got hobbles?" Choc asked.

"Yeah," Luther said, carefully checking the area as he reached back and undid the saddlebags.

"Hobble yours, I'll tie mine to your saddle horn."

Luther bailed off his dun and fixed the soft ropes around his legs. Then he loosened the girth to ease the pony while they searched ahead on foot. How far away was the source of that smoke? No trace of any in the air when he tried again to use his nose and find it. He removed the .44/.40 from the scabbard and slipped the lever down to check the chamber. The oily-smelling rifle was loaded to the gills.

Armed with a double-barreled shotgun, Choc took the lead and headed uphill. The smoke must have come over the ridge to reach them. Wind was out of the south, still, the source of it might be miles away. His boot soles tramped through the deep leaf mulch as Luther hurried to catch up. His man could outdo a horse on foot in the woods. He hoped Choc wasn't in that big of a hurry this time. When Ben gave a loud sneeze, Luther looked aside at him. They might need the general's services before this was over.

"Come on." Ben fell in with them in his usual aloft manner, stopping to inspect and piss on various items as he went along.

Choc held out his hand to stop them when they reached the crest. Smoke rose in a thin wisp from a well-made stone chimney. They lay on their stomachs side by side on the ridge. Luther used his looking glass to study the source. No sign of anyone around the outside, but the front door of the small, neat-built cabin was shut.

"Nice-looking place. It ain't new," he said, rolling over on his side to hand the glass to Choc.

"No, this place belongs to someone."

"You think Hart is squatting here?"

Choc nodded and looked hard through the eyepiece. "I've been here before. Didn't know if he was at this one. I think the only way out is the front door and that one window."

"Good. Will he surrender if he's in there?" Luther asked, sprawled on his belly beside the man.

Choc shook his head. "I don't know. Maybe have to stuff green leaves down that chimney and smoke him out."

"Fine, I'll give him a chance to surrender first before we do all that work. If we have the wrong place, they should tell us."

"Good idea." Choc smiled and collapsed the brass scope.

"Buddy Hart! Buddy Hart! U.S. Deputy Marshal Haskell here! Come out with your hands up!" A double echo of his words came back and he waited, the rifle ready. The bleached gray wooden door remained closed.

Ben sat on his round butt beside them and scratched his

right ear with a hind foot as if bored by their actions. Then he licked his upper lip and nose to complete his ritual.

"That damn dog acts like he knows he's down there." Choc belly-laughed at the notion. "Maybe Buddy knows you got Ben up here and don't want to get bit in the butt."

"If he's inside, he sure ain't answering." Luther saw the door barely open. The barrel of a long gun poked out the crack. "Get down!" he shouted, and they flattened out.

The shotgun blast roared and soon spent pellets filtered down upon them. Ben snorted his disapproval, rose, and went downhill behind them as if that would be a safer place.

Hard pressed on the ground, they scowled at each other over the reply. Rage swelled in Luther's chest. Hart wanted to play tough, they'd play tough, too. He would soon learn he'd messed with the wrong men doing a stupid trick like that. Keep up that foolishness and he might even go back to Fort Smith in a wooden box.

"He answered us," Choc said, on his elbows beside him.

"Yes, he did. How can we stop up that chimney?" Luther asked, still perturbed over the shooting.

"You watch the front door. I'll go gather some leaves. We'll smoke him out." On his hands and knees, Choc backed down the hill.

Luther wondered how his man would ever get them into the chimney, but it was worth a try. He set the rifle on the ground a little ahead of his body to be handy, then looked back at his partner and agreed with a nod.

Choc half rose as he retreated. With him gone, Ben crept up to rejoin Luther, his belly close to the ground, until at last he lay beside him. He panted as if out of breath.

"You getting braver, General?" Luther reached over and scratched the bulldog's scalp. A low growl curled out of Ben's throat and his brown eyes focused hard on the cabin.

"We need to get this one, old boy."

Ben sneezed, but quickly recovered and resumed acting on his guard.

Over half an hour later, Luther rose enough to observe Choc making his way from the decrepit shed toward the side of the cabin. No more actions from the occupant, only some noisy crows and a squirrel chattering overhead about their invasion.

At last he could make out that Choc carried something resembling a large ball. Uncertain of the nature of the man's package, Luther spoke for Ben to quit his whining. Then he cocked the Winchester. Beside the chimney's base, Choc swung the cloth ball on the end of a rope. He gave it a high toss. It landed on top of the stone and mortar structure and went out of sight.

Choc grinned as if pleased, then he moved to the right to stay out of the line of gunfire. Smoke no longer rose from the stack. Enthused about his man's success, Luther felt they were making progress at last. In a short while, the sounds of coughing from inside could be heard. Gray wisps seeped from around the top of the closed door. Getting bad in there, Luther decided.

At once the door burst open. A small woman coughing in her hands came out, waving a white kerchief, shouting, "Give up! Give up! No shoot!"

Still leery of what Hart might try next, Luther rose with the rifle in his hands. Filled with caution, he advanced down the hillside. After a curt word to control the growling Ben beside him, he saw Choc moving in from the right with his shotgun ready.

"Tell Hart to come out!" Luther ordered the girl. The next few moments could be crucial. Was he using her for a ploy? Luther stopped fifty feet from her.

The figure of Hart broke out of the doorway. With his wide eyes fiercely searching around, he spotted Luther and Choc. Before Luther could raise his gun sights, the fugitive disappeared around the side of the cabin. No chance for a shot by either man with her standing there.

"Get him, Ben!" Luther shouted and the eager bulldog jumped into hot pursuit. A blinding fury of white and black, he tore past her, made the corner on his side, issuing a roar to match a lion the whole time. She fell back screaming, though Luther knew the dog had missed the girl by inches.

Luther shouted for Choc to go the other way around the cabin and he took the left side. Running hard, he came around the house and spotted the fugitive in the forks of a small peach tree. The bush tottered with his weight, almost breaking it. Each time the angry General Ben McCollough lunged off the ground, he snapped his flashing canines like a bear trap only inches from any of Hart's body parts.

"Ben! Ben, get over here!" Luther ordered and slapped his leg.

One final try to sink his teeth in the fugitive's hide and Ben quit. With a look of disgust at his master, he came over to Luther, plopped his butt on the ground, and began to scratch his right ear. For Ben, his part of this arrest was complete.

The wide-eyed Hart looked like a man who had seen the devil and somehow lived through the ordeal. Acting as if unsure he was not to be eaten by the monster, he looked with distrust at the seated bulldog and clung to his tenable place in the waving peach bush.

"Get down," Choc said, armed with the handcuffs and ready to put the irons on him.

To Luther, Hart hardly looked out of his teens. The fugitive glanced one more time at Ben, then unceremoniously climbed down. On his feet, he said something in tongue to Choc, who locked up his wrists.

"I didn't kill that white man," Choc answered him.

The boy nodded as if he understood his half brother's statement.

"He blaming you?" Luther asked Choc when he joined them.

"He wanted to know what I would do if I were in his moccasins."

Luther agreed with a nod. Tough deal. If Hart had killed a white man in the act of a crime or with malice, then his chances were good of having a meeting with Judge Issac Parker's hangman.

In front of the cabin, Choc spoke to the girl about food. She looked even younger than the boy; Luther doubted she was more than fifteen. Her reply was in tongue.

"She has some fried bacon and corn bread," Choc announced. "We better eat it. May be dark before we can get back to the wagon."

"You have a horse?" Luther asked the prisoner.

Acting defeated, he shook his head and looked down at his worn out shoes without laces and socks.

"It'll be a long walk back to Moss's Store," Luther warned him, and started to leave. But a question rode heavy on his mind as he turned back and asked, "Were you drunk when you killed him?"

"Bad whiskey."

"Better think up a better defense than that," he said off-handedly.

Choc and the girl had gone inside the smoky cabin for the food. They soon returned coughing. Choc tossed his sack of green leaves out in the yard to smoulder. She put a skillet of burned corn bread on the porch stoop, then went back inside and returned with some browned bacon slices on a slab of wood.

After setting the platter on the stoop, she stepped away from it. Luther nudged the anxious Ben back with his toe. Then he walked up, bent over, and took a piece of the meat. A little salty to his tongue, but he nodded his approval as he chewed on it. Seated on the step, Choc used his jack-knife to slice the dark bread and dug out a crumbling piece.

"Ain't bad inside," he said, chewing on a large hunk. "Little black outside."

"Where do you live?" Luther asked the girl, who stood with her hands locked in front of her skirt.

"Here," she said in English.

"No," he said, busy trying to get some bread out of the pan, but it kept breaking up and crumbling apart with his efforts. "Where is your home?"

"My folks—live—on—the—Grand River."

"Will you go there?"

She shook her head vehemently.

"Where will you go?"

"Fort Smith."

"To wait for him?" In defeat, he stuffed a pinch of crumbs in his mouth, then raised up. Her nod told him she would follow her man like he expected. The poor girl would go live in Shack Town, do whatever she had to do to sustain herself during the months ahead. In the end, they would probably hang her lover. By that time, she would either be a drunken whore in the alleys of Fort Smith or have drowned herself in the muddy river water.

"Why don't you go home—to the Grand River!" he said louder than he intended, sick to his stomach and feeling depressed by the ugly picture of her demise.

"I am his woman," the resolute-sounding girl said, her eyes dark as diamonds, shing hard in the flickering sunlight coming through the overhead leaves.

With disgust, he looked at her, wanting to say something powerful enough to change her mind, then without a word, he turned on his heels. "Come on, Ben, we need to get the horses."

"More food here," Choc said, squatting beside it, busy feeding his face. He gave the bulldog some of the corn bread, which Ben lapped up.

Luther never answered his man, but kept walking up the slope. He wanted to be on their way back to Moss's. His hunger had turned to nausea at the thought of the girl's bitter future. And all because of the supposition he had framed from Hart's own information; how some white men sold that boy bad whiskey. A really good reason to kill him. Yeah. Would he ever learn how these people thought?

The next morning at Moss's, they prepared to leave the shackled Hart chained to a pine tree behind the store. The Indian girl, who called herself Martha, promised to feed the prisoner and bring him water. Choc cautioned her not to try to free him. She agreed. The two lawmen rode out with Ben trotting behind on the heels of their horses.

"Will he be there tonight?" Luther asked when they were out of her earshot.

"Yes."

He nodded in approval. Choc knew the limits and the ways of these people. Without a jail facility, chains and irons were the only method of restraint they could use while they went out to serve the other warrants. It forced Luther to leave his prisoners in irons each day and in care of someone to see to their needs.

"Did Buddy kill that man over bad whiskey?" Luther asked as they rode beside the rail fence that protected a healthy-looking patch of knee-high corn.

"Bad whiskey or no whiskey. He was drunk. Probably wanted more."

"Had no money?" Luther asked.

"Probably was broke. Whiskey does terrible things to some Indians."

Luther agreed and they pushed their horses into a long trot down the dusty road. It hadn't rained in a week or longer, and the last of the moisture had evaporated in the stiff winds from the south that this time of year usually brought thick clouds to the Nation. All spring, the winds had only delivered hot weather even in the mountains, where one could usually escape some of the high temperatures.

They headed for Ellis's sawmill. The warrant Luther wanted to serve was for an Indian, Smoky Kline, charged with stealing an Army mule. He hoped the day's planned arrest would be a quiet one. Most of their apprehensions went well because of his Indian partner's presence. Choc was familiar with many people in this district, who knew him as a no-nonsense, tough person. In Luther's book, the breed being along saved him many serious out of hand altercations with the red men they arrested.

Mid-morning, when they rode off a steep hillside into the wide clearing, Ellis's vast mill operation bustled with activity. Smoke spewed from an iron chimney in a great column that marked the sky. The scream of the blade digging its steel teeth in the wood fibers filled the air. A powerful smell of turpentine pine and sour oak sawdust hung like a heavy perfume. Men labored to unload log wagons, and others with mules skidded single cuts to the main mill. A mountain of bark slabs rose beside the steam engine, which huffed like a great fire-breathing dragon under a shake-roofed open shed, providing belt power for the saw.

A short white man dressed in waist overalls, long-sleeved shirt, a weathered cowboy hat, and holding a great brown oil can came out and nodded to them over the noise. Luther tried to read the man's look. He showed no great pleasure over their presence. Obviously, he knew they were not there to buy lumber.

"We're looking for Smoky Kline," Luther said, and dismounted.

"You the law?"

"Yeah, U.S. Deputy Marshal. I have a warrant," he said, loud enough over the clatter and whine for the man to hear him.

"What did he do?" the white man asked, as if troubled by the matter.

"Sold a U.S. Army mule to a man at Van Buren," Luther read from the bad handwriting by the clerk on the warrant.

"Well, he wasn't very smart then, was he?" The man laughed, which broke some of the tension between them, and shook his head in disappointment. "Hell, anyone dumb enough to sell a branded mule like that sure deserves to be arrested, don't he?"

"He work for you?"

"Oh, yeah. I don't figure he'll give you a minute's trouble." Ellis took off his felt cowboy hat and scratched the thin hair on top of his head. "Hate it. Pure D hate it. He's a good worker. Family man. Wonder why he ever did that for. Hell, you two don't know the reason why. You're just serving them papers, right?"

Luther agreed. They soon found Kline stacking lumber and handcuffed the tall Indian.

"Boy! Why in God's name did you sell a U.S. branded mule for?" Ellis asked the prisoner.

The broad-shouldered Kline shrugged and shook his head. "He was lame and I couldn't ride him anymore."

"Still, that was pure D dumb of you, boy." With that said, he left them, wagging the oil can, headed across the yard for his steam engine.

Late afternoon, they arrived back to the store and added Kline to the chain with the dejected Billy Hart. Martha cooked them two chickens she had bought earlier from a nearby farmer with Luther's money. She also fixed a big kettle of brown rice for their supper. The sun was about to set when they finally ate the meal.

The first food since daybreak in Luther's mouth drew the flow of his saliva. Martha's chickens looked a little blackened on the outside, but the leg he twisted off tasted good enough.

To get their attention, Ben stealthfully crawled up on his belly and began making snorts and grunting sounds out of his flat nose. Luther ignored him. The bulldog could be a real pest at mealtime.

"That dog's begging again," Choc said between bites of the chicken breast in his hands.

"Don't pay him no mind," Luther said.

"Who we going after tomorrow?" Choc asked, turning his head to the side to eat more meat off of the bone.

"Two White Crow brothers. Josh and Tag."

"What they do?"

"I think it's robbery."

Choc nodded. "They will be at Red Springs. Maybe making whiskey."

"You can get in trouble drinking it or making it. Good food, Martha," Luther said to the girl as she gathered up the tin dishes. "You can give Ben some corn bread, if you've got any left."

She nodded in the firelight and looked back at him. "I'll feed him."

"Go on with her," he said in a head toss to Ben.

The bulldog rose, stretched his back, and then plodded off into the growing night after her. It drew a laugh from Choc.

"He understands English better than my own children."

"Ben understands eating," Luther said, and chuckled.

After their breakfast of reheated rice with chicken, they set out on Texas Road for Red Springs. Luther left Martha with seventy-five cents to buy something to cook for supper, promising to return by evening or past. He and Choc trotted their horses away from Moss's Store.

The coolness of the predawn felt good to ride in. He knew it would heat up again by late afternoon. Each day grew hotter than the day before. Besides, they wouldn't be in the mountains after these two. The place, Choc mentioned, Red Springs lay in the foothills.

Mid-morning, they rode up a rutted path. In Luther's book, it could hardly be called a road. Simply two ruts that wound around and up a narrow draw. Riding in the lead, Choc twisted in the saddle often and frowned with displeasure at him. A profuse growth of head-high saplings lined the way blocking their view of everything.

When Luther checked on Ben, the dog acted normal, padding along under him. He could smell and hear better than either of them. Luther felt easier that they weren't riding into an ambush, though one could surely spring out of this mess of brush at any moment.

At last they rounded a bend and reached a clearing with several open fields. Ahead of them stood a brush arbor housing several wooden barrels beneath it. At the discovery of their appearance, three fat Indian women began screaming in panic; they ran away, each in a different direction. Ben rose to the occasion with a deep-throated growl and started after one of them.

"No! Ben! Get back here!" Luther shouted, unholstering his handgun and dismounting. Far more concerned about the possible presence of their men than the fleeing females, he searched around as he dismounted.

"I'll catch one and bring her back," Choc said, and sent his roan after a woman who was headed down the weedy field and still in view.

"Ben!" Luther said again to halt the dog, and viewed the shack to his left. He hitched the horse, looking around, trying to familiarize himself with the layout.

A wonder they hadn't been shot in the back. Had anyone been inside that raw board house, they'd made a perfect target. The front door either stood open or was gone. It may never have existed. On close examination, he saw no hinge marks. Cautiously, he put his boot on the front stoop.

Ben whined, then stuck his head inside past the casing. The bulldog tested the air, then satisfied, went ahead of him. Without any interest, he crossed the large open room and Luther watched him go into the lean-to on the side. A few housekeeping items, plus some bed ticking and old blankets were all he could see. Newspaper wallpaper and tattered calendars covered the walls.

Sneezing, Ben soon returned, and Luther nodded to him.

"Good boy. They ain't here." Relieved, he started for the front door opening.

Coming across the yard, Choc marched a rather fat squaw by the arm ahead of him. He stopped in the bare dirt space and let go of her arm. His release drew a nasty look from the woman and some guttural words under her breath.

"What's your name?" Luther asked, looking around for any other signs of their men.

"Josie."

"Well, Josie, where are the White Crow brothers?"

She folded her arms over her amble bustline and with her dark eyes dared them to make her talk.

"Maybe a noose around her neck would help her remember?" Choc asked.

Warily, she cut her cold gaze around at the posse man and mumbled, "Gone."

"Gone where?" Luther asked her.

"To sell whiskey."

"Where do they sell whiskey?"

"How should I know!"

Luther wanted to laugh. Obviously the brothers did not take her on such sales trips. He removed his hat and wiped

the sweat out of the band with his kerchief. They had to
be somewhere in the area.

"Josie, when will they be back?" he asked, looking at
her and spinning the hat on his hand.

"When they sell all the whiskey."

"Yes, I understand. You do know making whiskey in
the Nation is against the laws of the government?"

She shrugged, as if that made no difference to her. Those
were white man laws. She was Indian. This was the same
way most of the native people in the Nation felt.

"You know I need to find the brothers?"

A slow nod was all she allowed herself.

Luther decided his line of questions with her was going
nowhere. They best bust up the liquor making operation,
destroy their supplies, and move on.

"Josie, you call those other women back here. If you
three help us break up the still and barrels, I won't arrest
you or them." All he needed was three fat women to take
back to Fort Smith. Besides, there would be children somewhere to be concerned about. No, his amnesty offer would
be the best way out of this situation. Then they could get
on with finding the White Crow brothers. The sooner the
better.

"You heard him," Choc said, giving her a not-too-gentle
shove. "Go get them and don't be long."

"Maybe they are gone?" Her brown eyes flew open in
disbelief he would demand such a thing.

"Too hot. They won't run far," Choc said, and pointed
in the direction they left. "Hurry or you can sit in jail."

She gathered her long dress and headed toward the
southeast. The once-upon-a-time cornfield was infested
with a profusion of waist-high green weeds. Her route
looked direct, and Luther felt certain the others were hiding
in the woods on the far side. Choc was right. The first ones
he saw were like her, too fat to run very far in the heat.

Would she really find the others, come back, and help
them? He looked at Choc and they both nodded. Better get
to work. No telling about their help. At least they wouldn't

have to take back any women prisoners, especially fat ones to load and unload out of the wagon.

Choc found an ax and used it on the stinking barrels full of souring mash. Like chopping open a ripe melon. A few whacks, the staves split and the strong-smelling contents flew out on the dirt.

"Some hogs may get drunk tonight," Choc said with a horse laugh. Then he reared back and bust open another. The heavy intoxicating odor of soured grain soon filled the air.

Busy emptying two bottles at a time, hearing Ben's throaty growl, Luther looked up to see the threesome of women coming back through the weeds.

"No, Ben. They won't hurt us," he assured the growling dog. "Hey, Choc, we're going to have company." His partner nodded and the dog dropped his head back on the old rag rug he was bellied down on.

When the women arrived, Luther told them to dump all the mixed bottles of white lightning. They looked around suspiciously at the two of them, and stepped wide of the growling dog to obey his orders.

"Cut this coil up?" Choc asked, meaning the coiled tubing, which was how the product was distilled.

"In little pieces," Luther said, taking a small half pint to save for evidence. He stowed it in his saddlebags.

"Now break all the bottles," Choc ordered the women. That way they would have to go collect more "new" bottles to start up their operation again. It might slow them down from setting up very fast, but he doubted it. There were more stills in the Nation than mushrooms in the springtime, and they had a fair share of the fungus each year.

Midway on their return ride to Moss's, Choc thought of a place the Crow brothers might be selling whiskey.

"There's a big church meeting this week on the grounds over on Dead Fish Creek. They maybe over there selling whiskey," he said at his own discovery.

"A church meeting?" Luther gave him a frown. You

didn't sell the stuff at a revival. Sounded like a poor marketplace for whiskey to him.

"Oh, yeah," Choc said with a chuckle. "Lots of people go there for an excuse to meet other people. Some go for religion, some to visit, and always some attend to get drunk."

"How far away?"

"Maybe ten miles."

"We better go check it out." Luther knew the detour would make them late getting back to their own camp, but they had wasted the entire day so far without results. He didn't consider the destruction of the Crows' still such a great feat. He couldn't count the time he'd lost from enforcing the law and serving warrants in the territory in their destruction.

At the next crossroad, Choc motioned to ride west. When they topped the rise above Dead Fish Creek in late afternoon, heat waves rose off the dry, powder road from ruts previously cut by many hooves and iron rims. Spread under the cottonwoods and ghostly white sycamores up and down the valley were hundreds of wagons, picketed horses, mules, and makeshift tents. Camp fire smoke swirled about.

Children rushed around in play, their shrill voices cutting the air.

"Big revival," Luther said, impressed. "Ben! Get over here."

The dog had already begun scratching the ground like an angry bull anticipating all the dogs for him to whip in this place. His stub of a tail pointed straight up; no doubt he was ready for war.

"Damn it, Ben McCollough, we don't need any dogfights here." Luther searched for him under his dun. Locating the bulldog, he gave him a large scowl of disapproval, which Ben ignored; Luther sat back up in the saddle.

The camp's yellow and black mongrels began a chorus of barking at the discovery of strangers, especially ones with a new dog. Choc took the lead on his roan and headed up the lane through the middle of the camps. Many dark eyes looked up from their cooking to stare at them.

Ahead, Luther could make out the wilted leaves of the branches that formed the roofs of the shades set up for the revival. Obviously the people were on a break, for no shouting or hallelujahs came from the brush arbors. Twisting around in the saddle, he looked over the individuals while a woman bent over a cooking fire stared at him. A band of small children wide-eyed with suspicion followed them.

"Hello, my brothers," he said with a dignified manner about him. His dark beard and full mustache were laced with gray; his eyes, black as coal, glinted as he looked them over.

"Good day," Luther said, checking around and resetting his dun to make him stand still. "My name is Luther Haskell. I hate to bother you, but we represent the federal court in Fort Smith and we're looking for some men."

"Name's Windgate. I am the spiritual leader of this camp. Who do you seek?"

"Josh and Tag White Crow."

The preacher shook his head, as if their names were unknown to him. "There're many people here for this gathering, but those two are not familiar to me. You sure they are amongst us here?"

"They sell whiskey," Choc said, and booted his roan closer to the man. He wasn't missing a face in the crowd that had gathered to see about this intrusion.

"I don't allow—"

"Preacher Windgate, they won't ask you for permission to sell it."

The man agreed with a solemn nod, then held his arms up to gain the crowd's attention. "These men seek whiskey peddlers. They are here on business and want no trouble with God's children. If any of you know of two men by the name of White Crow, tell these men where they are." Pained-looking, Windgate searched their faces as he waited for someone to give them a word. The row of head shakes told Luther enough. Not a soul would come forward.

"Sorry," Windgate said. "No one here knows of them. But you may light and be blessed by our togetherness with the Lord on this hallowed ground."

"Thanks, Preacher," Luther said, and nodded to Choc. "But we must ride on."

Then one of the bolder camp dogs could no longer resist challenging the invasion of the spotted devil under Luther's horse and made his move. Dodging around from behind two squaws' skirts, he bolted into Ben with the roar and fury of a panther.

Spooked by the charge under him, Luther's horse threatened to buck him off. Fighting the dun, the pony shied sideways and bumped and spilled into several startled people close by. The war was on, with Luther so occupied with controlling his upset horse, he couldn't even shout to stop it. Both dogs reared up on their hind feet, snapping and snarling for a hold on the other. Then Ben clamped on the other dog's leg. The cur settled for Ben's short ear, but the tremendous pressure of Ben's iron jaws upon on his foreleg caused him to quickly release it and begin to wail in pain.

"Ben! Ben! Let go!" Luther shouted from the midst of the crowd, his horse at last behaving. People crowded in to better see the fight and pushed the dun around to escape being stepped on.

"General Ben McCollough!" The full force of his voice directed at the persistent bulldog who still had not released the screaming mongrel's leg from his jaws. Filled with rage, Luther bailed off his horse and handed the reins to a full-faced woman. He waded into the open space and kicked his hardheaded dog swiftly in the rump.

At that point, Ben released his grip and the three-legged mongrel raced for safety. Through the laughing crowd he went helter-skelter, running into people, and after one collision, falling down on his butt. Quickly looking back with disbelief written on his face over his misfortune, he left the vicinity in even greater haste.

Head down and wincing in dread, Ben finally looked up

at his master. Luther turned on his heel and went back for
his horse. He'd had enough nonsense for one day. He
mounted the dun, swung his leg over, and yelled at Ben.

"Get over here!" he ordered, then nodded to Choc that
he was ready to leave. "Sorry about the fight," he said to
the preacher.

"Why, Marshal, your fine bulldog did not start it. Is that
his name, McCollough?" Windgate asked.

"Yeah, that was my father's commander."

"Good man, sir. Ride with the Lord, my friends. Sorry
that we're unable to help you."

Choc was chuckling to himself when they topped the
hill and looked back. The sun was red and fiery orange on
the range to the west. Smoke cloaked the valley in a fog.
Luther twisted in the saddle to shake his head at the amused
breed, who was hardly able to hold it in.

"What's so dang funny?"

"Bet that damn worthless cur don't jump another bulldog."

"Bet he don't see another," Luther said, still edgy about
the dog fight. "Ain't that many of them around."

"That's true. You got anything to eat in your saddlebags?"

"Some crackers, dry cheese. Why?" Luther asked, considering their contents. Sure not much, and not very fresh.

"I figure them White Crows are around here somewhere.
If Windgate knew they were here selling whiskey, he'd
bring fire and brimstone down on them. But he don't know
everything that happens in the vicinity of his camp meeting."

"You want to stay here a while longer and look around
for them?"

Choc bobbed his head until the eagle feather twisted on
his hatband. "I'll bet them White Crows ain't missing such
a good place to sell their whiskey."

Luther stepped down on the ground and unbuttoned his
shirt in search of the creature crawling over his skin. He

plucked a large red Lone Star tick from his chest and crushed it with his fingernails.

"Even the Christians have ticks in their valley," he said, buttoning his shirt. Then he swung back into the saddle. "Fine, let's circle around and look for them."

Choc wanted to wait until the camp meeting started back in full swing. Then with all the true believers involved in services, they could easily scout around for the spirit peddlers. Made sense to Luther as he considered the gathering darkness and the day's oppressive heat. A good breeze to stir the stillness would certainly help, but none appeared forthcoming.

Eating dry crackers and drier cheese with tepid canteen water to wash them down, Luther turned an ear to the voices singing hymns that carried on the hot night air. Seated on the ground with his legs crossed, he wondered how long he'd be out in the Nation chasing fugitives this time, before he could return to Fort Smith.

In the last of the twilight with Tillie on his mind, he thought about her smooth perfumed skin, and their physical relationship. That new outfit she wore made him chuckle. Why, she'd just as well be nude. Her hardheadedness niggled at him the most. She wouldn't leave that two-story house, not even for a preacher's words. He had offered her his hand in marriage. She'd refused him, saying she could never be a wife. He found no way to change her firm decision, so he looked forward to seeing her when he could and knew she'd never be his alone.

"You ready? We better go on foot." Choc stood up and stretched.

"Coming," Luther said, considering his next move before he rose. "I'll tie up Ben."

"Yeah, he might cause us some trouble with them camp dogs."

"Ben, come here," he said, and barely snatched him by the scruff of the neck. At last with Ben secured on a rope leash and with finger-shaking orders for him to stay there, Luther started after Choc.

They kept to the woods, skirting to the south of the camp. Making his way after the posse man and stumbling on an occasional unseen object, Luther felt certain Choc could see as good in the night as in daylight. Twice in the darkness he found himself trapped in a dense briar patch by his own doing, and had to backtrack to catch up. As the breathless night wore on his nerves, sounds of the enthusiastic evangelists carried across the valley.

"Ho! Ho!"

Luther caught up with Choc at the edge of a clearing. "That ain't no revival sound," he whispered.

Choc nodded. Camp firelight illuminated several men shuffling around. Obviously they were drinking spirits and enjoying themselves.

"See anyone we need?" Luther asked, relying on his man's recognition of the brothers and others.

"Too dark, but they're probably there."

"You got your shotgun ready?"

"Yes."

"Go in from the right, I'll come in from the left. We get in place, you fire a round in the air and that'll get their attention."

Choc agreed and slipped off to the right side. Luther drew his Colt and went the other way. He hoped the ones he looked for were in this group. The commerce of spirits in the Nation was prohibited, and part of his job was to enforce that law.

"Hands up!" he shouted at the men dancing around the fire. Choc's shotgun shattered the night, and the drunkest man in camp awoke with a loud, "Huh!"

"You're under arrest!" Luther said with a show of his pistol.

He estimated the number of men in camp at eight or nine. But his hold on them for the moment was tenuous. Only the fear of being shot by either lawman held the drunks in place, but how many could they shoot?

The only light was the fire's glare, which cast large shadows beyond their raised arms. Luther recognized the

older of the White Crow brothers, Josh, who looked wild-
eyed and about to flee. If he broke away, so might the
others. Luther leaped to the man and stuck the gun into
Josh's cheek with his other arm gripping the Indian's shoulder.

"Tell them that if they run away, you die!" To enforce
his point, he shoved the Colt harder into the man's face
until the muzzle was jammed against the Crow's teeth.

"Wait! Wait!" Josh shouted to the others, and the fight
went out of them.

Choc disarmed them, tossing knives and firearms aside,
shoving them into a covey against the wagon in the firelight. Luther swung his man around to be certain that no
one came out of the dark and snuck up on them.

"You not take me!" someone shouted. Luther saw the
flash of his white sightless eye. It had to be Curly Meantoe!
Luther had not realized the one-eyed outlaw was among
them. Before he could swing his gun around and shoot at
him, Meantoe ducked beneath the wagon. There was no
chance of Luther firing it without hitting one of the others.
Meantoe fled on his hand and knees, and Choc rushed
around to stop him.

"Stay there!" Luther warned the others, and leveled the
Colt at them. He shoved the brother hard toward them and
felt he had things under control.

Choc came back in a few minutes. "Got away."

"It was Curly Meantoe."

"Yeah," Choc said, sounding disgusted over their loss.
"I didn't know he was even here in all the confusion."

"How many we got here?"

"Five of them that you got warrants for."

Luther smiled at the news. He should have brought Ben.
Then they'd have Meantoe, too. His next concern was how
many allies these men had in this camp who could cause
them problems? People were no longer singing and shouting. They must be coming to see what the shooting was
about.

"Let's get them in irons and be on our way," he said.

"Good idea," Choc agreed, hancuffing them in a chain. He used his pairs and Luther's two cuffs, which was barely enough to make a chain.

"We heard the shots," Windgate said, coming through the ring of onlookers.

"No one is hurt," Luther said. "But I do need their whiskey bottles busted up."

"Yes, we can gladly do that. I am sorry that I did not know these men were here, or that their purpose was not to serve the Lord."

"Big camp," Luther said with a nod. He felt grateful so far that the others did not appear hostile over the arrests. "You bust up the whiskey. It will be payment enough. We will take these outlaws to jail."

"God be with you. Let's do what the man asked," the preacher said to those gathered.

The matter of destruction to be handled, Luther nodded to Choc. Time to make their exit. They started the men toward their horses in the inky night. The inebriated Indians complained and stumbled as they were forced to march.

Filled with growing impatience, Luther figured it took them an hour to get the string of drunks back to their horses. After he released the snorting, happy Ben, he checked the big dipper and guessed it to be past midnight. At this rate, they'd not get back to Moss's before daylight. Oh well, they had several more prisoners this time.

"Both Crow brothers, Yicky Brown." Choc named them off as they rode their horses and led the moaning string of fugitives on a rope. "Taylor Brown is his cousin, and Hankins Farr."

The chorus of complaining drunks staggering along forced Luther to turn around and go back to them on his dun. He checked his horse before them.

"Next man moans or can't stand up, that bulldog of mine's going to bite him in the ass. Do you hear me?"

"Hmm," came their reply in unison. But his threat shut them up and they began to walk a little faster.

*   *   *

In the morning light, Luther went over the rest of the warrants. Seated on his butt, enjoying the coolness of the day, he read off the remaining ones with Choc, who sat cross-legged across from him. They savored Martha's fresh coffee and listened to the birds coming alive in the trees around the grassy place behind the small store.

"Apple Nuggent?"

"He went to Kansas," Choc said.

"He use to live down here?" Luther looked at him with a frown.

"Got in trouble over a woman. He was in bed with her when her husband came home. Decided to change climates." Choc chuckled. "Damn good idea, 'cause her husband would have killed him."

"Louie Benneau?"

"He may be dead."

"What killed him?"

"Had a knife fight at a stomp about a month ago." Choc nodded as if the matter was settled. "He's dead."

With a pencil, Luther wrote *deceased* on the warrant, then read the last two. "That leaves Curly Meantoe and Owen McCantle. You know him, don't you?"

"Sure, Owen McCantle is a big rich man. What did he do?"

"Counterfeit money, it says here."

"He lives at White Soap."

"We better rest today. I didn't get enough sleep last night. Go after him tomorrow."

Choc agreed. "You arresting him? McCantle?"

"Kinda hope he's willing to promise to go in by himself."

"He's a big man." Choc shook his head in disbelief.

"Marshal Williams mentioned that he felt we should handle him with kid gloves."

"He know about it?"

"McCantle?" Luther shook his head. "Guess not. Usually rich men like him have a lawyer warn them, and surrender before the warrant is served."

"Yes. Wonder why—"

"Damned if I know anything about it. Just what Williams said."

Choc pinched some grass off and tossed it into the wind. "You think Williams sent you 'cause you and him don't get along?"

"You think he thought I'd have trouble with the man?"

"You and your boss aren't close friends."

"We've had our differences."

"He didn't like the way you brought in that rich man's son belly down over that horse."

Luther looked away toward the high mountain range in the south, recalling the arrest. "Little smart-mouthed bastard. He wouldn't come peacefully."

"His dad was a banker."

"Yes, in Little Rock. That boy was lucky I even brought him back alive."

Choc nodded and busied himself pinching off more grass.

"Williams got mad, too, 'cause you shot up them Goats."

"Fred and Chester Goats."

"After they ambushed you and you had two bullets in you. My, my, what a shame you had to shoot them both."

Luther exhaled and shook his head. "Yeah, me and the boss don't always get on the greatest." He considered the issue of the rich man's arrest for a long while, then he nodded his head. "He may have sent me after McCantle on purpose."

Choc let the pieces of grass slowly drift one or two at a time. "I was only thinking."

"Yeah." He would, too.

The rest of their day of leisure was spent resetting the shoes on Luther's dun. Several of the prisoners' wives showed up in wagons and cooked for their men. Some even brought clean clothes for them to wear. There were tents set up, tarps strung between trees and wagons. The entire area around Moss's had become a damn circus, to Luther's disgust, but there wasn't a thing he could do about it. This was the way his business went in the Nation.

"When you go Fort Smith?" a big woman demanded, blocking his way.

"Soon," he said, and his answer appeared to satisfy her. She moved aside for him to pass her. He glanced back, wondering how his simple answer appeased her so quickly. It couldn't be *too* soon for him. Maybe this time he could convince Tillie to marry him . . . but deep in his heart, he doubted it. He went over to join his partner in the shade.

"How do you arrest a rich man?" Choc asked as if the problem of taking in the property owner still perplexed him.

"Just do it."

"You think he's guilty?"

"The grand jury decided he must be tried."

Choc nodded as if he understood.

The following day they rode to the White Soap Community. Past noon, they approached the two-story brick house set on a knoll under some giant oaks and pines, in the midst of McCantle's vast fields of cotton and corn. Men, women, and children, busy hoeing in the fields, looked up at them with blank looks.

Concerned about Ben getting into a fight, Luther spoke sharply to him each time some sharecropper's mutt challenged him from the safety of a shack.

They reined up before the big house and Luther dismounted. He looked around the manicured grounds. This must be the finest place in the district. McCantle had to be married to an Indian woman to possess this much land in the Nation. On several occasions, he had seen the man in Fort Smith and knew him on sight, and that he was white.

A tall black servant came to the front door.

"Mr. McCantle home today?" Luther asked.

"Yes, suh. Who may I say is calling?"

"U.S. Deputy Marshal Luther Haskell."

"Very good, suh. I's will tell him."

Luther looked around at the many flowers in the beds and shared a nod with Choc, who waited at the end of the walk with Ben and the horses. He heard the black man returning.

"Come in, suh. Mr. McCantle will see you in his office."

"Thanks." Luther removed his hat, which the man offered to take. He refused, and carried it in his hand.

The polished wood floor sparkled and the sun coming in the tall windows washed the room with light. Fancy, was what Luther called the French sofas and tables made of rich wood set upon Iranian rugs. A huge glass bookcase loaded with volumes lined one wall. Crossing the great room after the man, he glanced up to consider the huge crystal chandelier over his head.

A woman came out on the balcony. Tall and willowy, dressed in a fine blue silk dress, her long dark hair hung unbraided past her shoulders. No doubt from her dark coloration, she was the Indian of this grand house. He gave her a nod.

When he entered the office, a familiar face with a gray mustache and beard rose from behind a desk cluttered with paper. Serious and brooding, the man forced a smile, then extended his hand, which Luther shook.

"Good day, Marshal. What brings you here? Business, no doubt. Have a chair."

Luther handed him the warrant and remained on his feet.

The man picked up a pair of gold wire-rimmed glasses and hooked them behind his ears to examine the paper.

"Go ahead and sit down," he said, and busied himself reading it.

Luther stayed on his feet.

The man set the warrant down, unhooked his glasses, and leaned back. "You're here to arrest me?"

"Yes, but I have considered the matter. If you will agree to ride to Fort Smith and surrender yourself to the chief marshal, I could save you a wagon ride."

"I understand. Fine, Marshal, I will set out for there in the morning. Is that satisfactory?"

"With me, yes. You understand that if you fail to appear, I will come back and physically arrest you?"

"Perfectly. May I offer you food or drink?"

"No, sir."

"My compliments to your boss, Marshal Williams."

"I'll tell him, but you will no doubt see him before I do."

"Oh, you are making arrests in the district?"

"I am. Good day, sir." Luther prepared to leave. He turned the felt hat around on his hand. The band was damp from his perspiration and felt cold to the touch.

"Randolph will show you out."

"No need. I can find my own way."

Luther left the office, nodded to the woman still on the balcony, and hurried across the polished floor, wondering if he wasn't marring the surface with his boots. A current of distrust ran through his thoughts. Maybe the fact that McCantle would never sit for a minute in the hellhole called a jail in the basement of the federal courthouse bothered him the most. Some big lawyer would have his bail set immediately and then wrangle the rich man out of the charges, guilty or innocent. Why someone of his apparent wealth would even mess with counterfeit money was beyond his comprehension. And he might even be innocent, though he found the grand juries empaneled in the federal court usually had sufficient evidence of a felony having been committed before they issued an arrest warrant.

Good to be able to listen to a mockingbird, he decided, outside in the sunshine. He drew a breath of fresh air. Somehow he felt he had emerged from an alien world. At the dun's side, he checked his cinch.

"He in there?" Choc asked in a soft voice, motioning toward the house.

"Yes, I talked to him." Luther swung in the saddle. "He's going to turn himself in."

"What'll they do to him?"

"With a good lawyer, probably dismiss the charges."

Choc nodded and they rode off. Before it was out of sight, Luther twisted and took one more look at the big house. Some place.

"Where's Meantoe gone to?" he asked his posse man.

"Maybe to hide in his big fancy house like McCantle, or to give himself up." Choc laughed. Luther joined him. He could imagine the one-eyed breed living in such an elaborate place and informing him how he would surrender with his lawyer in Fort Smith. Sure would be funny. Only thing, it was true about McCantle and would never be for the rest of the accused they searched for. Two worlds, Luther decided—them that have and them that don't.

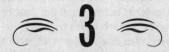

3

Governor John Sterling paced across the carpeted floor with his hands clasped behind his back. Major Gerald Bowen concluded the meaning of Sterling's headlong thrust and the rapid foot pattern on the oriental weaving, meant that something had the governor thoroughly upset. This was nothing new in their relationship. The major knew that the man would soon have an ulcer from all his worrying about things that went wrong in the Arizona Territory. Even before the two of them devised the secret Territorial Marshal Task Force, Sterling had fretted about something every time he summoned him to the mansion.

After the legislature turned down Sterling's request for rangers, the lawmakers, of course, left the lucrative county by county sheriff law enforcement system in place. The Arizona Territory needed an arm of the law that went beyond the sheriff's individual fiefdoms to ever curb the criminals, therefore the marshals. Then to avoid the ire of the legislators, he and Sterling had to be secret and named them as officers of the state court system. A very loose way to avoid controversy, or—they hoped it worked that way, with the governor issuing the agency's wages and expense money from his federally funded court budget.

"You've heard about the hanging of those three ranchers in Christopher Basin?" Sterling demanded.

"It's been on the front page of the *Daily Miner* enough." The Major lit his cigar and sat back in the chair. "Yes. They say that vigilantes hung the three men. It is assumed the victims were rustlers in the area."

"One of them was Theodore Dikes, the son of a very large political contributor from New York State. His father has contacted President Hayes, and the fat is in the fire over his son's lynching. Sheriff Rupp was up here an hour ago. Of course, he's already sent two of his best deputies up there to investigate it, but he says the trail by this time is way too cold to ever learn anything."

"I agree. What else does Rupp think about it?"

"Well . . ." Sterling made a wry face. "I believe Rupp is an honest man. He's maybe one of the few such men wearing a sheriff's badge in the Territory who is honest. Frankly, he thinks the mystery of who did it will go unsolved."

"That means the locals probably know who hung them and won't tell?"

"Yes. In most of these cases, he says they do know and they will protect their own."

"If the president had not wired you?" The major looked hard at Sterling, wondering what would have been his response without pressure from D.C.

"I don't know. His secretary contacted me about the urgency of it, and I have to answer him immediately with my plan."

The major set his cigar down and rubbed his temples with the tips of his fingers. "If Rupp can't learn anything up there, then we need someone to go in there undercover and try to find out who did it."

"Who could do that?" Sterling cast a troubled look at him.

"I'm thinking he needs to be a cowboy or stockman. Needs to fit in with those people and then try to find a crack in their wall of silence."

"How long will that take?"

"Months, I suspect."

"Oh, no, that won't work. I need an answer today about what I am doing out here."

"These Dikes must be powerful people." The major drew his head back and gave him a frown. Why did Sterling always expect immediate results that were impossible?

"They must be very important." Sterling threw his hands in the air. "This may be the most serious thing we do."

The major agreed. "I'm afraid I need to go and find the right man for this job."

"Where?" Sterling blinked his eyes in disbelief.

"Fort Smith, Arkansas."He nodded to himself, pleased with thinking of the place as a source for his new marshal. That should be the spot to find him.

"Why there?" Sterling frowned in disapproval at the notion.

"Judge Parker's court has jurisdiction over western Arkansas, the unassigned lands, and the Indian Territory. His chief marshal has lots of U.S. deputies. Several of them, I understand, have a southern drawl. Most of those ranchers up in Christopher Basin came from Texas, right?"

"Yes, but Fort Smith—that's weeks away from here." Sterling looked frustrated and beside himself at the prospect of more delays.

"Those three men's graves are cold. Another week or so won't hurt them."

"This new marshal that you're going to hire—"

"John, I don't even know his name."

Sterling clapped his hands on both sides of his face. "What will I tell—"

"Tell the president that the local law is working on it. Fire off a letter to that U.S. Marshal Bloom in Tucson."

"Him!" Sterling shook his head. "He'll tell me that lynching isn't a federal crime."

"Good," the major said, on the edge of losing his temper. "But you can tell Washington you have even asked the U.S. marshal to look into it."

Sterling frowned impatiently. "You know Bloom won't do a gawdamn thing."

"I'm going to do something. I'm going home to pack my bags. I'll be at the railhead as fast as I can and catch the first train east. I'll wire you from there."

"Fort Smith?" Sterling crossed his arms and held them. He dropped his gaze to the floor, as if he couldn't fathom the plan.

"That will be our best option to hire a man who can fit

in up there. Perhaps, I say, perhaps . . . he can break the silence."

Sterling squeezed his beard and looked hard at him. "Damn it, doesn't it go against your grain to hire someone you know was a former Reb soldier?"

"Not if he can get the job done."

"It damn sure would me. It would absolutely scald my backside to have to hire one. Oh, go find the man and then we can sit around here and stew until he learns something."

"Sterling?" The major waited. "This will not happen overnight. That man has to worm his way in up there. Don't expect an open and shut door."

Sterling held his hand out to stop him. "I understand. Do it your way and I will face the consequences." He shook his head in disbelief. "We'll have to do it that way. We've no other choice."

"Right. I better go pack."

"Yes, be careful, Gerald. I understand that Fort Smith is even wilder country than Arizona."

"I don't know how it could be," the major said, and left the mansion.

The major had a lot to do. As he made his way downhill to the Walnut Creek Bridge, he considered his new alliance with Ellen Devereau, the madam who ran that high class house of ill repute, the fancy two-story brick Harrington House on the hill. It would do to speak to her about this matter. Women like her learned more in ten minutes than some diligent lawmen could in a month. He would do that upon his return. First, he needed that man in place up there at Fortune, and all this arranging might take as long as a month. So poor Sterling's upset stomach could last for that long. The governor would simply have to wait, if Sheriff Rupp's men didn't turn up anything more in their investigation.

At the house his wife, Mary, helped him pack his bags and acted concerned. "You need to be careful. You aren't a boy anymore."

"Oh, an old man at forty-three, am I?" he teased her.

"You aren't in authority either. You're a retired military officer."

"You're saying I still act like an officer?"

"Well, you aren't one."

He hugged her and laughed. Then he kissed her on the cheek. He would miss her. It was a shame they never had children to share their lives. Wasn't to be, the doctor said. The famous physician they sought back east really had few answers then, and after years without results, they gave up looking forward to ever having any offspring of their own. At different times, they kept several orphaned Indian children, but each one was later claimed by relatives.

He could recall their saddest ordeal, when the squaw came and asked for Betsy Sue. Then they lived in officers' quarters at Fort Bowie. Fine two-story house, and the young Indian girl made it come alive. At her age, which they guessed as seven, she had proven a delight to Mary. Then one day her aunt showed up at the front door and asked for her.

All the Chiricahuas were being sent to the San Carlos Agency. Her aunt felt Betsy should go and be with her people there. When Mary asked Betsy Sue what she wanted, the child, close to tears, hugged her and whispered, "Go with Nan-Nah."

The separation proved hard on Mary. She never spoke of another adoption or caring for a child again. It was like she shut her heart away until they moved to Prescott and she found a new pursuit: her blooming flowers, which were the talk of the town. It pleased the major that she had found a new love to take up a portion of her loss.

The stage for the railhead at Ash Fork left Prescott at four in the afternoon. The driver put the major's bags in the back compartment, spoke cordially to him, and motioned he could get aboard, if he liked. In the flurry of activity around the stage office, the major climbed inside and took the back facing seat.

A long purple ostrich feather came at him first. Like a

shaking bird's head, it probed the inside of the coach. Then the young woman under the hat blinked her long black lashes at him.

"Is that seat taken?"

"No, ma'am."

"No," she said, standing in the aisle and switching her skirt around her narrow waist until it satisfied her. "My name ain't ma'am. It's Lily Corona."

"Lily Corona." He tipped his hat. "Gerald Bowen."

She plopped down beside him in a great show of petticoats and high-top buttoned shoes. Then she pressed her skirt down and turned to smile at him.

"I'm going to St. Louis, Gerald."

"Business or pleasure?"

She gave him a wicked wink. "I do both, Gerald. What do you do?"

"Retired military. I work for the governor."

"I would love to be retired," she said, and looked at her fingernails. They must have satisfied her, for she quickly put her hands down and half turned to look at him. "What do retired people do for the governor?"

"I work for him because I can't live on the money that I retired upon."

"Do interesting things?"

"Like go to Fort Smith to hire a man."

"I've been there," she said, sounding amazed. "I worked in Molly Mather's Cathouse right there on the Arkansas River."

"Guess you saw the seedier side of Fort Smith from there."

"No, not really. I met some really nice marshals when I worked there."

"Did you say lawmen?" he asked. She might know one who would work. He weighed whether he should continue. With her leaving the territory, she couldn't be too great a risk and might even know the man he needed. "You knew some of the marshals that work for the court?"

"A few," she said, and pursed her lips as if satisfied with her intuition.

"Ready to roll," the driver said from on top. He kicked the brakes loose and hurrahed at the horses. The major realized that they would be the only ones on the stage for Ash Fork. In a lurch, the conveyance left Prescott, tossed him from side to side with Lily. The stage cornered the block and headed for Chino Valley.

"Any of these lawmen you knew were real cowboys?" he asked, looking out the open window at Thumb Butte to the west.

"Yeah. One I knew was a drover. Luther Haskell. He's the real thing, if you truly need a drover and a lawman."

"How old is he?"

"Thirty, but he's hard as nails and brings in lots of prisoners. They say he can ride anything with hair on it." Then she laughed aloud at her words and he felt his face grow red.

She slapped his leg. "I didn't mean to sound so rude. You will forgive me?"

"Of course."

"Luther originally came to Fort Smith to sell cattle to the Indian agencies. But them agents was so crooked, he gave up on that. He wanted no part of them. Why, they were giving them poor starving Indians old tough beef they bought dirt cheap and pricing it to the government like it were good stuff."

The major looked out the side window as they passed through the jumbled malapia rocks of the Dells. Luther Haskell might be a man to look up and talk to when he reached Fort Smith. He would keep the name in mind.

"Yeah, he's a real cowboy." She smiled as if there was more unspoken about the lawman. "Good-looking, too."

"Guess that counts," Gerald said, to make conversation.

"Oh, yeah. My, it does. You sometimes get guys that are ugly as a bear. Have to shut your eyes tight. But now Luther's took up with me girlfriend Tillie McQuire." Lily nodded her head as if that were the fact of the matter. "She wrote last week in a letter all about how a couple of months ago him and her captured some marshal killer over in Shack Town."

Gerald nodded. Why in the hell did he have a dove along with him going after a killer? That would be suspect of poor judgment in his book. Yet Haskell was still a lead.

"She said she drove the buggy to run down the scudder, and he jumped off and got him. Must have been hair-raising, don't you think?"

"Must have been. You worked in Preskitt?"

"Naw, I went up to the Crown King district. To the mines. I dealt some cards. But there ain't much money or gold floating around up there. Not like a real gold camp, where them good old boys find some in their sluices every day and come to town every night to spend it. Whoopee! Why, a girl can get rich in them kinda of camps."

"You didn't get rich at Crown King?"

"Naw. But I made some money. Only, you have to be there on the first and fifteenth—that's when the workers get paid at the mine." She made a face like those dates must have posed real work for her. "Like I said, there weren't many good old boys with pokes of gold up there."

"You found one, though?" He chanced aloud what he suspected.

"Yeah, I did." She leaned forward and looked at him as if to say "How did you know?" "That's why I'm going home to see my momma in St. Louis. She ain't well."

"Sorry to hear that."

"Well, she's never claimed me for the past ten years. Mad that I was working in them cathouses and dealing cards. Said it ruined the family name. Hell, I never used that name. Now she's sick and the rest of them worthless kids say they can't help her, so she calls on me." She shook her head. "Wouldn't think she'd want my soiled money, would yah? But she does."

They soon arrived at the Chino Valley relay station and the men came hurrying outside to switch horses. The major felt grateful for the still portion of the ride at last. The driver popped open the door and stuck his mustached face inside.

"Only be here five minutes. Facilities are out back and coffee's inside."

She looked pained at the major, removed her hat, and put it on the vacant seat. "Better go use it," she said, and in a rustle of skirts and petticoats bailed out of the stage. "Be right back."

He swung down to stretch his already sore frame.

"Nice night," the driver said, standing on the porch, cradling a cup of steaming coffee in his hand. "We should be there on time."

The major thanked him, his mind set on the woman's referral. Luther Haskell, a man he wanted to at least talk to at Fort Smith.

The Frisco, more properly called the St. Louis and San Francisco Railroad, made a passenger run out of Monett, Missouri, to Fort Smith, Arkansas, twice a day. The tracks ran north to south over the Ozark Plateau, a familiar land where the major commanded troops during the last three years of the war. The puffing locomotive plowed southward through a recently completed tunnel at the top of the pass in the Boston Mountains, raced over several high wooden trestles, and stopped at Van Buren, then rumbled across the wide muddy Arkansas on a high bridge and arrived at the stone station on the riverbank, where the conductor called out, "Fort Smith, Arkansas!"

Not bad, four days later and he made his destination. This whole United States grew smaller by the minute. Using a handkerchief to mop his neck and perspiring face, he had forgotten about the high humidity of this land.

"Get them bags for ya, suh?" a black man asked.

"Yes. Which is the cleanest hotel?" he asked, surveying the blocks of new multistory brick buildings that lined Garrison Avenue standing against the afternoon's blue sky.

"I's never stayed in one, suh."

"Oh, I see. Take me to the one you think is the best. What's your name, by the way?"

"Dan. Dan Tuney."

"Good, Dan Tuney, you're the man."

"Yes, suh, you's follow me." The lanky built black picked up both bags and started up the grade to the street.

"Where's Molly Mather's place?" he asked, looking around.

"Oh, you's wants to stay there?" The man frowned with concern and confusion in his eyes.

"No." The major chuckled at his reaction. "Later I want to speak to a young lady there."

Dan raised his shoulders in a shrug. "It be down there on the river. Folks goes there for lots of reasons. I guess you can talk all you wants to one of them if you's got the money to pay her."

"I do." The major looked around. Brick streets and gas lights, very impressive layout. Fort Smith's recovery since the war looked impressive. Plenty of traffic. This place was really buzzing.

He hurried to keep up with Dan in the congested sidewalk traffic of men in sea caps from the riverboats, cowboy hats, derbies, and stovepipes. Several Indians wrapped in blankets moved about. Some sat dejected in alleys, obviously having consumed too many spirits. Barkers shouted about the cheap prices and good deals of their respective saloons. Commerce in the city looked full steam. He stayed on Dan's heels.

The Diamond Hotel lobby's hardwood floors shone from a wax polish when the major walked in off the street. An aloof young man behind the desk primped and acted very important. He adjusted his bow tie before he greeted them.

"I need a room for a couple of days," the major said, and looked around at the potted ferns and sofas.

"Has someone recommended you to our establishment?"

"You need that to stay here?"

"We require it, sir."

"General Tecunseh Sherman did."

"Oh, yes, sir. That will be adequate." The clerk opened the register, fanned the pages, and turned the book around for the major to sign.

Smug over his quick answer, he shared a sly smile with Dan, then stepped up. He scratched his name and address on the line and the man produced a key tagged 224.

"That's upstairs and to the right, sir."

"Dan? Let's go," he said. Motioning for him to go first, he fell in behind the black man. They hastily climbed the flight of carpeted steps.

"I's sorry, Major, I never knowed about the recommendation needed stuff. Ain't many of my customers stays in this fancy place," Dan whispered over his shoulder near the top.

"That's fine, Dan. And by the way, I may need a guide. What do you charge by the day?"

"Dollar be a good sum?"

"Fair enough," he said, unlocking the door. "I will be downstairs in half an hour, and you be ready to show me some places in Fort Smith."

"You need a buggy, suh?" Dan put his bags on the bed, opened them, and begun to hang up the major's clothes on the rack in the corner.

"Perhaps later. For now we will use shank's mare."

"Oh, yes, suh, I sure be waiting."

The major tossed him a quarter. Dan caught it double-handed with a clap that drew a wide smile of white teeth and pink gums.

"Half an hour downstairs?"

"Yes, suh-ree."

When he came from his room and stepped out front, he found his man waiting and on his feet. Dan informed him that the best food in town was at the Cotton Cafe. Of course, they parted company at the front door of the resturant. Dan waited outside, for no blacks were allowed in the place. The major ordered southern fried chicken, mashed potatoes, fresh greens, soda biscuits, and iced tea. He called the waiter over before he finished his plate.

"Wrap me two drumsticks and two biscuits in a napkin. My driver will be starved."

"What is his name, sir?"

"Dan. He's out front."

"I will have him come to the back door in the alley and we will feed him whatever you request."

"The whole thing and a slab of apple pie," the major said.

"Very good," the man said, and went to the front door. Through the front glass windows, he could see the waiter talking to Dan. The lanky form took off at a run. Satisfied his man would be fed, he went back to enjoying his own food. The railroad fare had been bad, but this delightful meal restored him.

He finished with a large slice of the apple pie under thick cream and a succulent cup of hot coffee. In no rush, he noticed the grinning Dan had returned out front, busy picking his teeth.

When the major came out, Dan nodded to him. "It sure be okay food and I sure thank you much."

"Good. I need to see the chief U.S. marshal now," the major said, looking up and down the bustling afternoon sidewalk traffic. Attractive ladies with parasols in the latest fashion strolled by. Amongst the crowd, he noticed children dressed in fashionable clothing and other youngsters in rags begging as they went, and quick to dodge a intended kick or clout from an angry drunk.

"Chief marshal, he be at the courthouse." Dan pointed west. "Two blocks that way and two blocks south."

"Good."

"Ah, yes, suh. That was sure good food. Best I done had in a while. Thank you."

"You looked hungry. Tell me about this court business," the major said as they strode down the sidewalk, weaving through traffic.

"That old Judge Parker, he holds court all day and half the night. He be a workhorse, you could say."

"Parker?"

"Yes, suh, Issac C. Parker. He hangs them killers too. Sends them others off to the Detroit federal prison by the carloads. They going to have to build wings on that place pretty soon, he done send so many up there."

"Is he fair?"

"I's don't know. What be fair? Them guys his deputies bring in, they all rough as bears. One guy says that they didn't do that, but they sure enough done did ten things worse than that." Dan laughed and showed his large teeth.

"Do the deputies get paid well?"

Dan shook his head like he wasn't certain. "They gets two dollars an arrest, some mileage and money for food, but they don't get no salary."

The major nodded. He had heard they were only paid for what they did, very similar to what his man had told him. Good. Then the right candidate could be hired for what he could offer him in wages. One hundred fifty a month, and expenses. The task would be picking the right man.

Dan waited for him at the base of the stairs of the federal courthouse. Obviously he did not feel like going up the flight to wait at the white doors on the second floor. Climbing them, the major recalled the Army using these facilities for official business during the war. He entered, removed his hat, and spoke to the receptionist, a young man busy with many official-looking papers spread across his desk.

"Chief marshal in?"

"Who may I say is calling?"

"Major Gerald Bowen."

"Oh, I am sure he will see you, sir." The boy popped up and hurried down the hallway.

In minutes he returned with a bare-headed man who wore a walrus mustache. The man struck out his hand.

"Major, I'm Carl Williams. What may I do for you?"

"Good day, sir. I need a few minutes of your time. In private, sir."

"Come back to my office. You live near here?"

"No, Arizona."

"I knew your face was new to me. Come on in." The man showed him inside a spacious office. Cases of rifles and shotguns lined the wall. A picture of President Hayes and one of George Washington hung on the other wall. Light came in from some high windows and the office felt sweltering.

Williams motioned for him to take a seat and dropped with a creak into a wheel-back, wooden chair behind the cluttered desk.

"I work for the territorial governor of Arizona, John Sterling. I am in need of a man to hire as special undercover agent who is unknown in that region."

"I have some good men. I'll put out the word."

"No." The major reached out. The man didn't understand. He hadn't come over a thousand miles to let the whole damn world know his purpose. "I can't afford for this to leave this room. It might jeopardize the man's life. There are rumbles clear to the White House over this case. Do you understand?"

"Oh, I understand. Sounds like a serious matter."

"That's why I came by myself instead of wiring you. The man I need must be above reproach and he needs to be a cowboy."

Williams sat back in his chair and shook his head in dismay. "You're sure asking for a lot."

"You have any deputies like that I could speak to?"

"A few."

"Which one would be the best one?"

"Nate McMillan."

"Who's he?"

"Served in the Confederate army, sergeant's rank. Has a wife and three—"

"Won't work," the major interrupted him. "He won't want to go out there and be away from his family."

"Guess you're right. I'll have to think on it some more." Williams shook his head, as if he could not recall any other possibility.

"Fine, I am at the Diamond Hotel." The major rose and

handed the man his card. "If you get the name of a possible candidate, let me know."

Strange that this Texan whom the dove spoke about, Luther Haskell, didn't come up in Williams's conversation. Was there something about Haskell he should know about? Maybe he wasn't the man he needed. The notion niggled him as he prepared to leave Williams's office.

"I've got lots of men working for me. I'll go over the roster and see if there's one fits your needs." Williams stood, and stretched his back. "If there isn't one here, where will you go next?"

"Fort Worth."

"Plenty of cowboys around there."

The major agreed and left the chief marshal. Outside, he joined Dan at the base of the stairs. "Where's that whorehouse?"

"My, my, Mr. Major, you sure didn't have much business in there."

"No help in there." He glared at the column of smoke coming from a paddleboat's stack chugging upstream. The notion struck him that he needed to be careful in this town. Some rebel or bushwhacker from the war days might recognize him and still hold a grudge.

"I bets they done got someone up at that place what can sure help you." Dan chuckled to himself and slapped the knees of his wash-worn trousers. "Yes, suh, I bets they sure do."

"Maybe," he said, letting a small grin play in the corner of his mouth.

They walked the four blocks and Dan pointed to the front door of the two-story house. Half a dozen steps led to a wide porch. The sun died in the west, spreading blood-red over the rippled water of the wide Arkansas. A fishy smell hung in the air. The major could hear a tinny piano inside when he reached the door to knock.

"Good evening, sir, and welcome. Come inside. Our rules are no guns, no knifes allowed. Check them here in the hall, then you may go in the parlor," the buxom woman in a green silk dress said. She waited while he unstrapped his holster and wrapped the gun belt around the .45. "I'm Miss Molly."

"Gerald Bowen."

"Fort Smith?" she asked over her shoulder.

"No, Preskitt, Arizona."

She turned back to blink at him. "You are a long way from home, sir. Anything in particular that you have in mind?" She waved to an assortment of girls sitting on the couches with smiles for him. Most were dressed in very little clothing and looked to be teenagers.

"I need to speak to Tillie McQuire."

"Oh. Why, she's upstairs resting, but you may go up and knock on her door."

"Which room?" he asked with his nose full of her potent perfume.

"The last one on the left. Down the hallway."

"Thanks," he said, and started for the staircase.

"You do know your left?" she asked.

He raised that hand and nodded to her with a grin. The woman's words drew a snicker from the parlor girls. He ignored it and climbed the worn steps. At the end of the hallway, he stopped at the open door on the left.

A young woman lounged on the bed wearing something like a black mosquito netting. One exposed white leg cocked up. The other draped over the side. She fanned herself with a funeral-home issue on a stick.

"Excuse me," he said. "You Tillie McQuire?"

"Yes," she said, batting her eyelashes at him between swishes of the fan.

"Lily Corona said that you could help me."

"Lily? Why, she's way out west." She dropped her leg, sat up, and placed them together, which only made it worse because he could see everything through the net material.

"Yes. She said you could introduce me to Luther Haskell."

"You have business with Luther?"

"I need to talk to him." He lowered his voice. "Privately."

"He's supposed to be coming in the next few days," she said, fussing with the filmy material, smoothing it out over her shapely legs.

"He's not here now?"

"In Fort Smith? Oh, no. He's gone to the Kiamish Mountains to serve some warrants." She gathered her long brown hair in both hands and twisted it over her shoulder. "But he will be here by Friday. He promised to take me to supper then."

"Guess he won't disappoint a pretty girl like you?"

She wet her lips and smiled at him. "You're very nice." With an intent glare, she looked him up and down. "You aren't going to hurt him, are you?"

"No, ma'am, I have a business offer to discuss with him. I understand he knows about cattle."

"You don't look like the treacherous kind, anyway." She wrinkled her thin nose to dismiss that. "Oh, yes, he was raised on a ranch, drove lots of them to Kansas."

"My name is on this card. I am staying at the Diamond Hotel. Ask him to contact me."

She took it and shook her head back to loosen her hair. Then she looked up at him and licked her lips again with the tip of her tongue. "Now, what else can I do for you?"

"Nothing. This is for you." He handed her a five-dollar gold piece. "You tell Luther Haskell that I want to talk to him."

"My, my, for this I could sure . . ." She closed one eye seductively. "Let's say, entertain you."

"Not tonight."

"I know," she said, sounding disappointed. "He needs to see you at the hotel."

"Thank you. Is there a back way out of here?" he asked.

"Yes, I'll let you out the back stairs."

"Thanks," he said to her again.

Grateful to at last be out in the still night air, he started down the long flight. Over in the dark inky river, a boat pilot blew a sharp horn. He waved good-bye to Tillie and bounded down the steps. The alley stunk of rotten garbage. He soon made his way to the street and found Dan.

"You leave without paying them girls?" Dan asked, frowning at his appearance coming from the other direction.

The major laughed, then clapped the man on the shoulder. "Where can a black and a white man have a drink together?"

"Blue Aces be the place. You must have sure had a good meeting in there?"

"I did, Dan."

"Well, where we going next, it ain't much of a place—what's wrong?" Dan asked when the major stopped, swept his coat aside, and shook his head. "I need to go back and recover my pistol."

"Oh, you gots in such a hurry, you left it?" Dan laughed some more.

"Something like that."

At last with his hardware retrieved and strapped under his coat, they hurried along the river front to a dive called the Blue Aces. Dan warned him that the crowd might get a little rowdy, but he would't let them shanghai him. The major found that amusing, but didn't doubt it happened in the dimly lit barroom. The floor was hard-packed dirt. At the bar, they enjoyed some halfway cool beer in a tunnel of smoke.

On a small stage under flickering candlelight, a black banjo picker played fast riverboat tunes on the strings and sang some of them. A mulatto teenager in a short red dress pranced and twirled around the musician showing her skin and most of her private areas to the roaring crowd.

Considering his presence in this rather obscene setting, the major wanted to laugh aloud. Mary would never believe him that such a place as this existed. The fact it was only a block or so away from the organized business district and that such a seedy dive could even operate there amused him.

"Hoy, Dan," a big bearded white man said, and pumped

Dan's hand. From under a flat-brimmed wool cap, his greasy, curly locks hung in his brows. He looked intently at Dan as they shook.

"Meet the major here, Scotty," Dan said.

"I be proud to make the acquaintance, mate." The big man's paw felt firm and strong enough to break necks if needed. "Infantry or horse soldier?" he asked.

"Horse."

"Horse, huh? Ah, you ever knew the likes of Georgie Armstrong Custer back then?"

"A time or two. Our paths crossed."

"Ah, may gawd rest his soul good, laddie. At Fort Lincoln, he put me arse in the guardhouse and went off to the war against the bloody Sioux without me. It was a bloody damned shame for me, huh?"

The major toasted him with his pewter mug. "He might have won that battle of Little Big Horn with the likes of you along."

"Hoy, Dan." The Scotsman indicated the major. "He's a helluva great chap for an officer. Where ya been ah-hiding him?"

"Just found him today." Dan beamed a big toothy smile. "Hey, Major, where else ya been?"

"With George Crook in Arizona."

"Aye, I seen him, too, once in Montana. Don't like to wear uniforms, does he?"

"No, he doesn't. Rides mules, too."

"Ah, yeah. See you two. I got to be running away. Got me a little sweet thing from Shack Town waiting for me outside. You boys be good."

"Tomorrow," the major began, "rent us a rig. Fifteen years ago, at the end of the war, I was in Van Buren. I want to see it again."

"Yes, suh, Major. I will show you this whole country if'n you got's the time."

He didn't want to tell Dan that he was only waiting to talk to one man: Luther Haskell. No need to act anyway but interested in looking around. Williams had not acted too eager about giving up any of his men to him. If he failed to find a suitable marshal here, he'd have to go to Texas to get one.

"Say, you seen that head marshal? Tomorrow we can go by and speak to the best black lawman there is over at Van Buren. If him be home. He's really a big lawman for him being a black."

"What's his name?"

"Bass Reeves."

"He's the best?"

"For a black man, he sure be."

"I'd like to meet this Reeves." He might know someone.

The major ordered another round of beer for them. He rather enjoyed Dan's company, and relaxed for the first time since he left Arizona. Sitting in a room full of thugs, pimps, whores, and even stranger individuals, he still felt safe enough with Dan and the Colt under his coat.

In the golden sunlight flooding Garrison Avenue, Dan pulled up the buggy before the Cotton Cafe. The major noticed his arrival, while still eating his breakfast and enjoying a rich cup of coffee. He sent the waiter out to tell Dan to go around back and get his food.

After breakfast, they drove out of Fort Smith, through the farms to the free ferry and crossed the river to Van Buren. The major could see from the landing how much the town had grown since his post-war days in the village. Before they went to Van Buren, Dan planned for them first to drive down in the bottoms to this black lawman's place. Mid-morning, they reached Reeves's neat farm.

The major watched the big man rein up his team of sweating mules, tie off the reins, lay down his double shovel, and come striding over to Dan. His shoulders were wider than most lumberjacks' and he had arms that looked like hams on draft horses. The man's even white teeth sparkled against his clean-shaven jaw.

"Dan, what brings you out here?"

"The major here, Bass. He wants to meet you." Dan

wrapped the reins and jumped down to let the major off.

"Major Bowen. Nice to meet you, Marshal Reeves." He shook the man's huge callused hand. It felt like the black could crush an arm or leg in his powerful grip. The skin of Reeves's palm felt tougher than rawhide from an old bull's hide.

"My pleasure. How can I's help you?"

"I need to hire a marshal to do some work for my agency. He needs to know cattle and ranching."

"That be Luther Haskell."

"Someone else came up with that name." The major considered the man's quick reply. He wanted to ask why Chief Marshal Williams hadn't thought of Haskell. Did he not know his own men that well?

"They done gave you the best name." The big man crossed his massive muscular arms over the faded blue shirt and galluses.

"Why didn't the chief marshal mention him when I asked?"

"Well, that be simple, Major, suh. Some of them boys kinda crowds closer to the chief. That Haskell, he ain't no bootlicker, Major, suh."

"I need a tough man, not a bootlicker."

"That's Haskell. He be plenty tough. I served some warrants with him, down among them black Seminoles, 'cause I could tell them apart." A wide grin crossed his dark shiny face. "Luther's plenty tough. Saved us getting killed when he jerked up the leader of this gang and says to him, 'You got two choices: Tell them throw down their guns, or they better have them some good clothes to wear to your funeral.' " Reeves shook his head and laughed aloud. "Them boys never had no dress clothes, I guess, 'cause they shucked them guns like dry peas in a sheller."

"Thanks," the major said with a smile, and shook the man's hand again. "Sounds like Haskell is the man I'm looking for."

"You needs a real one, he sure is."

"I do, I do. I would appreciate you not saying a thing about this."

"My lips are sealed, suh."

"Good. Dan, let's go see Van Buren. Oh, yes, and many thanks for your help. You still marshaling?" he asked the black lawman.

"Oh, yeah." Then with a knowing look, he said, "They finds a little more work for them white marshals. Course, they ever got a two-headed snake, I gets to go after them. Besides, this corn of mine needs laid by."

"Good-looking crop." The major saluted him and got on the buggy.

Next Dan showed him the bustling river town of Van Buren. From the war shattered village the major recalled from over a decade before, there had been much recovery. In and out of several shops, he looked for some geegaws to take back to Mary. At last he found four crystal salt cellars and had the clerk wrap them well in newspaper for him to carry back. Afterward Dan drove him to the ferry and they arrived back at the hotel close to suppertime.

"I guess until the man returns, we can sightsee," the major said.

"Yes, suh, I be here with this here buggy come morning."

In the next few days, the major and Dan visited the communities around Fort Smith. Out in the Indian Nation, the major even happened to meet an ex-noncom who served under him, Jasper Thornton, who came close to tears when he discovered the major's identity.

With each passing day, the major grew more restless with his waiting. In his letters to Mary, he mentioned the high humidity in the river valley and how he missed the dry, cool air of Prescott. In his writing, he almost spelled it Preskitt, the way the residents pronounced it. Even the Arkansas nights were saturated with humidity. Bathing didn't cool him—he finished each bath sweating worse than before. He looked out the open window of his hotel into the street below. Not a breath of air stirred.

In the distance he heard what sounded like cannon fire. He listened closer and then saw the flashes on the western horizon. A storm was headed toward Fort Smith. Maybe a good rain would cool things down.

He mopped his sweaty brow and turned away from the window. Any relief would be nice. Perhaps this trip would all be in vain. Poor Sterling must have walked a hole in his carpet fretting about him and how to handle the Christopher Basin lynching.

Where was this Luther Haskell?

4

The distant peal of thunder drew a hunch in Luther's shoul-
ders as he drove the team. Already he wore his canvas
duster against the threat of a downpour. He dreaded the icy
cold of raindrops penetrating it, along with the grave dig-
gers that danced across the entire western sky. Those elec-
trifying bolts from the devil had claimed some good
cowboys, friends of his, on cattle drives to Kansas.

He reined up the team at the top of the bank. A slow
grin crossed his face as he rubbed the itchy beard stubble
around his mouth with the back of his hand. There before
him across the inky Arkansas River sat the queen city of
Fort Smith. Ben raised up from the floor, put his paws on
the dash, and sneezed at the sight of it.

From his position, Luther made out the lantern lights on
the ferry and heard the putt-putt of its steam engine coming
across the channel to the west bank landing. No one else
waited on his side. He turned and looked back at the zigzag
pattern of lightning in the western wall. No way he could
get across that river and to the federal courthouse before
the sky opened up. His luck wasn't that good.

"We're going to get our butts wet," he said to the dog.

With each sudden cool gust, the smell of rain grew
stronger than the fishy odors of the Arkansas. He checked
his eight chained prisoners seated in the wagon bed, and
satisfied they were all there, he clucked to the team. Then
using one hand on the brake handle to control his descent,
he started down the slope to the place where the ferry
would soon rest. One of his wards in back had a coughing
spell as the wagon rumbled over the layer of logs.

Luther's thoughts were on Tillie, who waited for him
across the murky river, a bath and a shave away. His pa-

perwork could hold off until morning. The clothes on his body were ready to stand up by themselves. No telling the ticks and chiggers he had attracted in the brush. He might need to take a bath in kerosene to extract the vermin. It would be heavenly to lie in a real bed, eat something besides that Indian girl Martha's burnt cooking, and feel clean again. Whew. He would have to pinch himself to believe those three weeks were finally over.

Eight prisoners, at two bucks a head. The mileage at ten cents. A buck a day to feed them, he might make thirty dollars for his efforts. Plus he needed to collect Choc's posse man wages for a dollar a day and send it to him. He drew back on the reins and set the brake to scotch the wheels. At this rate of pay he would be plumb rich, just any day. He tied off the lines and jumped down to limber his stiff muscles.

The ferry drew closer. There were rigs aboard the barge and he left them enough room to let their rigs off and past his.

"Hey, that you, Marshal Haskell?" the deckhand, Charlie O'Toole, shouted, jumping off and securing the lines as the pilot nosed it up tight.

"Yes, it's me, Charlie. We're about to get wet."

"I'd say so. Be ready for you to board in a minute."

"Fine." Luther studied the first buggy coming off with a hesitant horse, but it was too dark to see who drove it. In a bolt, the startled horse leaped off the ferry. The poor driver cursing and trying to haul him down went bumping past him up the corduroy slope. The other customer drove a pair of mules and wagon, a teamster, a real one. The man coaxed them off the ferry over the growing wind and thunder onto the landing and past Luther's rig.

Leaves and branches rattled in the trees overhead. The storm drummed closer. Rain came in huge drops. Luther jumped upon the wagon, undid the lines, and drove his team with his dun horse hitched to the tailgate on the deck. His outfit at last was on board. The deckhand scotched the wagon wheels for him. Luther climbed down to stand on the deck in the driving rain.

"How many you got this time?" Charlie asked, over the growing storm's fury.

"Eight."

The pilot reversed his engine and they snaked away from the bank. Waves sprayed over the sides and Luther's team stomped around on the hollow-sounding deck. He and Charlie turned their backs to the growing force and the sky opened up.

Docked at the end of Garrison, with jagged streaks overhead and booms rattling the air, Luther drove off the ferry in a blinding deluge. From the main street, he turned the rig south and soon drew up in front of the federal courthouse. Ignoring the complaints of his wards in back, he went up the stairs in the roaring downpour.

"I've got eight prisoners outside," he said to the captain of the guard seated behind his desk.

"Well, are they drowned?" the man asked, rising and slipping on a rubber raincoat.

"Half," Luther said.

The captain buttoned his rubber coat, then drew down a sawed-off shotgun from the rack and went outside with him. Lightning struck close by. The flash was blinding, and the thunder was loud enough to deafen Luther for a moment. He ordered the soaked prisoners to disembark. They needed little encouragement. Holding wet blankets over themselves and their chains, they looked around like they expected to be struck dead any moment.

All eight were finally inside the shelter of the basement. The jailers searched each man, then unlocked their leg irons one at a time.

"I'll make you a receipt for them," the captain said.

The building trembled with a loud strike outside. That one was close. Ben tore into the alcove like something had chased him. He dropped to his butt and then sneezed.

"Your bulldog's got him a cold?" one of the jailers asked, making conversation and looking him over.

"No. He don't like the smell of this jail."

"Have to admit it damn sure ain't roses."

Luther laughed with the man.

An hour later, with his three horses stabled at the livery, he left Ben for the night with them. It beat having to pull him off the strays that slunk around Garrison. In the drizzling rain, Luther made his way for the bathhouse. Delays, delays, delays. He wondered if he would ever get to Tillie. That was the part of his return he looked forward to the most. First things first. No way that he could go to see her smelling like a wet horse. He took the stairs into the basement shop two by two.

"Damn you, Chink!" The words sounded tough as Luther pushed in the door. A bell tinkled over his head.

"You highway-robbing yellow bastard!" The man's back was turned to Luther. He had the Chinese owner of the bathhouse by a fistful of his kimono.

"Hey," Luther said with a frown. "What's your beef with Chang?"

"Mind your own gawdamn business." The man jerked Chang up and halfway across the counter. "I ain't paying for no damn—"

Luther whipped out his .45 and with all his force, laid the barrel on the edge of the man's head. Like a poled steer, he went down to his knees and let go of the short Chang. The second lick sent him facedown on the cement floor.

"Oh, very sorree!" Chang shouted. He boosted himself up to look over the counter at the moaning man.

"Who in the hell is he?" Luther stuck the Colt back and put his hands on his hips to appraise the situation.

"Man's name is Hopkins."

"Go get a policeman. Hopkins needs to be locked up. I can smell liquor on him."

"Madman, him say we ruined his clothes! No payee for washing them."

"What happened?"

"All rotten. Fall apart when wash them. No can help it." Chang held out his small hands in defeat. His poor wife huddled, moaning in fear the end of the world was about to strike them both.

"I understand. Go and get a patrolman. He can handle him."

"No want trouble with law." The small man shook his head vehemently.

"Okay, I'll handle him." Luther realized the poor Chinese man felt any dealing with police would turn out badly for him. The Chinese were to be seen and not heard. Poor Chang probably already paid a hefty weekly *business fee* to one of them on the beat. Luther reached down, collared the disoriented drunk, and half dragged him to the door.

Then in the dowpour, he hustled him up the stairs by the coat collar. Once on the street, he looked around. Never a policeman around when you needed one.

"Who the hell are you?" the drunk slurred, and swung his arms around loosely.

Luther didn't bother answering him. He shoved his prisoner in the direction of Garrison. Surely there would be a cop there. Under a gas lamp and on the main street, Luther could see the rain coming down diagonally.

"Police!" he shouted. Then with growing anger, he searched the wet night. Someone was coming in a hurry. Maybe a cop.

"You—" The drunk never got his threatening words out. Luther spun him around and drove his head into the lamp pole with a clunk. The man fell face down.

"What's happened here?" the policeman demanded, brandishing his billy club.

"This drunk ruined my bath. Threatened law-abiding citizens. Throw him in the tank and sober him up."

"I guess you'll be filing charges."

"Not tonight." Luther looked at the man like he had lost his mind.

"We can't hold him—"

"Just lock him up," he shouted, with water running like a river off the brim of his hat. "Take my word for it, he's drunk and disorderly."

"In his present state . . ." The policeman shook his head as if there was no way for him to handle the matter.

"Then let's say I shoot the sumbitch. Then what can you do?"

"You're one of them bloody marshals, now ain't yeah?"

"It's going to be bloody around here in few minutes if you don't do something."

The cop held out his hands. "All right, all right, I'm taking him in."

"Why couldn't you do that in the first place?" Luther turned on his heel and headed through the downpour the block back to Chang's. Damn. He'd wasted enough time arguing with that dumb cop to take two baths. And Tillie was still waiting. My heavens, he hoped so.

Hours later in her room, he lay for a long while on his back in her bed and studied the tin ceiling panels in the lamplight. Memories of their very physical tryst drew a smile on his tight mouth. The smell of her new perfume imbedded in his nose, he swung his legs over the side of the bed and went to the smudged window to look out. A faint crack of dawn had begun out there. His brain still in a daze from their torrid activities, he looked around to see her return, wrapped in the black net robe. Why she even bothered wearing it he couldn't decide. He could see through it like she had nothing on. Cooler in the summer to wear it, she claimed.

"Oh, yes," she said, standing in the doorway. "A Major Bowen over at the Diamond Hotel wants to see you."

He blinked and hauled up his pants. "What's his business?"

She went to the dresser, picked up a card, and read it. "Only says that he's a retired major on this."

He padded across the pine flooring in his bare feet. Taking the card, he held it to the lamp. Bowen, all right. Prescott, Arizona Territory. Who was he?

"Must want to see you badly. He paid me five in gold to tell you that."

He backed up and dropped his butt on the bed. Then,

shaking out his sock, he smiled at her. "Didn't he want any other services for that price?"

"You can believe me or not. I think he was embarrassed to be here." She shrugged her shoulders under the netting, then leaned her face against the edge of the door. "He was very nice. I let him out the back way."

"What does this major look like?"

"Stocky, but shorter than you. Sandy brown hair. Maybe in his forties, but he stands very erect." She threw her shoulders back and her exposed breasts pointed through the net material.

Luther shook his head in amusement and laughed. "He damn sure must have impressed you."

"Hey, he wasn't some bum off the sidewalk."

"When does he want to see me?"

"I guess when you got back." She shook her head in disapproval. "I figured it was too late last night to go see him when you got here. Then I about forgot him."

"Major Gerald Bowen, huh?" he said it more to himself than to her. "Guess I better go see him."

"Ain't you ever going to sleep? I'm so tired, my eyes won't stay open."

"You can do that anytime," he said, and with his boots on, he stood.

"Not me." She moved in front of him and ran her palms over the hair on his chest. "Kiss me and don't come back for a while. If you're leaving, I'm going to bed."

He kissed her. "I may play some cards for a while if he ain't up yet." Then with a playful swat on her heinie, he sent her toward the bed.

Luther started the four blocks to the Diamond Hotel. The temperature felt cooler than in weeks past, and the rain had freshened the air. Things were beginning to stir on Garrison. Mop buckets of slop were being unceremoniously dumped off the curb; sounds of a tinny piano carried to his ears.

"Wait! Wait!"

Luther turned and looked around. A lanky black man hurried to catch up.

"What do you need?" Luther asked. He certainly didn't know him. What was his purpose in stopping him there on the street?

"You be Luther Haskell?" the black asked, out of breath

"I am."

A warm smile filled the man's dark face. "Lordy, that major, he's sure going to be pleased to see you. I'm Dan, Dan Tuney."

"Dan, you're the second person told me that today," Luther said, and the two headed up the sidewalk.

"Ah, you been talking to that girl he seen at Miss Molly's?"

"Yes. You work for him?"

"I sure do and I'm sure going to miss him when he leaves."

"What's he like?"

Dan shrugged, then went to bobbing his head as they walked. "He's a big man. And he don't mind to have a beer with a black man in a bar. You'd know what I means? He done shook hands with Bass Reeves like he was someone."

"Bass *is* someone. What was he seeing Bass about?"

"About you's, I reckon."

"Where is he, this major?"

"Right in there." Dan pointed to the Cotton Cafe window. Then he clapped Luther on the arm and nodded to the man inside. "This him, Major. This him. I found him for you."

Luther thanked Dan and went inside the restaurant. The sandy-headed man did look stockily built. He felt the major's keen eyes inspecting him as he crossed to the table.

"Have a chair, Haskell," the major said, standing and extended his hand.

"Obliged," Luther said and took his place.

"You come in during the storm last night?" the major asked, waving a waiter over. "You haven't had breakfast yet, have you?"

"No, but anything's fine." Luther held up his hands in surrender.

"Bring him a large platter," the major ordered, and the waiter poured Luther's coffee into a china cup from a silver urn. "Where were we? Oh, yes, the storm?"

"I almost got my wagon here, but it caught me."

"I was told you have been off in the Kiamish Mountains serving warrants?"

Settled in the large straight-back chair, Luther considered the man's erect posture and take-charge manner. He could be a tough man to cross or to anger. What was his business? More than that, what did he want with him?

"Bass Reeves says you're a tough lawman."

"You know Bass?"

"Dan, my guide, does. I spoke to Reeves earlier this week."

"You need a lawman?"

The major quit cutting his ham and raised his gaze. "I need a tough one."

"Sounds interesting enough."

"Interesting enough to go undercover for several months to ferret out some killers?" He waited for a reply.

"Who, why, and where?" Luther blinked in disbelief at the platter of eggs, ham, biscuits, gravy, and grits that the waiter delivered. He nodded to the man.

The major looked around to be certain no one was listening, then began to explain the details of his territorial marshal force. After completing the explanation, he told him about the triple lynching and the political ramifications for the governor.

"That trail, like the sheriff said, is sure cold by this time," Luther said, wondering about the low chances for his success.

With a forkful of egg, the major paused. "You know, in every chain there's one link weaker than the rest. You would have to find that link."

"And let's say that after a few months I can't make a crack in the case?"

"Then we'll have other enforcement matters for you to attend to. The job of cleaning up this territory is endless, as far as I can see. Eat your food. It's getting cold."

Luther agreed. He took a bite of the soda biscuit. It melted in his mouth and filled it with saliva. One other thing the man had not mentioned was money.

"You've never been to Arizona?" the major asked.

"No. Drove a herd of cattle into eastern New Mexico is close as I ever came to it."

"Good, then maybe we can keep your identity concealed. Job pays one fifty a month plus expenses."

Masticating the biscuit, Luther nodded slowly, considering the excellent salary. Sounded a damn site easier and better paying than being a deputy U.S. marshal. It came as a quick reminder of the past three weeks making various arrest of hard cases, caring for the prisoners and all the rest. Arizona couldn't be worse than the Nation.

"I'll take it. When does it start?"

"I first need to arrange a cover for you. I think we can make a connection with a cattle broker. Then you can ride into the Christopher Basin country with a reason to be there. You do know cattle?"

"I made a living buying and driving them to Kansas, till the railroads put me out of business. Where do you need me?"

"Winslow, Arizona, for a jumping off place. It's on the Kansas Pacific tracks. Give me two weeks. And, Luther?"

"Yes?"

"Don't tell a soul where you're going."

"I understand. You'll send my orders here?"

"Yes. I will send you your orders here. So you stay in Fort Smith until I can arrange everything out there."

Good. Luther nodded that he heard the plan, then savored a bite of the sweet, smoke-cured ham. That would give him time to sell his team wagon and stock and maybe find a good buyer for them if he wasn't rushed. The major had it all lined out. A new job in a new land. Posing as a cattle buyer shouldn't be too hard. He looked over his plate of food. He had hardly put a dent in it.

The major went on to tell him about the other marshals in his force and their operations. He concluded with, "You can see with only Sam T., John Wesley, and you, we're a small force. The politicians and sheriffs wouldn't take to the notion of this marshal business if they realized the full extent of our operation, but that's too damn bad. We're officers of the court. Our job is to enforce the law. Be polite, but firm. Let them have the headlines. Some will work with you. Others may even be in with the local out-laws."

"Why hire me?" Luther paused in his eating.

"Your reputation. You have some good referrals. Bass Reeves was one. Another a young lady, Lily Corona, whom I met on the stage to Ash Fork."

Luther nodded. "That's different. A black man and a whore recommended me." He chuckled to himself.

"You know why I put so much weight on that?"

"No."

"They both had nothing to gain by telling me the truth."

"I can savvy that, Major."

"A man once told me, don't hire a boy when you need a man." The major's brown eyes were hard set in expectation when he said it.

"Must have been my paw." Luther smiled and nodded in agreement. "Now tell me something. You never asked about my military?"

"Did I need to?"

"No, but I figured you wore a shiny blue uniform."

"You're wondering why I'd hire a former reb?"

"Lot's of folks are prejudiced." Luther shrugged, taking another forkful of eggs.

"Including the chief marshal?"

"I said, lots of folks."

"I needed a man for the badge."

"Good enough."

"And, Luther, those two other marshals served under me

during the war. I knew them well. But you won't be any less a member of this force than them. We've got a big job to do together. It's a new war and a tough one. It's either us or lawlessness will prevail."

Luther slumped back in the chair and slowly nodded. He liked this man who didn't mince words. Major Gerald Bowen might be all right to work for. He felt an edge of excitement and anticipation. The territorial marshal job? Yes. It would be all right.

5

Fluffy clouds gathered along the towering rim. It would rain somewhere in Christopher Basin by mid-afternoon. Matt pushed the buggy horse in a long trot on the Fortune road through the pines. Dropping down the grade, he could see the open meadow country. A horse and rider waited ahead. He recognized Charboneau's big gray horse. The man appeared to be by himself.

What was he up to? Drawing closer, he noticed the gray's shoulders were dark with sweat.

"Good morning," Matt offered as he reined up his single footed horse. The squat man in the saddle removed his Stetson and wiped his face on his sleeve.

"That sheriff he sent two deputies up here."

"To count cows and up our taxes?" Matt grinned to make a joke of the matter.

"No. They're asking lots of questions about those three." Charboneau's eyes darkened and he frowned. "I mean they're asking tough questions."

"Let them. What can they learn?"

Charboneau shrugged his thick shoulders. "I don't know, but I don't like it none."

Matt waved away his concern. "They can't prove anything."

"Unless someone talks."

"No one is that foolish."

"You better be sure to button Porter's lip. I think he might explode about it." The hard glare in the man's dark eyes told Matt enough.

Charboneau was upset about Reed Porter's mouth. Matt considered the man's words for a moment. "You know anything about Reed doing any loose talking?"

"No, but I think we better gawdamn sure watch him. He ain't very strong. They press him, he might talk." Charboneau shook his head ruefully.

Matt nodded. He understood the man's concern. He would have to do something about Reed Porter to keep him quiet. They all had way too much at stake to let one of their numbers talk.

"Where are those deputies now?" he asked.

"Riding all over. I ain't seen them since yesterday."

"Who are they?"

"Hank Killiam and Wylie something, I can't recall his last name." Charboneau's gelding stomped his hind foot at a fly.

"Don't know them."

"Hey, they're tough enough. Not some cow counters like he usually sends."

"In a week or two they'll lose interest," Matt said to settle some of the man's concern.

Charboneau ran the web of his hand over his drooping mustache. "I sure hope you're right, but the word is out that the Dikes family is offering a big reward for the arrest of his hangmen."

"Hasn't ever been anyone tried for that in the territory yet."

"Listen, Matt, I don't want to even be near a courtroom."

"You won't. I'll handle Reed Porter."

"You better. See ya." Charboneau turned his gray and headed north across the meadow. Matt watched him disappear into the trees, then he flicked the reins at the bay. Charboneau acted much more concerned than he'd expected. Up until that moment, he considered the man a safe bet, but if those lawmen upset the Frenchman that badly, they could push Porter off the brink. What next? He had planned to have his lawyer, Grayson Bond, start the paperwork on procuring Dikes's place. That better wait.

Matt reached Fortune at noon. His plans were to have a drink first, then take some lunch. He drove the bay past the weed-crowded shipping pens and up the single street lined with houses, false-front buildings, and the two-story hotel.

The town's farrier was shoeing a horse in front of the livery when Matt passed. Several ladies graced the boardwalks and porches. Matt tipped his hat to them and reined the bay around the side into the shade of the Texas Saloon.

He hitched the horse and paused on the boardwalk. A small boy with a bucket of foaming beer parted the doors. He raised his blue eyes to look up, then said, "Got to get this to them workers," in an Irish brogue that brought a smile to Matt's lips. He watched the bare feet churn up dust off the hard-packed street as the boy flew away to wet down his charges.

"What'll it be, Mr. McKean?" the barkeep, Earl Duffy, asked, making a swipe with his rag to polish the surface.

"Double rye," he said, looking around. A few cowboys sat at a back table playing cards. They must be out of work to be in there that time of day. None of his business. He certainly didn't need any more men on his payroll.

Matt paid Earl two bits for the drink and in two tosses had the dust-cutting whiskey down his throat. The sharp liquor also warmed his ears and settled his stomach.

"Got lunch out," Earl offered, meaning the food on the sideboard. Boiled eggs. Crackers. Pickled herring and cheese.

"No, thanks. Where's Lincoln today?"

"Took the day off. Business is slow in midweek."

Matt hated the fact that the bar's owner wasn't there. Lincoln Jeffries knew everything that went on in the basin. Matt had hoped to learn more about those nosey deputies from him. The lawmen would be by sooner or later to question him, since he was the leader of the party that cut them down.

Strange, they hadn't been by his place so far. He shrugged off the notion. Lots of difference between being a suspect and proving the fact. What could they find out? Nothing. He thanked Earl, said he'd be back, and went across the street to Lonigan's Cafe.

Matt sat at the counter. Farnam Brown, the long drink

of water who recently married the cafe owner, Mary Sue, stood with a toothpick in the corner of his mouth and brought him a stained white cup full of coffee.

"We got pot roast today," Farnam offered.

Matt agreed that would do, familiar with Mary Sue's tasty dishes. He cradled the cup in his hand and watched the former ranch hand's slender figure snake his way to the back for the order. Lonigan died a few years earlier of a busted appendix. Farnum hung around until Mary Sue said yes, then he quit cowboying to help her run the place. Most folks thought her cooking would fatten him, but he must have tapeworms, Matt decided, because Farnam was still the skinniest guy in the basin At six four, he made a string bean.

"How's the cattle price holding?" Farnam asked when he came back from the kitchen and used the toothpick to explore his back molars.

"Ain't certain. Last I heard, you could contract some for last year's price. You into cattle?" Matt asked.

"Yeah, I got a few head."

"You register a brand?"

"Bought one, Seven Y."

"I ain't seen it."

"Aw, all I got is half a dozen head of sorry heifers that I got down in the valley. But I aim to have me a herd of my own someday." Farnam bobbed his head as if in deep thought about the matter of his future livestock empire.

Why, Matt wondered, did every old ranny want to be in the ranching business? Burned him to a crisp, but he shielded his feelings.

"How much's that Teddy Dikes's place worth?" Farnam asked.

"I ain't got half an idea. Not much." The notion of Farnam's interest in Dikes's outfit formed a ball in the pit of Matt's stomach. Only days before he thought the whole thing would work out smooth and in a few months he would have control of the place. Now Farnam wanted in on the deal.

"Figured that it should sell cheap." Farnam took the toothpick from his mouth. "That way, maybe, Mary Sue and I could afford it for a starter. We've got some money saved."

Matt felt grateful for the sight of the buxom Mary Sue as she brought him the plateful of meat, potatoes, carrots, onions, and plenty of her sourdough bread. Gave him an excuse to shut up about the matter.

"You all right, Matthew?" she asked.

"Fine, Mary Sue. Better now that I have some of your good food."

"Need more, you just send the plate back." She gave him a friendly smile.

"Aw, this ought to fill me fuller than I need to be."

"Good to see you," she said, and went back in the kitchen.

"Keep your ears open about that place for me," Farnam said.

"I will," Matt promised. "I sure will." Matter of fact, he planned to see Grayson Bond, his attorney, when he finished his lunch. No time to be respectful about buying Dikes's place, or some other rat would pop into the vacant nest.

Grayson's cubbyhole was behind the assayers' and claims' office. The lawyer looked up from his notes when Matt walked through the door. Coatless, tie loose, with his sleeves rolled up, Grayson appeared busy. He acknowledged Matt, then turned back to the papers before him.

"Be a minute." Grayson held up his left hand. "Take a chair."

"Must be important, you're that engrossed."

"Point of law. Searching for an answer." At last, Grayson made the effort of tearing himself away from the page and looked across at Matt.

"What's happening with you?"

Matt considered their privacy, then leaned forward. "I want you to quietly get hold of Dikes's place for me."

"The boy that got lynched? His place?"

"Yes, that rustler that they are all crying over. Listen, Grayson, I intended to let the ruckus die down, then contact his parents or buy it at a sheriff's sale, but there is some kind of damn land rush up here."

"Yes, there is."

Matt frowned. "Who else wants it?"

"Some cattle company out of the valley contacted me yesterday."

"Who the hell are they?" All he needed was more competition for the short grass and water.

Grayson went through his papers. "I never heard of them. Here it is. Flat Iron Cattle Company." He held up the stationery and studied the signature. "John O'Malley, president."

"They're planning on moving cattle in the basin?"

Grayson nodded. "More than likely. They're probably looking for a headquarters to set up in. How bad do you want that place?"

"Get a price, I'll see if I can swing it. We damn sure don't need some big cattle company in here, too."

"I'll do that. May have to go to Prescott to get all the details."

"Whatever." Matt rose; his stomach churned over his latest discovery. "And let me know what you can find out about this Flat Iron outfit."

"I will," Grayson agreed as he stood up. They shook hands and Matt left the office. He wanted to go back to the saloon and drink a tub of whiskey.

For a long moment, he stood outside the office in the warm afternoon sun and considered his next move. The distant roll of thunder made him look up at the encroaching dark clouds. In a few minutes, there would be a monsoon shower, like every summer afternoon somewhere along the Mongollon Rim. Better find himself a dry place for a while. The upsetting news about another big outfit moving in his range niggled at him all the way to the porch of the mercantile.

Then he recalled that Jakes had told him he needed horseshoe nails.

Rain drummed on the tin roof of the mercantile. Robert, the son of the proprietor, weighted him out ten pounds of nails and put them in an empty keg. Robert then asked if he needed anything else.

"No, put it on my bill. I guess as hard as it's raining, I need to stay in here until it passes." Matt indicated the roar of the downpour on the roof over them.

"Sounds like a real one," the boy said, and finished marking down the sale. He held the receipt out for Matt's inspection.

"Your dad gone today?" Matt asked as he approved it with a nod.

"Gone to Flag to get new stock."

"He may be getting wet."

"We can always use rain in Arizona, so I guess it won't hurt him."

"How right you are," Matt agreed with the youth's wisdom, and went to the front door to watch the slashing storm. It spilled off the porch eaves in sheets. He hoped some of this would fall up on his range and not in some small circle around the town.

He needed a meeting with the others. What could they do about a big outfit moving into their country? It was all public domain, belonged to the government; all they had were the small claims to their places. Still the unwritten law was . . . he paused. It belonged to the users. If that Flat Iron moved in, they'd be users, too.

A bright flash of lightning blinded him for a second. Thunder boomed overhead close enough to make him duck. He saw a heckuva wreck coming if that new outfit pushed more stock in this range. Better hold a Basin Stockman's meeting. He would need the others. Deep in his concerns over the latest turn of events, he absently scratched an itch behind his right ear.

What could they do? More thunder boomed close by.

Two men in yellow raincoats rode up, dismounted,

hitched their rain-slicked horses, and ran onto the porch.

"Whew," the shorter man said, looking back at the downpour from the safety of the porch.

"Afternoon," the younger and taller one said to Matt. His blue eyes looked him over critically. Matt decided they were the lawmen. "Name's Hank Killiam. This is Wylie Green. We're Sheriff Rupp's deputies. You're Matt McKean, right?"

"Yes, I heard you boys were up here."

"You were with the party cut them down, Mr. McKean?" Killiam asked.

"Yes, I was there that night. Not a nice scene."

Killiam nodded, then used his thumb to force his sodden hat up higher. "You have any idea who did it?"

"Vigilantes, I guess."

"Vigilantes have names behind those masks," Green cut in.

"I wasn't there for that. I did my duty as a citizen and helped cut them down." Blinding lightning flashed over the buildings across the street and thunder crashed on top of them.

"Oh, we never said you were there for the lynching."

Matt frowned at the younger man. "I wasn't there."

"Mr. McKean, you're a big man in the basin. Have lots of cattle wearing your brand. You ever know of any rustling by those three men?"

"There's been plenty of rustling up here. But no, I never saw any of them rustling my cattle."

"You see any blotted brands?"

"A few."

"Guess you think this lynching will end the rustling in the basin?" Killiam asked.

"The lynching?" Matt frowned at the pair as they unbuttoned their slickers before him.

"Right. Those three weren't hung for picking their noses. It's easier to sleep nights with them rustlers gone, isn't it?"

"I don't hold with taking the law into your own hands."

"Mr. McKean, some folks in this country did that,"

Green said with a hard set to his eyes. "Can you furnish us any names?"

"I told you, I was at the dance when word came they were hung. I did my—"

"Civic duty," Killiam butted in. "We've talked to lots of folks done that, too. You know, without any proof that them three rustled any cattle in this country, it surely makes their deaths out-and-out murder."

"I guess that's your jobs to prove it," Matt said. An edge of impatience creeping in his voice that he found hard to restrain.

Killiam nodded. "That's right. You don't have any idea who hung them?"

"None whatsoever."

"Damn strange to me," Green said with a hard frown. "Three men were hung in broad daylight, and ain't one sumbitch knows a living thing about it in the entire country."

The clouds began breaking up. Sunshine glistened on the wet pine needles. Thunder moved over the ridge. The last drips off the eaves splashed into the puddles on the ground. A rig coming down the street sliced though the watery slop.

"Tell Sheriff Rupp that I send my greetings," Matt said. They needed to know he had contributed money to the man's last campaign. Those two acted a little out of line to his notion.

"We will, Mr. McKean. And if you think of anything else about the lynching, let us know. We'll be stationed up here at Fortune for some time," Killiam said.

Matt left the porch. He wanted a drink, and bad. He turned back at Robert's calling after him, "Don't forget your horseshoe nails, Mr. McKean."

"I won't," he promised as the wetness soon soaked through his thin, handmade boots crossing back to the Texas. He glanced down in disapproval at the brown mud on them. More concerned about his answers to the pair than his footwear, he tried to reappraise the interview. Had he given them anything to go on? No. But those two were tough enough. They might get someone to talk. Let something slip, and they would pounce on it like a hawk on a mouse.

The best example of someone with a weakness would be Reed Porter. How had he done with them? No telling, but so far the two lawmen probably knew very little. He needed to keep it that way.

6

"So you're just up and leaving me?" Tillie McQuire asked with her hands on her hips.

"I could probably send you money in six months to come out there." He gave her a pained glance over his shoulder. Blocking the light from the window, he appeared engrossed with the view through the dirty glass. "The first part of my new job is undercover work. I wouldn't have a way to meet with you."

"Undercover?" What does that mean? Tillie wondered. Sometimes he made little sense.

"I'm going to be a spy," he said with an edge of impatience.

"Oh. Isn't that dangerous?"

"All law work's got its share of danger to it. The secret is not letting them figure out who you are." He shrugged his shoulders under the galluses crossed behind his back.

"What are you spying on?"

"I really can't say."

"You are leaving me . . ." She fought back the knot in her throat. "And it's so damn secret you can't say a thing?"

He turned on his heels and looked at her with a new-found hardness in his silver eyes. They were more like steel than blue. She felt them like daggers stabbing her aching heart. She wet her lips and clutched the chenille robe tighter around her body.

"Tillie, we once promised to be honest with each other. You have your job." He held out his hands and spread his fingers as if in surrender. "I have mine. You didn't want to give this up and become my wife."

She agreed to his statement about marriage with a nod. The deep-rooted sentiment she felt at losing him could not overcome her fear of being a scrubwoman on her knees. That was being a wife to her. No. She would take her chances on her back in this bed. Housewife. Slave. No. Never. She closed her eyes to the idea of him leaving her and tears ran down her face.

"I've offered to find a preacher."

"You did, b-but I never counted on losing you!"

"I told the major I would take this job." He closed his eyes and shook his head. "What do you expect of me next?"

"It must pay well?"

"Yes. There's a good salary. We could live well on it."

"Get out!" she screamed, unable to control her remorse a moment longer. "Go be a spy—I don't know what . . ." She pointed to the door and stomped her foot. "Get away from me!"

"Tillie?"

"Don't Tillie me!" In a rush, she grabbed all his things, handed them to him, then shoved him out the room and slammed the door in his face. She braced her shoulder against it to hold it shut, in case he even tried to reenter it. Tears streamed down her face. There were no sounds beyond the thin door. She pressed her ear to it—hoping he would come back. Beg. Plead with her. Relent his plans to go out there. Nothing. Then her knees buckled and she crumpled to the floor.

The one man in her life who never lied. Who had even offered her respectability and she had rejected it. She'd sent him away and he'd left her life . . . forever. Why had she told him no?

She knew the answer was in the bitter memories of her mother's dreary life, and her own growing up. Bitterly she recalled how her mother slaved over wood fires, beat clothes clean with rocks, carried crying babies on her hip, and did without food, dry shelter, and adequate clothes. Did without those things that Tilie's profession provided. Sure, she and her sisters in this house of sin were an abomination in the eyes of society, but where were those church sisters when all that she had to eat were her own tears?

In the depth of her self-pity she paused and heard her own wails that sounded like a pack of wolves over the ridge. Her body felt far removed from her mind. She knew her soul must be riding on a cloud, the one she rode as a girl to escape the brutal lashes of a peach branch that her father delivered at the slightest notion.

"I'm a going to drive the devil out you, Tillie May," he would say, then roughly bent her over his knee. Those words stung her as hard as the lashes did on her bare legs. Her mother's protests were far away and ignored. Afterward, her mother got a severe whipping as well for interfering.

An empty belly and shivering cold was how she recalled her life growing up in Ohio and Kentucky. If her father ever grew a good crop, she couldn't recall it. They had hail, grasshoppers, tornados, floods. She saw more of their summer-long efforts washed away than she could ever recall harvesting.

Moving, always moving to some better place that was usually a sorrier one than the last. Rats wouldn't have lived in some of those hovels. A crippled mule to farm with, they never had anything worthwhile in her entire life. Never had a single thing anyone would want to steal. She and her mother worked all day making firewood and having to sell it for pennies to buy food and not having fuel of their own to cook with or for heat.

She found a kerchief in her robe pocket and blew her nose, loud enough to bring her back to reality, and to the fact she was upstairs in Molly Mather's Cathouse, sitting on the floor. Someone was knocking on her door above her head.

"Yes?" She waited. Hoping, expecting, to hear his deep reply.

"It's me, Bonny. Are you all right?"

"He's gone?" Tillie asked.

"Ain't no one out here but me. Can I come in? You sound upset, Tillie."

"I'll be fine, Bonny. But, Bonny?"

"Yes?"

"Thank you."

"I's just concerned about you."

"I know. Thank you," Tillie said, unable to face anyone over her losses. For certain she couldn't talk about it to another whore and not cry some more.

She gathered herself up and threw herself across the bed. How could she bury herself in it? Deep enough, be far enough away, she would never think of that hard-bellied cowboy ever again.

A knock on the door awoke her. It was dark outside, she sat on the bed. How long had she slept? Dull minded, she pushed the loose hair from her face.

"Yes?"

"It's me, Molly. I have a man out here."

She went to the door and cracked it. In the flickering hall light she could see his bald head. The banker, Arthur Coyle. She wet her lips and cleared her throat.

"Why, Arthur, how nice of you to come by and see me," she said.

Looking uncomfortable standing at Molly's side, he forced a smile on his round shiny face. Tillie strode out in grand style, took him by the arm, and led him back into her room with a nod to her boss that she would care for the little man.

"How have you been?" she asked him, closing the door.

"Oh, except for the complaint in my leg, fine." He stood looking around.

"Well, little Arthur, let Tillie look at that sore leg." She began to remove his coat.

"Yes, yes," he said gleefully, allowing her to undress him like a child.

Tillie drew a deep breath up her slender nose. He smelled of talc and barber's aftershave. After he left her, she knew he would go and take another bath. No doubt so that his dowdy wife could not scent out his transgressions. Poor Arthur. He needed a mother and a mistress, a role that, according to him, his wife avoided like the plague.

"I was so afraid you would be busy," he said in his little-boy voice.

"No. Never for you," she cooed, unbuttoning his shirt.

Grateful for the distraction of this customer, she looked with longing over Arthur's bald head at the starlit windowpane. Wherever you are Luther Haskell, I hope you're happy.

7

"Any word from the sheriff?" The major stood before the governor's empty desk and lit a cigar. Fresh upon his return from Fort Smith, he felt anxious for any news of the latest events in Christopher Basin.

Sterling paced the Oriental rug, hands behind his back looking glum. "No. I spoke to Sheriff Rupp two days ago. His men have not had any success at all. The entire community has closed ranks on these killers according to him."

"I hired a man to go in."

"I guess knowing his name is not important," Sterling said, pausing and looking hard at him.

"Luther Haskell. He's Texas enough to go in up there. Tough man, but I need a cover for him as a cattle buyer."

Sterling frowned.

"Don't you have an acquaintance in that business, who we can trust enough to confide in? Let them send Haskell in there as a buyer."

"Gerald! I can't think of a soul who does that."

"Then I'm headed out again in the morning. Perhaps some of my connections with the railroad can help me find one."

Sterling looked vexed. "How will you do this?"

"I'll find someone I can trust to help me make a cover for Haskell."

"But how?"

"I'll find a way. Trust me, I only thought—"

"What?"

"That we—*you*, as governor, had friends in this territory who would help us."

Sterling asked, "What if you can't find anyone?"

"Sterling, stop worrying. I'll find an ally I can trust. Quit fretting so."

"Gerald, there are times I would submit my resignation to this job just like that." He snapped his fingers.

With a weary shake of his head, the major waved off his threat. "We still have lots of work to do here."

Sterling squeezed his beard and pulled on it. "It's a task that requires too much at times. Please politicians, Washington. I think this Dikes boy's parents are coming out here, too."

"Oh, they'll do lots of good."

"Doing what? Raising hell with me and the sheriff, I suppose?"

"I'm going to find Haskell a cover in the morning. Excuse me, I need to see my wife and catch up on some chores for her."

"Give Mary my regards. She ever needs anything in your absence, have her call on me."

"I shall." The major stopped and considered the exhausted-looking man. "We'll solve this matter."

"I know you'll try, but I'm afraid it will continue to fester." Sterling sighed. "Eastern newspapers have ahold of the issue. They're saying we're a lawless hellhole out here."

"That sells newspapers."

"Forms public opinion, too."

"I guess. I never had to worry about that in the military."

"That's why you got out," Sterling said, and laughed.

The major turned and nodded, pleased at the man's amusement. "It may be so."

After he left the mansion, he stopped and arranged for a stage ticket to the railhead. His business completed downtown, he started for his house. Wearily, he strode up the hill, when a voice called to him.

"Suh?"

He turned and a black girl in her teens came in long strides waving a piece of paper at him.

"Missy, she wants to speak to you."

"Now?"

"If you can come."

"Of course," he said, looking around and then falling in beside the girl.

She hurried up the stairs of the two-story Harrington House and opened wide the front door for him. Inside, she indicated for him to stay in the vestibule, then in a flash of dark legs she wildly took the curved staircase two at a time in search of her boss.

Ellen Devereau soon appeared on the second-floor landing and handed the girl her hairbrush. Dressed in a blue gown that exposed a great deal of skin and cleavage, she came down the stairs smiling. The major removed his Stetson.

"Why, Major, you have not been in Preskitt or even visible for some time. So good to see you again."

"Thanks," he said, rotating his hat by the brim in his fingers. "What can I do for you?"

"Let's go in there." She indicated the room off the vestibule, and once inside, closed the door behind them. "Have a chair. How about a drink of something?"

"No. I have things to do. Not to be in a rush, but what can I do for you?"

"Well. . . ." She drew a deep breath, motioning for him to be seated. "I wanted to know how I could repay you for saving me from that scoundrel Waddle who held me hostage."

"It was the sheriff and U.S. deputy marshal did that." He recalled the recent arrest of the counterfeiter and murderer Waddle who had moved in and taken over her operations. She had sought the major's assistance in Waddle's removal and arrest. It was over the resolution of that matter that they agreed to cooperate in the future.

"You are much too modest, Major." She shook her head to dismiss his words. "I know who arranged it all so discreetly."

"There is one thing." He leaned back in the chair. "This lynching over in Christopher Basin has many people upset. There don't seem to be any answers to who did it."

"I'll listen, but . . ." She paused and then lowered her voice. "Perhaps you should poke around the territorial prison."

"You know something going on down there at Yuma?" He frowned at her. What next? That would upset Sterling's entire day if he knew things weren't going satisfactorily in the construction of the new territorial prison at Yuma.

"A girl hears things." She raised thin eyebrows at him.

"Yes? Like what?"

"How things are so high-priced."

"Enough said." He considered the matter. There must be some collusion going on down there. Especially if Ellen Devereau knew about it two hundred fifty miles away in Prescott.

"I will listen for anything regarding the Christopher Basin matter," she promised. "In case I learn anything, you will be the first to know."

"Thanks, Ellen," he said, and rose to his feet. What was going on at Yuma? Damn, he needed to secure Haskell a cover before he could do anything else. Oh, well, Yuma could wait until his return.

At his house, Mary gave him a hard look when he mentioned he must pack. "You are leaving again?"

"A few days this time is all," he promised.

"I hardly have your clothes washed and pressed from the last trip."

His arm circled her shoulder and they walked outside to inspect her flowers. The red, white, yellow, and blue colors spilled over the fences and yard like a giant painting.

"You have a green thumb, Mary."

"My flowers don't leave me except in the fall," she reminded him.

"Perhaps someday we can move down to Hayden's Mill and that new town called Phoenix. They say down there that flowers bloom year round."

"Summers, they say, are much hotter than Preskitt, too," she reminded him.

"Much hotter."

"I'll stay here. Now I must iron some more so you don't look neglected. Where will you go this time?"

"Winslow. It appears to be the headquarters for the railroad and shipping."

"How long will you be gone?" she asked from the doorway.

"A week, I suspect."

His attention focused more on Ellen Devereau's information regarding someone overcharging at the new prison construction than being at his own house. Oh, well. He'd tend to that later. He looked across Prescott at Thumb Butte, a particular landmark of bare rock that stood up like its namesake. Lots to do. At the moment, worst of all, he needed a good cover for Haskell.

A day later, he sat in the office of the Kansas Pacific Railroad Division chief and smiled at his former military cohort. The man behind the superintendent's desk, Floyd Grimes, retired colonel, looked a little grayer around the edges and thicker set in his swivel chair.

"Damn, Gerald, you're working. This marshal business is what the territory needs. Why, there's more known criminals in this region than you can count. My personal railroad police are constantly arresting them."

"I have a particular problem. I need a man to go into Christopher Basin undercover and try to learn who lynched those three men. Actually, I have the man, I just need a cover for him."

"What do you mean?"

"I want him to go in there as a cattle buyer. I suspect the ones most anxious to rid the basin of so-called rustlers were ranchers, so I want to send him in as their ally."

"So?" Grimes leaned back and tented his fingers, tapping the tips together, engrossed in his thoughts. "This person can't be someone who talks either?"

"Correct."

"I have the man for you." Grimes rose from his chair. "He'll need a buyer?"

"Yes, I think so, and we can trust him."

Half an hour later they entered the office of the Kansas City, Chicago, and Ashland Livestock Company. A young man ushered them back to the large office. Behind the cluttered desk, a man with snowy eyebrows and mustache nodded.

"Bill Allen. This is a former army buddy of mine, Gerald Bowen," Grimes introduced them.

"Pleased to meet you, Bowen. Have a seat."

"Bowen needs your help and he don't need it all over town," Grimes explained.

"Fair enough."

Allen listened to his explanation, nodding and making notes. Then when the major finished his pitch for him to hire Haskell, Bowen added one thing.

"Luther is a former deputy U.S. marshal at Fort Smith, but he comes from Texas. He's put cattle together for several herds and taken them north." The major waited for the man's reply.

"He should fit in with them rebs down there just fine." Allen chuckled. "If you say he's all right, I'll sure try him. Why not? You're paying his wages."

The major felt a great burden lifted from his shoulders. "All this must be kept very quiet. Not a word to anyone."

"Won't leave my office." Grimes rapped his knuckle on the desk. "I wish you good luck with your organization, Bowen. If Arizona is ever to join the nation and become a state, we'll have to end our violent vigilante ways."

The major agreed, grateful his plan worked so smoothly this far. If the Yuma one went this well, he'd be pleased. He dreaded telling his wife about that trip. Hotter than hell itself, they said of the place.

"When's your man due in here?" Allen asked.

"As soon as I inform him to come here." The major considered his words. Luther Haskell might be riding into a certain hell, too. At least he had the man a legitimate cover; the rest depended on the Texan's skills to ferret out the truth.

"I'll send Haskell instructions to come see you and you can point him to the basin."

"This all might work out very well," Allen said, and nodded his head as if extremely satified. "A woman who claims to be a sister to one of those men hung has given me the authority to gather his stock and pay her the proceeds. Can Haskell handle that?"

"I'm sure he can."

8

"**Boys, we may be fixing to get new neighbors up here,**" Matt told the others in the back room of the Texas. He searched around the table at the grim faces of the three ranchers.

"Who?" Charboneau asked with a frown as he paused to light his fresh cigar.

"Outfit from the valley, called the Flat Iron Cattle Company."

"Never heard of them."

"Ain't no sign they won't bunch up a couple thousand cow brutes and send them to us."

"They ain't got a crew or nothing?" Crain asked in disbelief.

"Boys, you can hire cowboys like ants. There're hundreds laying around drunk, or digging ditches between here and Fort Worth. One loud call and you'd have an army of them hired."

"You certain about this?" Charboneau asked.

"Certain enough that I called you here."

"What can we do?" Reed Porter asked, looking around.

"I'm going down to Phoenix and try to find out what they plan to do."

"Good. Hope to hell it's all rumors." Charboneau sat back and drew on his cigar.

"Me, too," Matt said and took a seat.

"Those damn deputies are still nosing around," Porter said, and all eyes turned to him. "I mean those two asked lots of questions of everyone."

"They stopped me this morning," Matt said. "They're pretty sharp. Like to ask questions to backtrack you over what you said. I told them I helped cut them down. They wanted to insinuate I was there when they swung."

"I asked them why they wasn't counting cows." Charboneau laughed and coughed on his cigar smoke. "I figure they'll get tired and leave."

"Sooner the better," Crain said, sounding upset. "They're like smoke. Show up and don't take the front gate in either."

"Asked me if I had any proven cases of rustling against any of them," Matt said. "Why didn't they go ahead and ask if I hung them?"

"Yeah, and if you'd showed them those bastards' handiwork, they'd charge you with their hanging," Charboneau said.

"Keep mum. They'll go back to Preskitt in a few days."

"Can't happen too soon for me." Porter's shoulders shuddered under his coat.

"Don't tell them anything," Matt warned, edgy about the man's resistance under pressure.

"I won't," Porter mumbled.

"Whiskey or cards?" Matt asked, cutting the seal off the new bottle with his jackknife.

"I ain't in no mood for cards," Crain said. Porter agreed with him. Charboneau shrugged.

"Then let's have some whiskey," Matt said, trying to raise the room's spirits.

They broke up early, in no mood to do anything but go home and sulk until the worrisome deputies left the basin. Matt waited till all had left but the downcast Porter.

"You better do your drinking from now on up at one of your line shacks," he said, sharp enough so that Porter batted his eyes at his command.

"I—"

"You've been drinking a lot. Worrying the others. Do it up there for all our sakes."

Porter agreed with a dejected nod.

"I'm not picking on you. But you don't need to get loose-tongued with them deputies around."

"I'll go up under the rim to do my drinking," Porter said obediently. "You know where the shack is if you need me."

"Yeah, I know. It'll be for the best. This thing will pass. Don't worry so."

"I'll try not to."

"Good."

They parted and he watched Porter ride out of town. If only his fatherly advice worked. If not, he'd have to do something about him. Still concerned, Matt went to the livery for his buggy.

Finding a few showers en route home, he drove his rig back to the ranch to arrive in mid-afternoon. Henry took the horse when he pulled up.

"How's the horse breakers coming along?" he asked, looking in the direction of the pen where his son and Lefty were saddling a bald-faced colt.

"They got two of them saddle-broke. That proud cut Baldy, the one they've got now is a real fox, though." Henry shook his head warily.

Matt knew the man talked about the colt with the wide strip of white on his face. The colt's one glass eye made him *watch-eyed* in cowboy lingo, certain to be a spook in most westerners' minds. It was the main reason the gelding didn't get picked when he sold the best ones from the crop for forty apiece. That buyer from New Mexico didn't want him.

Headed for the house with the developments of more cattle coming in the basin still eating at his mind, he stopped at the base of the porch. He looked in time to see his son bail in the saddle and Lefty jerked off the blinds. Baldy bolted ahead in long leaps with Randy sawing on the bosal ropes. The colt piled up short of the corral fence, sucked back, turned inside out, and Randy never lost a stirrup. Soon he began to whip Baldy with the lines forcing him to lope around the pen.

Impressed, Matt raised his eyebrows. Not half bad. He exchanged a nod of approval with Henry, who had seen the ride, too. That boy might make a hand. It reinforced his notion about his idea to have Randy work out the string. Teach him responsibility and how to ride a damn sight better. Soon, there wouldn't be any more buck offs for him at roundup.

"You're home early," Taneal said, coming out on the wide porch as he reached the foot of the stairs.

"Need to go to Phoenix tomorrow."

"You better get a real night's sleep," she said, arms folded over her chest. "Rain on you today?"

"Between here and Fortune." He looked back over the country for the nearest clouds. A bank formed in the south where the moisture gathered from far off in the Gulf of California and worked inland, to rain on the cooler mountaintops.

"We could sure use some soaking moisture. Been raining everywhere but on us."

"Yeah, I better have Jakes recheck our major springs this week."

"How old is he?" she asked.

"Sixties?"

"Closer to his seventies. You ever watch him get on a horse in the morning?" she asked.

"Not lately."

"He's in such pain when he gets up there."

"Still the best riata man—"

"I think he needs to be retired. Have him do less."

"You want to shoot him?"

"No, I want some sympathy for him."

"It would kill him. Taneal, he rode with my daddy in Mississippi during the war."

"I ain't saying you don't owe him. I say he's showing his age."

Matt shook his head. She'd never really understand a man. It was why the two of them fought so about everything and she slept alone. In the coolness of the house, he felt the breeze sweep through the open doors and windows.

Whew. It would be hot down in the Salt River Valley. Still, he needed to check on this Flat Iron business. He drew a gourd of water from the hanging ollah. The sweetness flowed down his throat.

He searched around for Lana. Probably taking a siesta. Nothing he could do about that. What was wrong now? He turned on his heel and listened to Taneal's screaming.

"It's Randy! Randy's hurt!" she shouted from the doorway, and fled in the direction of the corral on the heels of Lefty.

Hatless, Matt raced to catch up with them. He could see the corral gate was open, and Henry was standing above a form on the ground. Then he spotted the bald-faced colt, dragging his bosal ropes. Oh, the boy was probably only shook up.

The dusted face of Randall showed no response, where he lay sprawled on his back. On one side of him, Taneal clasped her hands, while Matt leaned down over him with his ear and could hear that Randy still breathed through his nose.

"Broke his leg," Lefty said, and Matt looked to see Randy's lower right leg wasn't straight.

"He alive?" she demanded

"Yes. Knocked out is all. Lefty, help me get that boot off. We better before it swells up."

"Swells up? Oh, God, don't take him. Please, God, let my boy live."

"He'll be all right," Matt said. Damn that hysterical woman; nothing wrong a sawbones couldn't set.

"Easy," he said, holding the leg while the cowboy fought off the boot.

"Coming hard. There. His leg broke?"

"Looks like it. Go get some sticks to make splints out of, and have someone hook up the wagon." Boot finally off, Matt eased the boy's leg to the ground. Obviously, it was broken below the knee, but he didn't know enough about exactly where or how bad.

His eyes half open, Randy mumbled something.

"Oh, Randy, don't talk. Don't talk," she pleaded. "Save your strength. You'll need all your strength. Lie still, son."

Out of breath, Lefty came stumbling back with an armload of sticks and boards. He dumped them beside Matt.

"Go get an old sheet that we can rip up," Matt said to the concerned Mexican girl who had hurried from the house. "Go hitch that team," he told Lefty. The rest of the crew was gone. He met his wife's worried look.

"Go and get a feather bed. Have Lefty help you load it. It will ease his ride."

"You sure this is the thing to do?" Taneal started to rise but waited for his reply.

"Quicker we can get him there, the quicker we can get it set."

With a nod, she rose and gave the boy a last worried look. "I'll be right back, Randy." Then with her skirt in hand she raced for the house.

"Take it easy, son. You're going to be okay," he said to comfort him, laying out the sticks.

"I about had him rode, Dad."

"Yeah, you've done real good." Matt looked around for something to splint the leg with.

"Only got him and that blue roan left to get the kinks out of."

"Yeah, you've done well with them."

Those words settled him; Randy lay back and his face showed the pain had begun. Matt thought about the laudanum in the cabinet. Before very long, Randy would need some. Broken bones hurt deep. The sticks Lefty brought him would work.

Where was Taneal? He glanced back toward the house and saw Lana running toward them with a wad of sheets.

Squatting on his boot heels, he shifted his weight to his other leg and drew out his jackknife. She held the cloth up and he made cuts on the side so it could be ripped into ribbons. In seconds she tore loose the first one and handed it to him.

"I must go help the señora," she said, huffing for her breath.

"Lefty can do that for her. You keep tearing them. Randy, grit your teeth. I have to lift that leg. It ain't going to feel good."

"Yeah."

The sticks lined up, Matt raised the leg to thread the bandage under for the wraps to hold them in place. On his knees, he worked as fast as he could. He heard the jingle of harness.

"Tell Lefty to go to the house and help her load that feather bed in the back," he said to Lana, not even looking up from his wrapping. Crude splint, but it should work. "Tell him to bring some laudanum, too."

Their eyes met for a long moment. Lana was opposite him on her knees, helping him bind the leg in the sticks. A stone formed in his guts and the contents of his stomach sloshed around it. Her beautiful creamy olive skin. The dark eyes that haunted him. The cleavage between her firm breasts. He was forced to breathe deep up his nose or lose his breath.

"He will be bueno?" she asked with deep concern for Randy in her eyes.

"Yes, yes. Muy bueno," he managed to say then. To escape his captivation with her, he went back to tying the ribbons to hold the splints in place. No doubt his son would survive this. It was only a broken leg. She hurried away, skirt in hand, to help them load the bed.

"That sure is pretty," Randy said about the splint, sitting up with his arms behind him for support.

"Better lie down."

"Naw, I ain't a sissy. Little light-headed is all."

The concerned look in the girl's brown eyes before she left them had not escaped Matt. His wife was on the way back with laundum in her hand. They already had the feather bed loaded. Wasn't heavy, just bulky.

"Here," Taneal said, dropping to her knees with the big spoon ready. She filled it with the pain killer from the brown bottle.

"I don't need—"

"Randy, take this!"

"Aw, hell—"

She forced him to open his mouth and she administered it. He made a bad face.

"That will help ease the pain," she assured him.

In a few minutes, they'd loaded Randy in the back of the wagon. Taneal wanted to ride there to comfort him. Matt climbed on the seat and took the lines.

"Lefty, tell the others where we are and we'll be back."

"Sure, boss. Wish I could have saved him."

"He'll be fine." He nodded to Lana. She replied with a like sign. Still the worry written in her brown eyes bothered Matt. Was his son also having an affair with her? Funny, he never thought before about Randy ever being any competition to him. Randall was supposed to still be a boy, not a man. The notion was sobering when he looked back and told the two of them that he was ready.

"Drive careful," Taneal said.

"I will." He clucked to the team of horses and headed them for the road. It would be a long dusty drive to Fortune.

Hours later, looking tired, Doc Harrigan, a balding man in his fifties, washed his hands in a bowl. He dried them deliberately on a cloth towel, then turned to speak to both Matt and Taneal.

"He stays off of it. Don't try to ride any more broncs for six weeks, should be good as new."

"You're sure?" Taneal asked, seated on the edge of a parlor chair.

"I set them all the time. He's young, and young people mend fast. Don't worry. Leave him here overnight and you two go get you some sleep. Both of you."

They looked at each other. Neither made a move.

"Thanks, Doc," Matt finally said, and rose to his feet. He offered his arm to Taneal.

"Yes, oh, yes," she said as if in a dream. She stood and put her hand in the crook of his elbow. "We'll be back in the morning to check on you," she said to Randy.

"Ah, I'll be fine." Pasty-faced, he grinned at both of them with his head on the pillow.

"Yes, I guess you will," she said, still sounding numb. "Good night."

On the boardwalk at Doc's front gate. Matt stopped in the darkness. Some of the light from inside shone through the windows; he needed to know her intentions. It might save a public argument between them that he would later regret ever happened.

"You hungry?" he asked.

"No. Not really. Are you?"

"No. You want one room or two at the hotel?"

"Why, one, of course," she said as if it was the only thing to do.

"Fine."

"I've been thinking about a lot of things since this happened today."

"Oh?" He started them for the Brown Hotel two blocks away.

"We don't act like a married couple anymore."

No, and they hadn't for years, but that wasn't news. He noticed a pair of riders coming up the street. Some cowboys come to town for something. Her hand felt so familiar on his arm, it reminded him of how long it had been since they shared a conjugal bed.

"You're certain about this?" He looked over at her in the pearly starlight. Still a handsome woman, he recalled her flat belly and silky long legs. The notion excited him.

"It can be our second honeymoon," she said, sounding pleased, and hugged his arm.

What had he done or not done for this? After years, she'd found him again. Why? Ever since the schoolhouse incident, she had turned so frosty, so foreign and distant. He would never be able to figure out women. Certainly not the one he was married to.

When they reached the porch of the Longhorn Saloon, someone stumbled out the swinging doors. He tried to straighten his shoulders, then turned unsteadily on his boot heels. Matt recognized his hat. It was Porter—and, damn, he was drunk again.

"That you, Reed?" he asked.

"Huh. Oh, 'cuse me, ma'am," he slurred, and whipped off his hat at the discovery of Taneal's presence.

"You all right?" Matt asked.

"Fine—just fine. I'll be okay." He took three steps sideways and caught the porch post. Then he broke out laughing. "Little in the cups is all."

"You going to be able to ride home like that?" Matt asked.

"Sure, sure, I'll be fine." Porter struggled to put his toe in the stirrup.

"You better unhitch his horse for him," Taneal whispered.

With a quick check around, Matt stepped off the boardwalk and undid the reins. He gave the man a boost and Porter almost went over the horse. If Porter didn't listen to his warning about his drinking in town . . .

"Oh, yeah, the most important thing. My reins. Thank you, Matthew."

"Don't fall off," he said, and studied Porter as he turned the horse and started up the street. Matt stood for a long while, watching him go and wondering, too, of the whereabouts of those tough deputies. In Porter's shape, they could get lots of information out of him. The fool fast became too large a risk for everyone involved.

"When did he start drinking like that?" Taneal asked in a whisper, taking his arm and shoving her firm breast against his biceps.

"Lately," he said, still looking after the man. Porter and his horse disappeared into the black veil of the night. In the cooling air, Matt wished that somehow Porter could be gone forever.

9

A cool north wind swept the dock at the Winslow Depot. The endless crystal blue sky made things too bright when Luther stepped down off the train leading Ben by a rope leash. He thanked the conductor and then squatted down and turned the bulldog loose. Ben hurried off to answer nature's call. The porter brought his war bag down the steps and set it down.

Luther paid him ten cents and the man thanked him. He could see his saddle and other things being unloaded from the baggage car on a dock wagon. He searched around, but the town did not look that impressive. A few false-front wood buildings, the rest adobe hovels, and no trees. Some straggly starts, tied and staked to prevent the wind bending them, but to a man who had spent the past four years in the dense hardwood and pine forests of western Arkansas and the Indian Nation, this place looked bald.

He made certain his gear would be secure inside the depot while he went to find Bill Allen, the man the major had written him about. With Ben on his heels, he started up the hard-packed dirt street. Small curls of dust on the wind crossed it like waves on water. He noticed some dark-eyed doves standing in their open doorways, plying their trade in the daytime from narrow side-by-side adobe cribs.

The Chicago, Kansas City, and Ashland Livestock Company wasn't hard for him to find. Luther made Ben stay in the reception area with the young clerk named Chip. In his private office, Bill Allen, a man in his fifties, introduced himself, extended a hand to Luther, and showed him a chair. Then he walked over and closed the door.

"Guess the major told you about the job?"

"Told me in his letter that I was to report to you as a cattle buyer."

"Yes. Well, I've been hired to gather T. G. Burtle's cattle. Your job is to round them up and to look for me some good three-year-old steers to ship this fall. Don't need any longhorns or lots of it showing. There ain't a market left for them anymore. I want half or better Hereford or Durham."

"Fine. What about this Burtle's stock?"

"I guess it's mavericks mostly. B Bar is the brand, on the right side, a notch lower left ear and a blunt end. And that's probably what they hung him over. The state brand inspector, Ira Strand, will work with you. Good man. He lives down there at Fortune. When you get them gathered, let me know and I'll tell you what to do with them."

"Hire some help?"

"Yes. You'll need it. That's timber country. Hire you some brush poppers and a cook. Should be enough who want work to pick men from around that area. I'll send a couple pack mules with you, and when you get the men hired, you can rent a remuda this time of year from one of the ranchers down there."

"How much you do want to spend on this roundup?"

Allen nodded as if pleased by his words. "I told his sister she could foot the bill for gathering them. She gets what's left after that. Let's see, cowboys cost thirty, plus thirty a month to feed them, then add on horse rent. Five, or six hands, and you. Six weeks, but first you go look over the country, find where most of the cattle are. You might do it in less time than that."

"No idea about the tally?"

Allen shook his head. "He had some cattle. His sister, I am certain, thinks there are lots more head than you'll fine."

"You say you have two mules?"

"Yes. You can get the supplies you need in Fortune. But those two mules will be handier than a chuck wagon in Christopher Basin. It's rough country."

"How far away?"

"Eighty miles south."

"What are the main ranchers' names?" he asked, taking out his pencil and small book.

"Dan Charboneau, Louie Crain. Oh, Matthew McKean, he's a big one and may bite your head off over a summer roundup. McKean ain't easy to get along with unless the cards are going toward him and Reed Porter—he has the best Hereford cattle. Those are the big four. But you have the authority to go and get them."

Luther rubbed his palm over his whisker stubble. "You know why I'm here?"

"Yes."

"You have any idea who hung Burtle and those others?"

"It would be speculation."

"And?" Luther looked at the man, feeling awed by the vastness of this new land. So much country here and all so foreign to him. He felt like a leaf afloat in an ocean.

"You might have their names right there." Allen indicated his notebook, then he walked to the window and looked out on the shipping pens beyond. "Who else had enough cattle you could easily steal from down there?"

"Makes sense, but proving it . . . well, that may be a different story. I'll go get a feel for the country, locate the B Bar branded stock and let you know about hands."

"Can't find them down there. Plenty of them on the free lunch up here."

"Good." They shook hands, and Luther, with Ben at his heels, left the office.

At the livery, squatting in the sunshine with their backs to the corral fence, Luther and the owner, Winston, discussed a trade. The animal in mind was a stout red roan gelding with an X7F brand on his neck.

"He's a mountain horse. Sure-footed," Winston bragged, aiming brown spit in the dust between his dusty boots. "You'll like him down in that Christopher Basin where you're headed. Got a good running walk. Broke to death. Ground tie. Mount him left or right. I'm telling you, he's a real pony. A bulldog just like yours." He motioned toward Ben.

"I'd give you twenty bucks with new plates on him."

"Can't take that. Cost me four to get him shod."

"Bottom dollar?" Luther asked.

"Thirty, no shoes."

"I'd give that for him shod."

"Them shoes ain't bad that he's got on."

"His feet's grown out. Got him sitting back on his heels." Luther rose and, hands on hips, straightened his stiff back. All that train riding had made him a cripple. "Thirty-two and you have him shod."

"Damn, you drive a tough deal. I can't get him shod till . . . have him ready in the morning."

"Daybreak, I'll be after him," he said, counting the money into the man's hand.

"You're a hard man to deal with," Winston complained. "I'd go broke doing business with you every day. Bill Allen must've known you were a tough trader to hire you for a buyer."

"You sold a ten-dollar bronc for three times the value." Luther shook his head at the man, but he felt proud of his buy. "What do they call him?"

"Cochise."

"Any reason?"

Winston shook his head. "Hell, they name horses after everything else, why not some dead blanket-ass Indian?"

"Just curious."

"You sell that bulldog?"

"Nope. I wouldn't wish that much trouble on anyone," Luther said, and laughed as he pushed out the gate. Ben didn't lose the opportunity to slip out of the pen with him, as if he didn't want to be sold either.

"I'd trade you that horse straight across for him."

"Not for sale." Luther had a lot on his mind. His gear, rifle, and saddle needed to be transported to the livery. He had to check on Allen's mules—how to get them and where

they were stabled. The man had also promised him checks
for his supplies, wages, and cattle buying.

Perhaps before he left, he would write Tillie a letter. Tell
her how he had become a respectable cattle buyer on his
way to a town called Fortune in the Christopher Basin.
Sounded like some place in never-never land from a wild
dime novel. The notion they hung three men there brought
him back to reality. It wouldn't be a Garden of Eden. The
Biblical story of Cain and Abel came to mind. Jealousy
caused many problems and misdirected many individuals.
Grateful for the cattle buyer cover, maybe in time he could
find the answers that Major Bowen expected. Who were
those vigilantes?

He hurried toward the depot. Lots to do before then.

The bay mules proved to be as good as Allen claimed they
were. They bonded with Cochise the first day, and after
that, Luther didn't need a lead on them. When he rode into
Fortune on the second day, he studied the small houses and
little farms that surrounded the village. He caught a doctor's
sign out in front of a white house with lots of flowers growing inside the white picket fenced yard.

The village covered two blocks, all clustered around a
second-story hotel. A few rigs were parked outside Issac's,
the largest mercantile. At the hitch racks, hip-shot horses
switched pesky flies. Several more sleepy cow ponies stood
in front of the saloons. One such dispenser of booze was
called the Texan, the other and smaller bar was the Longhorn. Spindly pines were scattered about, though he had
seen lots of good pine timber coming over the rim. The
vast holding pens looked in good condition, and that was
a relief, unless they were privately owned and barred other
folks from using them. Highly unusual for anyone to deny
the use of corrals, especially when they weren't needed this
time of year.

He stabled the horse and mules at the livery. Then he
and Ben went into the Texas, which looked the most pros-
perous. Saloons were the main gathering place for infor-

mation and news. In such an isolated place, he considered they would also be the point of most of the commerce in a town this size.

He stopped inside the wing doors and looked for the bartender. When the man raised his head in question, Luther said, "Got my dog with me."

The man peered over at Ben and laughed. "He's fine. Come on inside."

Luther crossed to the polished bar, ordered a beer, and went to a corner table. Ben crouched underneath it. Having already been involved in three minor altercations with the town curs, he acted ready to rest.

"You in town on business or pleasure?" the bartender asked, delivering the foam-topped mug.

"Business, I'm a cattle buyer. Anyone around here I could hire to guide me? Need to look for some that we've already bought."

The bartender cradled his elbow in his hand. "Maybe Hirk would suit you."

"Hirk?"

"Yeah, short for Hirkermere Silver, but no one calls him by that."

"I guess not. How do I find him?"

"He'll be in here any time now."

"He have a place around here?"

The bartender made a wry face. "Ain't much of one, but he's a good guy. Knows the country real well."

Hirk showed up half an hour later, sprouting a week's whiskers, and his clothes looked like they'd been slept in and rolled in the dirt. Luther guessed his age as close to forty. He stopped at the bar, ordered a beer, and conversed with the barkeep, then turned and gazed hard at Luther.

"Howdy. Hirk Silver's my name." He gave a head toss toward the bar. "Earl over there said you needed some help?"

"Mine's Luther Haskell. Have a chair," he offered, and frowned at Ben's growl. "Get over, Ben, and let him sit down."

"Who's Ben?" Hirk bent over and peered beneath the table at him. "Why, howdy, pard. You look like you could double bite a fellar. Hope you never get mad at me."

"He's fairly civilized," Luther assured him.

"What're you needing, mister?" Hirk dropped into the chair and slouched down, like his spine would hurt to sit upright.

"My boss is helping T. G. Burtle's heirs, and I'm supposed to round up his cattle for them."

"Looking for T. G.'s stock, huh?"

"We find enough, I'll hire a crew and we'll round them up."

"You're looking for a guide, then?"

"Yeah, I don't know this country."

"We going to stay out a few days?" Hirk asked as the bartender delivered two fresh beers.

Luther paid for them. "We need to."

"You got a horse of your own to ride?"

"I'll get my gear ready. When we leaving?"

"I planned to leave in the morning, early. How much a day?"

"Buck a day and grub."

"Yeah."

"Fair enough. Let's meet at sunup over at the livery. I've got two mules to pack our stuff on."

"Here's to cow hunting." Hirk raised his mug with the foam spilling over the rim. "May it all go smooth as glass."

Luther returned the toast and hoped so, too. He studied the older man's stained floppy hat, once a high-priced white one. A leather thong under his chin held it on. An expensive red silk kerchief was wrapped around his neck and he wore a tattered wool vest. His faded brown canvas pants were wash-worn and filthy, tucked in run over boots with a cap and ball pistol in his holster that completed his dress. He had to trust that this cowboy knew the territory. He sure wasn't hiring him for his sharp looks.

A big man in a suit came in the swinging doors, went to the bar, and ordered a drink. Luther figured from his appearance that he must be a businessman or rancher.

"Who's that?" he asked his new man.

"That's Matt McKean. He's a big rancher in the basin."

As if the man heard him, he came across and introduced himself to Luther, who stood and shook his hand

"Nice to met you, Haskell. Earl says you're a cattle buyer?"

In an instant, Luther saw the toughness in this man's dark eyes. He knew McKean didn't come over to talk to someone like Hirk. He came with a purpose, and that was to learn something.

"I work for Bill Allen in Winslow."

"He paying the top prices this fall?"

"Yes, for the right cattle. He wants mostly Hereford and Durham crosses. You have several three-year-olds?"

"Yes. What's the market, Mr. Haskell?"

"Luther," he said softly. "We're offering ten cents a pound this fall at the railhead."

"Needs to be higher."

"Always needs to be higher. While I want to look at some cattle, the main purpose I'm over here for is to gather T. G. Burtle's stock for his estate."

"Oh, well."

"I'll be talking to you and the other ranchers about reps after I decide how best to gather them."

"I can send a rep. Right now I'm headed for Phoenix. Be back in a week. Been trying to get there for three weeks. When will you need one?" He looked hard at Luther like he expected his intentions explained.

"Soon as I see how best to do the job."

"Let me or my foreman, Jakes, know." McKean never once even acknowledged Hirk or addressed the man. The rancher downed his whiskey and with a sharp nod to Luther, turned on his heel to leave. He parted the doors and was gone.

"Big man, ain't he?" Luther asked, hoisting up his mug for a sip.

"Hmm," Hirk snorted. "Like to sell that sumbitch for what he thinks he's worth."

"He got a big spread?"

"You'll get gawdamn tired of seeing his brand up here."

Luther set the mug down and dropped back in the chair. He had met one of the four biggest ranchers in the basin. What were the others like? All that tough? McKean would be a hard nut to crack. Besides, he no doubt kept a fancy-talking lawyer on his payroll. Another tough Scotsman to deal with. It reminded him of what he learned before he left Arkansas. That prosecutor in Fort Smith had dropped the counterfeiting case against McCantle. If he'd brought the man in in irons, he'd never heard the end of it. No, he'd handled that situation well. Christopher Basin might be a different story. He'd wondered and worried enough about it until his belly began to complain.

"Let's go find some food," he said to Hirk.

"You bet. You buying?"

"I guess," Luther said, still trying to sort out what he knew about McKean. Not enough, except that he was tough as granite. He glanced back. "Come on, Ben."

"That dog go wherever you go?" Hirk asked, watching Ben stretch his back and then fall in.

"Most places. Why?"

Hirk rubbed his whiskered mouth and nodded. "Looks like he had a bad wreck and smashed his face in."

"Yeah," Luther said, amused. He pushed open the swinging doors. "A bad one." He saw McKean bring his buggy around and with a nod of his head, the big man drove off. Lots of unanswered questions about him. He and Hirk headed for the cafe across the empty street. Plenty to learn, plenty to find out.

10

The major opened the letter. It bore the Winslow cattle buy-ing company's name on it.

Dear Gerald,
Your man, Luther Haskell, was here and left for Chris-
topher Basin to gather T. G. Burtle's cattle. I was im-
pressed, but it may be a wonder if he doesn't get his
self killed up there. I'll keep you informed of any de-
velopments.

Bill Allen

"Doesn't get his self killed." Those words made him drum his fingertips on the table. Nothing he could do but hope for the best for Haskell. The man certainly had plenty of experience dealing with tough criminals in Fort Smith. He had other things on his mind. Mid-morning, and he was headed for the Harrington House. He wondered if Ellen Devereau had learned anything new about the Christopher Basin lynching or the Yuma deal. The matter of corruption in the new prison construction bothered him. It might be the thing that sent poor John Sterling over the hill.

"Come in," a young girl in a flowing white cotton shift said, opening the front door for him.

Hat in hand, he stepped inside the vestibule. "I would like to speak to Miss Devereau, if she isn't indisposed."

The girl's face went blank, then like a light went on, it cleared, and she said, "Oh, I'm sure she's got clothes on. She don't never run around naked in the house. What did you call it?"

"I meant was she busy."

"Oh." The girl threw her hands to her face and covered the red blush fast turning bright crimson.

"Jollie Ann, who is it?" Ellen asked from the top of the stairs. "Oh, Major, I'll be right down."

"Yes, ma'am." He waved his hat at her. "No rush."

The next few moments, the girl stood before him, wetting her lips and looking around as if for a place to hide. "I better go see about . . . ah, something." She indicated the parlor.

"I'll be fine," he assured her.

"Oh, yeah." At that she fled through the empty parlor and was gone.

"Land sakes, what did you say to that girl?" Ellen asked, looking perturbed as she came down the stairs. The silky yellow dress made a swishing sound and her perfume soon filled his nose. She led him by the arm into the drawing room and shut the doors.

"Glad you weren't indisposed," he said as she poured whiskey into two glasses.

"Oh, no. I wasn't."

"Your employee misunderstood me."

With a frown, she turned, extending a glass for him. "I don't understand."

"The poor girl thought indisposed meant without clothes. She told me you never ran through the house like that."

Ellen closed her dark lashes, shook her head so the curls on her shoulder tossed, and laughed freely. "Oh, well. The word was too big for her."

She motioned to the two parlor chairs with her own drink in her hand. "She also didn't know that you always come on business."

"Yes," he agreed. Seated, he took a sip. Good stuff. Expensive, no doubt, and only for her best customers. "What do you hear about the lynching?"

"Nothing that would help you. My rancher customers all talk about it, but they aren't from there and I've never heard a word on who did it. They do approve of it."

"Yes, but that's why we have courts to decide. Rupp's

men are working up there. They say they can't find any evidence of rustling against those men that were hung."

"Whew," she said with a long exhale. "Then why—"

"Why, that's why I am asking you to listen."

"I will."

"The Yuma thing we spoke about earlier?"

She leaned toward him, so close he could see the small freckles on her deep cleavage. "Whiskey talk. A man named Arnold said the territory was paying for his night here. Needless to say, he spent several dollars. He's supplying material to the contractor, I understand."

"Thanks." He sat back in the chair and considered the whiskey in his glass. At last, he had a name to go on. He raised his gaze and met her green eyes.

"You must be a happily married man, Major?"

"If I wasn't, I would like to see you indisposed."

Ellen burst out laughing. Not some haughty loud obscene outburst, but the warm mirth of a friend sharing something humorous with another. Her eyes sparkled and in the end, shaking her head, she raised her glass to a toast.

"To your wife."

"To Mary," he said, and they clinked glasses.

"I will listen for any news coming out of the basin. It is usually fall, and fall roundup, before I see anyone from over there. Preskitt is not convient for them to get here and I suspect that we aren't on their list of favorite places."

The major finished his drink, thanked her, and left the Harrington House. It was a six-block walk to the mansion. He dreaded the notion of his trip to Yuma. Talking the matter over with Sterling would not be easy. The man jumped at anything wrong.

When he reached the mansion, Sterling was in a meeting, so he found a chair in the outer office and read the dog-eared issue of *Harper's*. The artwork showed savage Indians, much uglier than he had ever experienced meeting. The writer spoke about the Army's campaign into Mexico for the fugitive Apaches. He wasn't concentrating on the arti-

cle, when two men came out of the paneled door with
Sterling.

The governor introduced them as legislators from the
Salt River Valley. They looked like farmers dressed in suits
that made them appear stiff.

"We've been talking about a dam project on the Salt,"
Sterling said.

"It would make our valley a bonanza," the darker faced
one said.

"Sounds good," the major agreed.

Sterling shook their hands and wished them well.

"You a dam builder now?" he asked when the governor
returned.

"No, why?" Sterling closed the double doors and then
smiled. "They need one badly down there. But I doubt this
term of Congress does a thing."

"I didn't come to talk dams."

"Have a seat. What did you learn?"

"Haskell is in the basin. But it will take time."

"I understand. I spoke to Rupp again. He's leaving those
two deputies over there a while longer."

"Good. Maybe they can learn something. We're all after
the same thing."

"You think we should leave your man there, too?"

"Of course. We've gone this far." He shook his head at
Sterling's thinking. "I have full confidence that Haskell will
find the killers."

"The Dikes family, I understand, will be coming here in
a week or so."

What could they do, except raise more hell? The major
wanted to ask it out loud, but realized that neither he nor
Sterling could dissuade them if they tried. Too many cooks
spoiled the soup was his second thought. He hoped Haskell
found out something soon, but he doubted it. Investigations
like this took a long time.

"I need to go to Yuma," he said, to get onto his next
project

Sterling blinked and looked aghast. "Whatever for?"

"To get warm, I guess. They tell me it's a hundred and ten there every day. No, I have some information from an informer that there might be some bill padding going on at the new prison construction."

Sterling's slapped his own forehead. The major could almost hear his words before he spoke them.

"My God, Gerald, what next?"

"It may not be much, but I better check on it. I'm going myself. If I learn anything, I'll wire you."

"Good." Sterling exhaled. "How bad do you think it is?"

"No idea. It may be small, but I'll go see."

"Be careful, Gerald. I need you." A look of deep concern crossed the man's face.

"I will." They had a short drink and he headed for home. Mary would be the hard one to tell. On his walk back, a blue jay perched on a bough scolded him and he smiled. His wife might sound worse than that.

When the major informed her of his travel plans, she frowned, displeased at him. "You're going again?"

"I know," he said, hugging her. "But it is only to Yuma this time."

"I better get your bags packed."

"No. Let's sit in the swing and enjoy this lovely day for a while."

She looked at him and raised an eyebrow. Then with a shrug, she led him to the swing seat. The ropes creaked as they went back and forth. He closed his eyes. A cool breath of air swept over them as fat clouds gathered for the afternoon showers. Prescott could be heaven; Yuma would be hell. Dread clouded his relaxation as he hugged her closer.

The stage to Phoenix-Tucson left at sunup. The run to Phoenix required twelve hours, without a breakdown or holdup. In another half a day he could be in Tucson. Then he'd take a stage to Yuma, which ate up another full day, according to the agent. He recommended that the major stop over in Papago Wells and catch the Yuma stage there, rather than riding in and back out for Tucson.

All the major could decipher of this scheduling was that he had some long hours to spend on the rumbling coach. His valises stored under the canvas cover, he climbed in and took a backward-facing seat. Two other men joined him. Both looked like drummers. The thin-faced one named Benton held his sample case on his lap, and close to his chest, as if it was very valuable. The salesman called Gordon looked ready to nap, leaned to the side, used his hands for a pillow, and with his bowler hat pulled down, tried to sleep.

After the driver's loud, "Hee ha!" in the soft first light of morning, the coach started out of Prescott. Sounds of the chinking tug chains and harness accompanied the motions as he circled the coach around and headed for the Black Canyon Road. In a crack of the whip and more vocal calls the rocking ride began.

The torturous hills slowed the ride to a cautious crawl, then they flew across the flats to snake up another steep grade at a walk. In a few hours, when heat of the day fired up, the major saw his first giant saguaro cactus of the trip. Their great arms, like those of a dancer, swung out. Some said it was for balance, giving them an appearance of a graceful woman dipping and swaying to soft music. The giants clung to the slopes, leaving the lacy palo verde trees to populate the flats.

Brown grass tufted from between great beds of pancake cactus, some purple on the edges of the flat pads. Yucca bloomed in great white profusion and the elegant century plant with its great once in a lifetime stolon reached up with stair-step blossoms in an outline against the clear blue sky.

The major had time to think about his small force. Sam T. Mayes deep in Mexico with his two helpers, Jesus and Too Gut, searched for one of Quantrell's lieutenants. John Wesley Micheals after some ex-Army sergeant who'd went on a killing spree. Then there was Luther up in the basin. Far from a consolidated force and, considering all the broken mountains and rough land they passed through to the stage stop, they could hardly amount to more than a tick on a large dog.

At the next stop, he followed the two drummers off and stretched his legs.

"Money? You got money?" The beggar was a small young girl in a filthy, ragged dress. She held out her un-washed hand cupped for him. Her wild black hair whipped by the wind and uncombed hung in her face. He could see dirt on her cheeks.

For a moment he considered her. She probably was an unrepentable slut even at that young an age. Her bare, dust-coated feet stuck out from under a raveled hem. Unable to deny even such a suspect of falsehood, he found a dime in his pocket and paid her. He did this more to get her out of his path than in charity.

"You good man," she said. With her fingers closed tight over the coin, she shuffled away.

He went to find the facilities behind the station, his bladder about to burst. Amongst the buzz of flies and powerful stench, it took him no extra time in the outhouse. When he returned, he found the girl seated on her butt with her back to the stage stop wall and proudly eating a snowy flour tortilla filled with something.

Her cheeks bulging like a gopher, she grinned at him.

"She got anyone?" he asked the man who had finished harnessing the fresh horses.

"No." He shook his head and glanced at her. "Showed up here by herself a couple weeks ago."

"I'll give you the money, if you will put her on the next stage to Preskitt?"

"Yeah. What for?"

"My wife needs help in her yard. What's her name?"

"Lucy."

He nodded. Then he went over and squatted down be-side her. "Lucy, there's a lady in Preskitt needs some help. Do you want a job?"

She nodded and swallowed hard, as if taken aback by his offer.

He took out a pencil and paper, then he scribbled down Mary Bowen. He handed it to her. "You can ride the next stage there. Ask for the way to Major Bowen's house. They will tell you. Then go see her."

"Mary Bowen?" she asked, so exactly, it knifed him in the chest.

"Yes. She's my wife."

He straightened and dug out two more quarters. "Maybe take a bath first." He handed her the coins. She switched hands with the tortilla and took them.

She swept back the wild hair with her fist holding the quarters and quickly nodded that she heard him. No telling, he decided, what she would do. Perhaps take his fifty cents and go the opposite way, but he'd tried. With that done, he went inside and paid for her one-way ticket to Prescott. She would need no intro to Mary. His wife would know why he sent her.

His last sight of her, she waved good-bye to him with half of the tortilla guarded in her fist. The coach rumbled off for the New River station.

Later that night, in the pitch darkness, he half slept on a bench in front of an adobe hovel, outside the stage stop at Papago Wells. Soon it would be daylight and he would be grateful for it. His bags close by, he wondered about that grim place, with slinking cur dogs and snoring Indians on the ground sleeping off their drunkenness. Strong fecal smells lingered that even the pungent perfume of the desert's creosote bushes could not dilute.

A dead burro's bloated carcass lay near the rock-walled water tank a hundred feet from where he sat. His eyes dry and sore, he tried to rub some moisture into them. The air lay still and hot even at the final hour before sunrise. Despite the higher temperatures it would bring, he would feel better in the light of day, when he could see what was around him.

Since his arrival, a handful of riders stopped and came to the pool. They spoke in Spanish, watered their horses, and rode on. Under the pearly light of the stars, they didn't look worth the powder to blow them away. In his book, they appeared to be up to some kind of skullduggery. He never moved during the time they watered their mounts, and hence went unnoticed.

In deep thought about the matter, he considered Lucy. Had she gone to find Mary? How would his wife take to the girl? She would have said later, "You should have sent her to me." He had done that.

A Mexican came out of the station and raised his arms to the sky and yawned loudly. Then, as if he recognized him, he asked, "You want some coffee, señor?"

"Yes," the major said, and stood, realizing how stiff he had become. He picked up both bags and took them inside. In this dried-up land someone might steal them.

A small lamp shone on the rough-sawn wooden tables and benches. He found a seat and soon a thick-set woman brought him a steaming mug.

"Food?" she asked.

He nodded, satisfied his Spanish was too poor to suggest to her any concoction he might like to eat. Instead, he blew on the coffee and hoped his stage from Tucson got underway on time. Papago Wells was not his choice of places to reside for any length of time.

She delivered him a plate of eggs, parched corn, browned meat, corn tortillas, and honey. As if pleased, she smiled at him.

"Wonderful," he said, "Gracias." He took another sip of his coffee, which she refilled while he ate. The first decent food in a day. Involved with his meal, he looked up to scrutinize the four swarthy men who came in wearing serapes vests and straw Chihuahua sombreros. Floured in road dust, their large spur rowels rang like cowbells when they entered the station.

The woman knew them, or acted like she did. In Spanish they gave her orders for their food. She went back in the kitchen. The leader of the group came over and put his high-topped black boot on the bench seat opposite him.

"You saw anyone ride in here since you came?"

The major considered his food and the egg on his fork.
Was this a lawman? He saw no badge.

"What sort?" Then he carefully took in the food.

"Some men. Mexican. There were perhaps five riders."

"How long ago would they have been here?"

The man pushed his sombrero up with his thumb. His
eyes were dark as coal, and the edges wedged in a fashion
that gave him a look of powerful authority. "Perhaps they
were here an hour or two ago?"

"Some men watered their horses in the night. It was
dark, I couldn't see their faces."

"Muchas gracias," the man said, and nodded. He put
down his boot with a clink and started to turn.

"Those men wanted?"

The man turned, looked at him hard. "Sí, señor. They
murdered some innocent people."

"The law want them?" the major asked.

The man made a small nod. "In Sonora."

He put down his fork and considered his coffee. "I
savvy."

They shared a look of understanding and respect, then
the man went to join his compadres. No words were necessary. International borders should never hide criminals.
His own men went beyond them. When justice failed, then
men instituted it. The difference between metered out justice versus out and out murder rode a razor's edge. Still,
this swarthy man rode after killers—felons beyond his own
grasp to prosecute under the territorial laws.

After they ate, the four rode on. Eventually the stage
arrived from Tucson. The driver loaded his luggage and the
major climbed inside. He removed his hat, nodded to the
straight-back woman seated in the front bench, and took his
place on the rear one facing her.

"Good day," he said, settled and looking across the desert to the south. Heat waves distorted the saw-tooth mountains in the distance.

He guessed her age to be in her thirties. Her black hair
was pulled straight back and her nose was too long and

sharp. When she spoke, her too-small mouth formed the letters. "Good day, sir."

"My name's Gerald Bowen, ma'am."

He waited, but she did not reply. Obviously she did not wish to share her identity with him. A trip of eighteen hours across the Sonoran desert might force her to be more friendly. He only wished the coldness she extruded would cool off the increasing heat of the day. In an effort to escape some of it, he removed his coat and placed it on the seat beside him.

Miss Hmm, as he nicknamed her to himself, stared over his head. Perhaps there was some great painting he had missed in that corner where the ribbed roof met the back wall. A famous French artist's canvas must exist up there and he had not noticed it. He removed his hat, mopped his forehead on his kerchief, and replaced the head gear.

"Let's roll!" the driver shouted. The coach swayed as he climbed up on the seat. The major felt grateful; moving might stir the air some. Then he glanced at his fellow passenger. She looked very cool. Oh, well. In eighteen hours, he'd be in Yuma with more problems to solve than how to get a prim lady to be cordial.

"Hee-yah!" And they were westward bound in the rocking coach.

11

Luther and Hirk rode off the ridge and headed down the steep
trail. Here the pines were scattered and the bunch grass
grew knee-high on Luther's roan pony, Cochise. Real cow
country, the stock they observed looked in good flesh. Several of them wore Burtle's B Bar brand. The cowboy obviously had been busy. But most showed the looks of
mavericks. Many were staggy steers cut as past yearlings.
Wild-eyed heifers, some still with scabby brands, told Luther they hadn't been worked as calves. Maverick law let
anyone with stock on the range and a registered brand to
claim such unmarked animals.

"Is this the way to Dikes's place?" Luther turned in the
saddle and asked his man. Both pack mules followed, the
panniers under the diamond hitches going side to side as
they shuffled off the mountain.

"Yeah. It's in this valley." Hirk pointed to the clearing
far beneath them. "Could be some more of Burtle's stuff
down there."

Luther agreed with a nod, grateful for an excuse to see
the dead man's layout.

Ben made a short bark at a squirrel who teased him from
a few feet off the ground on a ponderosa trunk. After three
stiff jumps, the bulldog stopped. His charge was enough
that the squirrel raced upward and chattered at him from
high limbs. With a sneeze at him, Ben marked the tree and
quickly caught up with the roan horse.

"How many hands we going to need to gather them?"
Luther asked over his shoulder. He leaned back as the sure-
footed Cochise made his stiff-legged descent.

"Half dozen, if'n we got to hold them and round them
up, too."

"You're right." Luther's thoughts were on all the work involved in gathering them. Perhaps Allen should have waited until fall roundup to collect them when the others worked theirs in a joint effort These mountains and forest would be worse than the brush he knew in the Texas hill country to gather cattle. Actually he should be grateful. This cattle drive made his cover up there that much better. What would they find at Dikes's place? Hirk told him they'd be there in another half an hour.

When they reached the last slope, Luther could see a low-walled cabin of hewed logs nestled in a grove of jack pines. Several water tanks in a row dotted the flat valley, obviously fed by a strong source. Several resting cows and calves got up at their approach. A large white-faced bull made a deep bellow and pawed up dust on his shoulders to threaten any challengers to his harem.

"Ben," Luther said sharply, and the bulldog ignored the cattle, trotting along beside the roan horse. Some of the cows, defensive of their calves, gave him a wary eye.

He and Hirk dismounted at the house.

"Pretty nice place," Luther said, looking around.

"Yeah. Old man Manson built it. Him and his wife were workers. Him and her built this series of tanks from the big springs, too."

"They sell this place to Dikes?"

"Yeah. The old man got himself hurt bad in a horse wreck. Finally he died, and she wanted to go back to Iowa to her people."

"I guess we can look inside," Luther said, and started for the door.

"Yeah. Teddy won't care none."

Luther pushed open the door; Ben charged past him in wild pursuit of a pack rat. The race ended in a collision with the wall and the angry Ben barking at the hole the rodent escaped through.

The room looked untouched. Dishes had been washed and stacked. An iron skillet wiped clean sat all greased and ready on the range. The bed was even made up. A six-point elk rack hung over the fireplace and some working clothes hung on the wall pegs. It reminded Luther that Dikes had been headed for a dance, according to the major, and no doubt he wore a suit of his best clothes.

"Here's something interesting, I bet, if you can read." Hirk held up a leather bound book. "It's got writing in it."

Luther's heart stopped. He couldn't act too excited, but he needed an excuse to examine that book if it was Dikes's diary. The killers' names might be spelled out in those pages.

"Here, you can read it." Hirk chuckled and handed it to him.

"Guess we should, and then be sure his relatives get it."

"I'd kinda like to hear what he had to say."

With a slow nod for the man, Luther agreed wholeheartedly. "I'll put it in my saddlebags for safekeeping."

"Yes, sir. Sure ain't no sense in a pack rat eating it."

A loud sneeze of approval from Ben drew a laugh from both men. The feel of the leather cover in Luther's hands made his heart race as he opened the pages and turned them toward the light coming in the small window.

March 10th, cold crisp weather, rode over to T. G.'s. We shot a fat mule deer doe, dressed her, and split the meat. Spent the night at his place and I read some of Shakespeare's sonnets to him. For a man with so little education, T. G. understands William better than I do.

Luther looked up and saw the half-dozen volumes of Shakespeare on the shelf.

"He say much?" Hirk asked.

"Killed a deer."

"My, my, be plumb interesting." Hirk said, making a clucking sound with his tongue.

"It's late enough in the day. Let's den up here," Luther said.

"You're the boss. Kind of hate to quit in mid-afternoon,"

Hirk said with a sly grin. "I'll go put the horses in the corral and bring in our bedrolls."

"I'll start a fire and we can have some bread with our beans tonight." Luther indicated the cooking range.

"Whew. Be like having a wife," Hirk teased, and beat the side of his leg with his hat as he went out to tend to the horses.

Luther followed him outside. He scoped the mountains towering over the place. The ridges were covered in tall timber with some higher, craggier peaks to the north that formed the rim. Shame Dikes had not continued to live and enjoy the view.

In back of the cabin, he found the wood supply and busted up some kindling for the stove with the axe left in a stump. It was hard not to let everything go and simply read Dikes's diary front to back, but he didn't know yet where Hirk's loyalties lay. The man was a good enough cowboy but also a resident of the country. His loyalties to the home folks might be too great for him not to inform them. Luther swung the axe again and again. Soon the supply of stove wood looked adequate.

"You're a funny boss," Hirk said, squatting down and gathering the fresh split pieces. "Ones I've had in the past would've left the wood splitting to me."

"You ever work for McKean?" Luther asked, recalling the rancher's brusque manner and the way he acted toward the man.

Hirk looked up and made a sour face. "One roundup was all. You got to be desperate to work for him. He flies off the handle at everything. Got mad at me over nothing, I swear." He stood with his arms full. "I'll herd sheep before I'd work for him again."

"Sounds serious," Luther said, and looked down the canyon. More cattle moved in to water. He wondered what brand they wore. Maybe more of T. G.'s. But maybe there were McKean cattle here, too. More water in this valley than he'd seen since they forded Alma Creek, where Hirk

pointed out the thick tree limb supposed to have been the
gallows.

There had been no need for him to check the scene out.
The necktie party had been held over six weeks earlier, so
as not to draw any suspicion, they'd ridden on. He looked
once more at the series of water tanks that gleamed in the
sun like full moons, and the circles went far down the valley. Dikes owned something here. Yet the peril of all small
ranchers was that they never had enough income; then the
difference between mavericking and rustling became a thin
line. Maybe the diary would answer some of his questions.

"You read that book of his out loud and I'll make supper," Hirk said, on his knees, placing wood in the fire box.
"I make mean biscuits, big as a cat's head. Sides, I'm dying
to hear what he said."

"Sounds fair enough."

The first pages Luther read aloud were about Teddy
coming west.

*"I found the ranch in the valley. I have enough money
of my own to buy it. Oh, if heaven ever had a place on
earth, I am certain it would look like this ranch. The widow
woman acts grateful I am buying it. The house is small, but
well-built . . ."*

"Hmm," Hirk snorted, and looked up from sorting the
small rocks and sticks out of the dried beans spread on the
tabletop. "I'd smile, too, if I'd been her. He paid her twice
what folks thought the place was worth. Lordy, I could
smile over that."

Luther set the book down. "Who thought it was worth
that much?"

"I knowed McKean offered her five thousand."

"She didn't take it?"

"No. She didn't like him either. Been some bad blood
there. I ain't certain."

"So Dikes paid her what? He don't say in here."

"I heard seven thousand."

"Cattle, brand, and this place."

"Yeah. They'd proved up on three-sixty acres. It's a dry land homestead."

"Don't look dry to me."

"The rest of it is," Hirk said, and used the side of his hand to grade the good beans off the tabletop into his kettle.

"How many she-stuff did he get with the place?"

"She claimed three hundred plus, but there wasn't that many. Maybe two or two fifty, and then three calf crops. Never sell them till they're three."

"You worked for Dikes?"

"No. I worked for the stockmen's association on the roundups."

"Dikes belonged to that?" Luther asked as the man rose to put the beans on to cook.

"Nope. Only four men belong to it. McKean, Reed Porter, Chaboneau, and Crain. Of course, all the small outfits ride along at roundup time."

"Maybe those three had formed their own association?"

Hirk shrugged. "Maybe we'll know if they did by the time you finish reading that book."

Luther took the hint and went back to reading aloud.

"I went to Fortune today for supplies. Met a neighboring rancher by the name of McKean. Rather blunt man. Right on the street, he told me I was a damn fool for buying the place and that I would never survive in this country. Oh, well, Mr. McKean doesn't know how determined I am."

Luther glanced over at Hirk. "Bad blood?"

"Naw. It was McKean's way of welcoming him. He ain't ever nice unless it's a-going to favor him."

Satisfied, Luther went back to reading about Dikes being bucked off a tame horse, getting run over by an angry momma cow when he worked her calf, several rope wrecks. One took place on a hillside that Dikes claimed came within a hair's breadth of being his last, but he miraculously came out unscathed. Too sore to walk, he crawled home that night.

They ate supper and enjoyed Hirk's biscuits. Luther wished for some butter, but he still savored the treat of fresh

bread. Even their brown beans tasted better. No way to
have a meat source for two of them. Anything they butchered like a calf, deer, or elk carcass would spoil in the
daytime heat before they even started to eat very much of
it.

Luther read on. They learned about Dikes meeting the
other two men, as well as Charboneau and Crain. But several of the next pages became flowered with Miss Margie
Porter's presence. Obviously, Dikes became infatuated with
her on first sight. Some of it sounded intimate enough that
Hirk shifted around uncomfortably in his chair under the
lamplight.

"Nice girl?" Luther asked, looking over at Hirk's
whisker-stubbled face and his snow-white forehead shining
in the lamp's glare.

"Pretty." Hirk gave a jerk of his head. "A man'd be a
fool not to like her."

"Guess Dikes really liked her."

"Yeah. Go on."

"It bothering you?" Luther asked.

Hirk made a sour face. "It bothers me to be within a
hundred yards of that girl."

"Why, don't you do something about it?"

"Huh?" He scrubbed his bristled mouth with his hand
and shook his head. "Why, I'd not stand a chance in hell
with her."

"Why, cleaned up and little prodding, you'd be surprised." Luther leaned back and nodded in approval at his
notion.

"Don't tease me."

"I'm not."

"Oh, God almighty, Luther, I'd never sleep again if I
even thought I could hold her hand. My knees would buckle."

"She affects you that bad, you better do something about
it."

"Go on reading about Teddy." He waved at him with

his hands as if to shoo him away from the notion of him and her.

The next morning, they ate reheated beans and cold biscuits. Hirk repacked the mules, while Luther finished the dishes.

"Ben," Luther said, wanting to make a tour of the place on horseback, "you stay here. I've got cows to check."

The bulldog looked blank as he scratched his ear. With another finger shake to remind him, Luther set out on his roan. He trotted past several sets and noticed many of the cows wore Dikes's TK. But McKean had cattle there. Most of them carried longhorn blood, obviously out of stock he brought up from Texas. The calves showed to be three quarters Hereford or Durham, enough to block them out. He also noticed a few red Durham bulls, their polished white short horns glinting in the sunlight.

A couple of good white-faced sires hung around the tanks with their own harems ready to argue about territory. The bulls deep bellowing echoed across the valley. He looked up and saw Hirk coming with the mules and Ben.

Hirk suggested they ride on east. His plan was to make Burtle's place by dark. Luther noted a few B Bar stock there, too. Those six tanks had to be the main water source for the area, pivotal for all the livestock. How badly did the other ranchers need it? He booted Cochise after Hirk and the mules. Ben gave the place his final sneeze of approval and they headed for the next range.

At noon they paused to water their animals at a water hole in an intermittent creek Hirk called Beaver. Luther looked up from undoing his cinch to see a rider coming off the mountain, a rifle across his lap.

"We've got company," he said to Hirk, and jerked loose the cinch.

Mopping his forehead with a wet kerchief, Hirk straightened and frowned. "Looks like Charboneau, and he looks on the prod."

"We ain't done nothing to him."

"Don't have to. Watch him. He's got a bad temper."

Luther could see the rancher forcing the big gray horse downhill.

He shifted the Colt around. Be a good time to meet another one of the big ranchers, mad or not. He had enough high-handed business from his meeting with McKean—this one, too? The sounds of the rocks rolling downhill grew louder from under the gray's feet.

12

The envelope was postmarked Winslow, Arizona Territory. No
other address. No general delivery. Tillie turned it over in
her hand and then picked up the letter from beside her on
the bed and reread it.

> *Dear Tillie,*
> *I have a good job out here being a cattle buyer. I know*
> *that you have no desire to ever be my wife. I guess being*
> *a wife is too hard, or you can't stand to be with only*
> *one man in your life. Still, I want you to know that I*
> *love you. Maybe I should have said that before I asked*
> *you to marry me. Comes out hard. I never told another*
> *woman in my life that I loved her. That does not matter*
> *now. But I wanted you to know I won't ever get over*
> *you.*
>
> *Luther*

She closed her eyes and tears ran down her face. He
loved her. How could she have been so foolish? All those
times he took her places. Never ashamed of her, took her
along to supper, to gamble, even to capture outlaws like
Lyman. He did all that because he loved her.

A knot in her throat threatened to cut off her breath. Her
heart hurt so much that she thought it might explode any
moment. She dabbed at the rivers of tears with a kerchief.
Damn you, Luther Haskell . . . damn you.

How could she leave all this? The safety, the security of
this fine house. The only comfortable place she'd known
her entire life. The only clean sheets, good meals, people
to protect her from mean men, and the camaraderie of the

other girls, even Molly, who was the sharp-talking mother when someone did not mind her.

He loved her. He loved the whore who ran away from a horny stepfather, got raped by filthy thugs on the river dock in St. Louis, then gave her tender body to a grimy old man whom she first thought was her friend. Luther wanted her.

How bad could being his wife be? He was no failing dirt farmer who couldn't raise whippoorwill peas. He had a good new job. He could surely afford a hotel room for them. That would be like being at Molly's. Have clean bedsheets. But what was Arizona like?

She jumped up, rushed over for the small box in her dresser, and dug out the precious letters Lily wrote her. Quickly she scanned them for the information in her friend's words.

Dry—desert is hot, but no snow, except on the peaks.

How could there be snow and it be hot? Lily must have been drunk when she wrote that.

The rain came today, the first in months. Oh, surely, it rained more than that if anything grew.

What could she do? She had over a hundred dollars in savings. A knock on the door. She looked up. Who was there? She scrambled to put all her letters in the small wooden cigar box. The lid closed, she replied, "Yes?"

"Your friend is back."

He's back? Luther is back. She jumped to her feet and, wild with expectation, drew open the door. Nothing. Then her gaze dropped and she saw Arthur's bald head. She sent a quick glance at Molly and nodded dutifully.

"Oh, Arthur, my dear, do come in."

"I told Molly you really helped my sore leg, rubbing it."

"Why, sure," she said and closed the door after him. "Excuse me, I must put up my box."

"Oh, sure."

She hurried to the dresser, dropped the box inside on top of her silky things, and pressed the drawer shut, then she glanced at the open window. *Luther, wherever you are, I'm coming.*

The last dusty miles from Hayden's Mill to Phoenix, Matt McKean drove past the irrigated fields of alfalfa. There were acres of the new wonder crop called Johnson's Grass, which made, according to what he could read about it, the best mule and working horse fodder in the world. No need to even supplement the working animal's ration with grain. Must be powerful forage. In this warm valley with irrigation, it was possible to grow tons of the coarse grass per acre and fill many Army hay contracts. A virtual gold mine on the ground.

New citrus orchards dotted the land. Vineyards, cotton, and some Mexican corn tasseled and rattled in the hot wind. Arizona would soon be the horn of plenty for the nation, if they ever got a railroad built to serve it. Why, they could grow things in the Salt River Valley when the northern parts of the nation were buried in snow. Rails would be the answer. That might never happen in his lifetime, though. If he even thought it would, he'd invest in some of that farm land.

Beside the caliche road, ditch water rolled down a small canal until it turned off into a lateral one to feed rows of a dry bean crop. The Army was paying top price for them. All of soldiers stationed in the territory because of the Indian trouble made the local market endless.

He flicked the weary horse to keep him trotting. Dizzy from the heat, he looked forward to a bath and a drink in the Siebring Hotel's bar. Another hot gust of wind off the sunbaked roadway scorched his face. It would be better if the wind didn't even blow. Must be 110.

At last with the horse and buggy parked at the livery, he strode over to the Siebring and registered at the desk. A porter took his bags to the room and Matt ordered a bath and water brought up immediately. The hesitant clerk agreed and told him it would be there in ten minutes.

Matt stepped into the barroom and ordered a double.

Looking about, he didn't recognize anyone he knew. With a sigh, he turned back to his drink. Somehow, he needed all the information on this John O'Malley and his Flat Iron Cattle Company. He'd have to work through some other sources. His banker, Arch Collins, might know, but he couldn't afford to upset him with news of more pending competition for the range up there.

The bartender came back and Matt motioned him over. "You know a John O'Malley?"

"Yes, sir, he comes in here often."

"You seen him today?" Matt asked, looking around, then went back to resting his elbows on the polished bar. Damn, he was tired from the hard two-day drive.

"No, sir."

"Guess he's a big cattle man."

The bartender gave a "maybe" face. "Looks more like a banker to me. He dresses more businesslike than most ranchers."

"He does own a large cattle company?"

"They say he's got pens and stuff over at Hayden's Mill."

Matt wished he had stopped there and checked the large flour and grist mill on the Salt; it would be a good place to learn things. Especially since O'Malley was located there. Didn't sound like he was the kind to push in someone else's range; he'd expected a wiry Texas rancher with some gun hands to back him. Better reserve judgment until he learned more about him. Satisfied, he thanked the man and went to see about his bath.

The room's sweltering air gagged him despite the fact the windows were open. Coming to Phoenix at this time of year was absurd, and he would't be there, except for the threat of the invasion by more stock. Undressed, he slipped into the tin tub. Thank heavens, the water wasn't too hot. His mind still dazed by the day's heat and hours of it still left, he soaked away for a while.

He ate supper in the hotel dining room. The oysters were fresh, anyway. If they ever got a railroad into this valley, those ocean gems wouldn't be so high-priced. After his meal, he went back in the bar and joined two stockmen from near the Yavapia county seat. Dick Woolard and Josh Hancock ranched north of Prescott.

The three men sat at a side table. Matt wanted to know what they might have heard about the hangings around Prescott. Across from him, Hancock rolled a cigarette in his fingers, then licked it shut.

"How's the rustling up in the basin?" Hancock asked. Then he stuck the cigarette in his mouth and struck a pearl-headed parlor match under the table. It flared up and ignited the twisted end of the cylinder. Hancock drew it from his mouth in a puff of smoke. "Or did you boys cure it?"

"Someone did."

"Ha. Come on, you boys did what the rest of us needed to do. String them jaspers up."

Not to be pulled into the trap of admission, Matt nodded. "I owe them, I guess."

"Rupp sent up a pair of deputies, didn't he?" Woolard asked, looking over his tented fingers.

"Been up there a month or more. Ain't caught a damn rustler yet."

Everyone laughed and ordered another round of good whiskey. Matt didn't want the liquor loosening his tongue, so he sipped his slowly. The price of cattle was bantered around, and Matt brought the conversation back to this new buyer of Allen's that he was curious about.

"You ever meet his new man, Luther Haskell?" he asked them.

"Nope. Must be brand-new."

"I know Jasper Dalton, but never met this Haskell."

"Must have some drover experience. Allen sent him up there to gather T. G. Burtle's stock."

"Wonder why he didn't wait till roundup this fall?" Hancock said, busy rolling another smoke with his finger.

"I wondered the same thing," Matt said. Then he dropped back in the chair and reflected on all he knew about the new man. Obviously, Haskell had hired Hirk to help him. Worthless trash, but the man probably didn't know any better. He'd be a lot smarter after he started that roundup.

O'Malley never showed up. Matt had asked the bartender to alert him if he came in. Perhaps the man was out of town.

The next morning, Matt rose early. His head hurt, and coffee didn't clear it. At last, he went in the empty barroom and tried a double whiskey. No better, no worse, he planned to set out with his horse and rig during the morning letup in heat. Not cool, but nowhere near the oppressive daytime highs.

"Where's this Flat Iron Cattle Company?" he asked the old man at the livery.

"They've got pens south of Hayden's Mill a mile or so and some hay ground over there."

"New outfit?"

"Yeah," the swamper said, tossing the harness on his horse. "They've already got hands hired. I heard they were buying she-stock and steers."

"Paying a premium?"

"I don't know. Just talk I hear. You got some to sell?"

"Could have if the price was strong enough."

The grizzly-faced old swamper, who looked to be dying for a drink, spat in the dust and nodded. "Hell, it's all for sale for the right price."

Mid-morning Matt drove through the open gate. The black and white Flat Iron Cattle Company sign looked brand-new. He reined the horse up before the house under rustling cottonwoods. Hell's breath had begun to stir, and Matt knew it would be a furnace's blast in his face going back to Phoenix. He regretted not bringing his bags so he could head for home after he learned this outfit's purpose.

A lanky cowboy sauntered down to the yard gate, hushing the barking border collies. His red silk shirt and silk kerchief set him off as something besides a ranch hand. The tall crowned Stetson like new and a cross draw holster with an oily Colt that gleamed in the sun, told Matt lots about him. He wore his trousers tucked in high-top boots. He looked Matt over with suspicion in his narrowed eyes.

"John O'Malley?"

The man shook his head. "He's not here today."

"This is his place?" He searched around. Cattle in the pens. But he couldn't tell what kind or how many. He could see their dust as they milled and heard their bawling. Several head, he guessed.

"Yes. You an investor?" the cowboy asked.

"Could be. My name's McKean."

"Toot Burns."

"Well, Toot, you and I know you can't run many cattle on this farm."

"Shipping point. There's more than ten million acres good grazing out there waiting for our stock and free for the taking." He made a wave with his left arm meaning all around, but that included the basin in his toss.

"I understand O'Malley is considering Christopher Basin."

Burns folded his arms and nodded. "Plenty of grass up there."

"Tell O'Malley I dropped by." Matt lifted the reins. He suppressed the swelling of anger washing over him.

"I will."

"Then you tell him I said to keep his gawdamn cattle out of the basin if he wants to see them again!"

"You threatening—why, you sumbitch . . ." Burns's hand went for his gun butt.

"I don't need to threaten. He'll learn fast enough what'll happen if he makes a drive in that country."

"You sum—"

"Save your words for the damn funeral and don't come 'less you have your life insurance paid." Matt clucked to the horse and slapped him with the lines. Another minute, he'd jump out and pistol whip that Texas gunny with his own Colt. O'Malley would need tougher men than him. Hell, even Jakes could turn Burns inside out and hang his hide on the corral fence.

Matt swung the horse in a dust swirling circle and, as he completed it, saw a flash of the red silk shirt. On the run to stop him, Burns raced alongside as hard as he could, then he lunged for him. Matt raised his boot in time and planted it in the flushed man's chest. It propelled the hired gunsel backwards into the cloud of dust. Satisfied that Burns was down, Matt galloped the horse for the gate. Bent over the dash, he halfway expected any moment to hear Burns pop a cap or two after him.

No bullets this far. On the road at last, he slid the rig around and headed the horse wide open for Hayden's Mill. The gauntlet was laid. He could only hope his threat would dissuade O'Malley from his plans, but he didn't feel his effort went far enough . . . yet.

In deep thought about what he should do next, he spent the afternoon in Hayden Mill's Silver Bell Cantina, a thick-walled adobe building on Main Street that reeked of cigar smoke, cheap perfume and the sourness of booze. He drank beer that was not as cold as the small cocky Hispanic bartender said it would be.

In a side booth, so he could watch the door in case that red-shirted gunsel decided to trail him, he toyed with a *puta* named Minnie. In her teens, with wide innocent eyes and pouty lips, she wore a low-cut blouse and skirt. In anticipation of gaining his attention, she squirmed against him in the most heated, provocative ways. Sent his hands to her especially private places for him to discover that she only wore a blouse and skirt.

Entertained by her efforts and nimble fingers, he wondered about O'Malley and his plans. How he needed to establish a spy in his outfit to be certain they didn't one day simply show up there with ten thousand head. Her fingers soon undid his pants in her boldest exploration of the afternoon. She smiled up at him with a look-at-what-I'm-doing grin. Of course, in the dimlit barroom, with their probing hidden in the booth and beneath the table, who cared?

Yes, he needed a spy down there. Who could he send?

Her activities distracted his thoughts. Sweeney O'Brien, a real loner. He would do it for enough money. Say double wages for him. Matt tousled the girl's limp black hair and grinned at her efforts. He'd have to do that—when he got home.

"Where is your place?" he whispered, his heart pounding and his hips aching with need for her.

She tossed her head toward the back door. He downed his beer, looked around, and then slid out of the booth. He left some change for the beers. They went outside the back door into the oven hot alley that swept his face like a prairie fire. She dragged him into a filthy crib off the alley that stunk of a full night jar.

Inside the dark, stifling room, he saw a shrine to the Virgin Mary in the corner. Ribbons and bows were pinned up around it. Black beads of a rosary were draped on top of the statue. Even whores need their God. She began to undress him. The heat of the room or the beers made him dizzy—or was it his eagerness for her body? He paid her fifty cents.

Naked as Eve, she coaxed him onto a sunken rope cot. They rubbed their sweaty bellies together until he reached a conclusion. Afterward, he fell asleep, to awaken later alone in the sweltering crib in a sea of his own perspiration, with his guts and bladder complaining for relief. Clothes pulled on hard, they stuck to his wet skin. Out of his numbness, he realized to check for his money. As he suspected, some of the bills in his pants were gone. Close to fifteen dollars stolen, he decided after counting what was left. He jammed the remaining bills back in his pants. Damn her thieving ass!

At last, seated in the fly droning outhouse, he repeatedly went over the theft. Served him right for falling asleep. If he ever caught her ass, she'd regret it! Hell, he would never see her again. The others would hide her. Disclaim her. What did a man expect from a fifty-cent whore? Done at last, he hitched his pants and blinded by the light when he opened the door, fought his way outside into the airless alley.

One thing for certain, O'Malley would do more than that to him if he let him. Better get home and tell the others what was coming. Wilted by the oppressive temperature, he headed for where his horse and buggy were hitched in the shade. It had been a bad trip. When he passed the back door of the cantina, he considered going inside and raising hell about her thieving ways. Wouldn't do a bit of good. The bitch probably slept with the town marshal too.

He forced back the urge to gag. Better get back to the cool mountains before this damn heat killed him.

13

Nothing here. That was Luther's first thought looking around
the unkept one-room cabin. If T. G. Burtle had anything, it
had been stolen or never existed. The bed was a raw tick
mattress that showed several stains. Straw poked out of
some of the mouse holes. One torn, work-worn shirt hung
on the wall. A few dirty dishes sat on the table, old crates
for chairs, and some splintery boards nailed together for a
table.

His enamel wash pan was chipped like it had been
beaten with a hammer, and a wooden water bucket sat on
the dry sink with a spliced rope for a handle. The lone
window was curtained in cobwebs.

"Ain't much, is it?" Hirk asked, looking around with a
scowl.

"For a man with as many cattle as we've counted, it sure
ain't no place."

"Maybe saving his money. Got a fortune buried in here."

"You look for it. I'd as soon camp outside tonight as
stay in this den," Luther said.

"Hold on. I ain't that all fired anxious to stay in here
either. Money or no money."

Luther looked around the shack for the last time, disappointed there was nothing for him. Another blind canyon
was all he could think about and that answered nothing
about the man or his demise.

Hirk chuckled about alluding to Burtle's money in there
and still laughed as they went outside.

With a gourd dipper, they each drank from the cool
spring above the cabin. Luther noted how the mossy
wooden trough ran the water into a large rock and mortar
stock tank. The excess flow eased over the lip in a green

slimy streak and went into the large circle of muddy ground in front of it.

"Well, we've seen Burtle's home ranch."

"And Dikes," Hirk said. He headed for the mules and turned back to tell him, "we can see the third one's place tomorrow, then I think that we'll have seen most of the country we need to ride over for the B Bar stock."

"Yeah," Luther agreed. That might salve his curiosity some about the dead men. Burtle looked to him like a hard case from the condition of his cabin. A man who would grunt if he didn't want to talk to you. Someone hiding a past as well, though the major never mentioned it. Burtle might not even be his real name.

Through with his own investigation, and marking critical places, Ben found the mud. He bellied down like a fat hog in the wet spot, and lay there panting with his large red tongue out.

"Bet you don't have any trouble sleeping tonight," Luther said to him, and headed to help Hirk unload. His bulldog received a good workout keeping up with their horses each day, but Ben never wanted to be left behind.

"Tell me about Luke Stearn," Luther said, tossing down their bedrolls from the pannier on the second mule.

"Another one who drifted in a couple of years ago. He was a cowboy, never heard him say where he came from. Rode roundup two years ago for the stockman, then that summer he drove in some dairy cross stock, along with a few head of rough desert steers with his S brand blotched on them. Had it recorded. Must have bought them culls down in the Valley. You get a brand, they don't pay you any more to work at roundup."

"Even if you only have a few head?"

"Right. You got a brand, then you're a rancher and you've got to be represented on the roundups."

"Kinda keeps poor cowboys out of the business."

"Yeah, if you ever want any work."

"You reckon he used a long lope?"

Hirk looked up from where he was squatted on the

ground, starting a fire. "That's a matter of opinion. See, if you own a brand, then legally you can capture and mark unbranded yearling or older unmarked cattle with your own brand. That is, on the same range where you have stock."

"So a few head allows you to maverick?"

Busy with his fire start, Hirk nodded. "And that's rustling to the big boys. They figure them yearlings are theirs and they just were missed. I don't think any of them boys was dumb enough to brand a calf sucking a cow. That's rustling."

Hirk shared a look with Luther. Then the man continued. "I've probably said too much. But not a one of them four big outfits had a case of calf branding to show Sheriff Rupp's deputies. But they are still up here looking for the lynchers."

"If those three weren't guilty of rustling, then those who hung them are guilty of murder?"

"Hard to ever prove."

"Hard to prove," Luther agreed, looking through the pine boughs at the towering peaks. Slate-blue slopes shown on the steeper side. Nice country, and so far he was yet to find a tick on his body—something he recalled as being a plague in the Indian Nation. Being a spy was slow work, but the major promised he had other cases if this job ever hit a dead end.

In a few days, he would be gathering Burtle's cattle. That should spice up his life. He hadn't done that kind of work in a few years. Hands on hips, he stretched his back. What the hell was Ben raising Cain about?

He hurried around the shed. "Ben! Ben, get back here!"

Past the corner, he looked uphill. A large black bear was facing the raging bulldog, who was stopped thirty feet in front of her, challenging her with his ferocious barking.

"Ben! Ben McCollough! You crazy fool. She'll make ground meat out of you. Get back here."

The loud report of a rifle reverberated over the hill and back. Bark flew all over the bear, who decided the tree must have exploded. She shied and took off across the slope.

"Ben!" Luther shouted through his cupped hands, realizing Hirk's shot was to scare off the bruin and not kill it. The cowboy made another shot in the pine boughs over the black scrambler to speed her retreat. Ben came loping back like he had run off the intruder.

"Gritty little devil, ain't he?" Hirk said in admiration.

Still angry with him, Luther scowled at the dog. "And a damn foolish one, too. Why, that old bear would have eaten him in two bites."

"Probably give her some real indigestion." Hirk chuckled.

"Probably would. Ben, you either forget bear hunting or get ready for dog heaven. On second thought, you're going to the hot place. Lot hotter than up here." He left the panting Ben at his mud hole and went off to help Hirk cook the evening meal.

They found Stearn's half-walled tent in mid morning. At first, they reined up at the iron pump over the dug well and took turns filling the dry tank and watering their horses. Luther had seen several B Bar branded cattle in the area, so the roundup would be perhaps two weeks or longer. Of course, the ones they didn't get up could be cut out in the range wide fall gathering.

The tent stood on a knoll with a hitch rack and an iron cot inside, made up neatly. The inventory included a camelbacked trunk, a dry sink, a couple of captain's chairs, and a small table. The iron stove served for his heat and cooking, a rusty stove pipe went out through a metal patch in the yellowing canvas, which let in a mellow light on the contents. Well-worn carpet covered the floor, though Luther decided there was dirt beneath it.

"Find anything?" Hirk asked, sticking his head in the flap.

"No, I figured them deputies must have checked it already."

"They never found Dikes's diary." He waded over and threw open the chest. "Well, I'll be a horned toad." The cowboy reared back with a picture frame in his hands. "Here's Eve!" he said, and turned the painting toward Luther.

The canvas bore a well-endowed nude woman lying on a fainting couch. The picture was expertly done in oils, and the artist spared no details. She even wore a small smile on her face.

"Wonder what bar he stole that out of?" Hirk handed it to him and recovered another unframed one from the trunk. It obviously was an uncompleted artwork of cattle and mountains. "You reckon that Stearn did these?"

Beside him, Luther saw some more frames in the trunk and could smell the paint thinner and turpentine strong enough coming from the chest. He drew out another. It was of a naked woman wading in a stream. Her skin shone a stark white, but freckles were sprayed over her shoulders.

"Oh, damn!" Hirk slapped his hand over his mouth and his eyes widened in shock. "You reckon she posed for him?"

"You know her?"

"Hell, yes. That's Matt McKean's wife, Taneal, wading in Christopher Creek. Why, I'd know her anywhere with or without her clothes on. Oh, damn, you reckon McKean knows about this picture?" He tapped his finger on the hard-stretched cloth to make his point.

"No. He'd surely burn them," Luther said, taking off his hat and scratching his head. No man would have left his wife's nude picture for all the world to see, no matter how demure it looked. Stearn was an accomplished artist. Burtle understood Shakespeare and Dikes wrote of him. Three one-eyed jacks in these pastoral Alps with the singing pines, and all of them dead by rope.

Had McKean's wife posed for Stearn? Hard to ride up and ask a proper married woman that question. Stearn probably snuck up and spied on her. He wondered about Tillie. Sure would be hot in Fort Smith by this time of year. He kind of liked the cooling gusts of midday wind sweeping his face. The puffy clouds on the move northward promised an afternoon shower somewhere along the front of the rim country.

"What're we going to do about these?" Hirk asked.

"Leave them, they ain't ours."

They looked at them again, returned the paintings to the trunk and closed the lid. Both men nodded and went outside. Luther looked back. A strange enough deal, but none of his business.

He searched around for Ben. About that moment with an I don't-care-look on his face, the bulldog came around the corner. Good enough. He was fine. In the morning, they'd head back to Fortune and hire a crew. By his rough tally, there were over three hundred head bearing the B Bar brand. Two of the big ranchers remained that he hadn't met Reed Porter and Crain. Luther wondered what they were like.

In the evening shadows, campfire smoke swirling around his pans, Luther stirred the beans and looked at Stearn's half tent. A man could surely be surprised. He never expected to find impressive artwork inside it. Why, the ranny must have taken lessons. Luther had seen his share of barroom nudes painted to pay a bar bill or collected by the saloon owner for the mutual admiration of his customers. The largest one he could think of hung in Dodge City behind a famous polished bar whose name escaped his mind at the moment. He would never forget her open, suggestive wantonness nor her ample, nearly life-sized proportions. They called her Lizzie Dodge. He closed his eyes, recalling Tillie, then watched a line of cows and calves cross the valley headed east.

"Water up there?"

"Yeah. Over that ridge. They know where it is," Hirk said, lounging on his side and smoking a roll-your-own.

Plenty of water, too, near where Tillie resided, though by early July in most years the riverboats had to wait for a rise to get that far upstream. Shame he couldn't forget her. She wasn't the first in his life, nor he hoped the last. She simply made a bigger mark. He tossed a pinch of grass in the wind and heard thunder roll in the distance. They might need Stearn's tent before the afternoon was over.

"You decided if we should do something about that trunk?" Hirk asked.

Luther shook his head. "We better leave it all here."

Hirk nodded as if that satisfied him.

14

The stage left Papago Wells with a great jerk and shouts. A whip cracked and they were off in what the major considered his ride to hell. He shared the coach with the stiff-backed woman in her thirties, who last smiled when she whipped some boys in her classroom for putting a toad under some papers on her desk. No, he made up that part about Miss Hmm. In fact, at the moment, he knew less about her than anyone he'd ever shared a stage with.

He could recall between Tucson and Pacacho Peak how he unlaced a girdle for a lady rancher from Chino Valley, who was about to die in the confines of the newly purchased garment. A pleasant shady lady rode with him on the stage to Ash Fork, and then took the same train to St. Louis when he went on to Fort Smith to hire Luther Haskell. He wondered how Luther was doing in the mountains on his cattle buying business and investigation of the lynching.

"Going to get hot," he said to her, wiping his forehead with the kerchief that Mary had ironed. The drum of the horse hooves, wheels whirling, and the shouts of the driver all formed a rush that swept them across the flat desert that was studded with giant saguaros, great patches of prickly pear and the leafless weeping Palo Verde, the greenest of them all.

"I am told the army took temperatures of one twenty in this region at a place called Gee-lah-Bend that we will pass through," she said with a primness that he expected.

"Gila Bend is about halfway."

"You say Hee-lah."

"Yes. A Spanish word. G is an H sound."

"Oh, you must be proficient at their language to know that."

"No, ma'am. I'm still learning it. In the Army, I had a scout named Jesus who did all my translating."

"J's are H sounds, too?"

"Yes. You're going to Yuma?"

"I would know of no other sensible reason to ride this bucking bucket than to go there. It is an absurd abomination for anyone to have to ride in such conveyances. They tell me they are building rails to there, but they are not completed."

"Southern Pacific. They're coming along with it."

"Coming along! They should be shot en masse for not having those tracks finished." At that moment the coach jolted. It tossed them from side to side, then a dip caused her to suck in her breath. "Total abomination," she gasped.

"I take it you aren't a resident of Yuma?"

"Resident? No, no. I am going to see about my uncle's estate that he willed to me." She made a shocked face at the rotating cloud of dust that boiled in the coach from a dust devil. Then she pawed at the swirling dust with her gloved hands, all an exercise in futility.

"Sorry, I tried to miss that one," the driver shouted, and went back to urging on his teams.

"He can't miss the bumps in the road. How did he expect to miss that dust devil?"

The major found the question humorous and laughed. Then with a look of shock, her features melted and she managed a few chuckles.

"Are you not put out with this primitive mode of transportation?"

"Beats walking," he said, considering the oven-like conditions beginning to heat up with the sun's journey upward.

She rolled her brown eyes toward the ceiling as if looking for some celestial help from this dilemma. "But only barely."

"Barely." He smiled at her and wondered about the chasers and those being pursued, who were somewhere

ahead of them. Sure hoped they didn't end up in the midst
of their confrontation. Oh, well. He needed to learn about
the honesty of the prison contractors and solve that matter,
then get back to Mary.

"You live in Yuma?" she asked

"Preskitt," he said.

"Is that the capital? I thought it was called Prescott?"

"It's spelled like that, but up there folks say Preskitt."

"I see."

"When in Rome . . ." He looked across at her.

"Yes, you do as the Romans." Then she folded her arms
over her rather flat bosom. Squirming to find a comfortable
place on the leather seats stuffed with horse hair, she looked
at him about ready to give up even trying her facade of
"putting up with it all."

They made the Soda Springs stage stop and he helped
her down to allow her to use the facilities out back. He
went the other way and behind the adobe-walled horse corral, and drained his bladder in the coarse, thirsty ground.

What was contained in those purple saw-toothed mountains that edged his world at Soda Springs? Be interesting
to ride over and examine them. Pan for gold in the dry
washes. Read the strange crude signs on the canyon walls
that some ancient Indians had left a record of their time
spent in this waterless land.

Many times on an Army campaign, Too Gut, the Apache
scout with his company, led him up a deep canyon and
showed him the pictures of men, women, animals, and
weapons left by the "old ones" pictured on a rock face.
Some of the artists were good as modern-day ones. Others
drew crude children's art, but real.

"Who were the ones that did this?" he asked the smug
Apache who crouched down, always watching with his repeating rifle across his knees.

"Old ones. Part ghosts." The only answer he had for the
drawings.

He ambled back to the stage in the hot wind. Miss Hmm
was outside on the porch, fanning her face with a funeral

house fan. The first thing popped in his mind: Had she inherited a Yuma funeral parlor? She would be good at that.

The horse handlers and the driver fooled with a piece of harness on the outside horse of the second team. Obviously, immediate repairs were necessary. The driver sent one of the Mexican boys after something. He soon returned and the leather tug was replaced. Their actions drew another look at the sky from the jittery woman.

"Better get in. We're fixed," the driver assured them.

"I hope so," she muttered under her breath.

In late afternoon through the dust, Gila Bend's huddle of low-built structures looked blood-red against low sun. But the closer the stage grew to the main stop, it took on the weathered adobe hue of dirt. Rushing up the narrow streets, the major wondered why with all the worthless land about the place, they hadn't taken more room to build wider ones. Must be a Spanish custom, for Tucson, too, had the same cramped streets winding around it. Perhaps safety from the bloodthirsty bands of Apaches who raged over this land for two centuries led them to build such narrow ones. The Apaches had deprived the Mexicans, and the king of Spain before them, from ever making more than stabs at civilizing and drawing any commerce from the region.

The stage stopped in a clatter of brake blocks on the iron rims, which drew a moan from Miss Hmm.

"You can get a meal here," the driver announced. "Thirty minutes."

"In thirty minutes?" she asked in disbelief. Then she stuck her head out to examine the palm frond–covered, dust-floored porch. She accepted his aid to dismount, and skirt in hand, took the driver's directions.

The major wondered if the two sets of riders had reached that place. Nothing was mentioned at any of the previous change stations about them. He hadn't pressed for information, but even the chance of being in the middle of their final resolution with her along concerned him.

She joined him at one of the long tables. He felt she did so more because of her fears than wishes. Several sleepy-eyed Latinos loafed about. Some might have been Indians, but they all looked rather introspectively at the straight-backed lady in black. The kind of looks men gave a woman when they wondered what she would look like in the buff. He was quite certain they would find hers to be a rather angular form, shaped by bones close to the skin. They would be disappointed at their discovery, he decided as he drank the alkali-tasting coffee to pass the time.

The woman in charge served them each a tin plate of frijoles in a brown gravy and a stack of black-spotted corn tortillas. With some coarse salt on the table, he managed to season his enough to make them palatable.

"Those hot chilies in them?" She pointed at his food with a long finger.

"No, they aren't bad." He passed her the bowl of salt which had a grayish cast and was in chunks. "Crush some salt and try it."

"How?" she asked, looking in dread at the salt cellar.

"I used my spoon."

"Did they wash it?"

"Ma'am, you know as much as I do."

With a shake of her head, she used her dress to polish the dull spoon. Between bites, he watched her mash the granules and spread them over the beans on her plate. She made a great effort to stir them all around in delaying tactics he felt postponed the time she must orally accept them.

"You think they're all right to eat?"

"They aren't sour," he said, and toasted her with his next spoonful.

She took her first bite and issued the most disgusting sound he ever heard. He wondered if she'd swallow them. But with perseverance, she finally managed to choke the small spoonful down.

With a face that two lemons could not have made any more sour, she went, "Ah, bad."

To keep from chuckling, he wiped his face with his kerchief. Then when he thought he might have to go outside to control his amusement, she smiled at him and that gave him permission to laugh aloud. The rest of the onlookers seated around the wall laughed, too, harder than he did. They raised enough dust slapping their legs that it caused her to sneeze. It must have been the first sneeze a gringo lady ever made in that stage station, for it only added to their mirth.

Her hand shot out and stayed his hand. "I am certain this must be a mistake."

"The food?" he asked with a frown, after deciding their English was the foreign language in this remote place.

"No, we're in a lunatic bin." Frowning seriously, she darted her gaze around to indicate their company. Then she laughed freely and shook her head in defeat.

He nodded in agreement, then watched in approval as she fed herself several more spoons of the beans. No matter the quality of the food, he knew from his Army days one needed some form of sustenance to survive such trips.

Their stage finally went off into the crimson sunset in a clatter of hee-yaws and pounding hooves on the baked caliche. The desert swallowed the day into twilight. The sun's blast released its hold on the super heat and he wondered if he would be able to sleep the rest of the way.

But suddenly, there were shots. They sounded like Chinese firecrackers at first, and the Major scrambled for his Colt. Orange flairs lit the night. Angry words of Spanish filled the darkness. Orders to give up. More blasts. The driver gave a shout about being hit. Then the coach swung to the right, and the major knew they would turn off. He dropped his revolver and tackled her. Despite the screams in his face, he wrapped his arms around her, in a cocoon hoping to break part of their crash as the coach struck ground and skidded on its side.

Dust boiled in. The cracking of splintering wood sounded like shots. Some of the horses were either down or injured; he could hear their shrill, pain-filled protests. His head hurt where he had hit the divider by the door. In choking dust and darkness they slowly released their embrace and he looked closely at her ashen facial features.

"Anything broken?" he asked in a whisper. His ear turned to listen for the words and location of the highwaymen.

She barely shook her head, frozen in his arms. "How about you?" she asked in a hushed voice.

"I think I am fine. Need to find my gun." He raised with the side of the coach under him and the benches piled on top of them. They untangled slowly and he winched at his hip that he had hurt in the wreck. She wrestled with the seat and he used his hands to feel for the Colt. It had to be there. His fingers found nothing.

Outside in the night, there were horses coming hard, and voices. Words spoken in a tough dialect he didn't underhand, but they told him enough. They were the outlaws.

"Where is it?" she hissed. Feeling anxious over his loss, he shook his head. Crouching, they moved the seat cushions and remained low enough not to show themselves above the sides.

"Must have fallen out," he said under his breath, still on hands and knees hoping against hope it was there somewhere in the inky darkness. He closed his eyes and his heart sank when he heard one say. "Hands up! Get out here!"

15

"Oh, damn," Tillie swore under her breath, already hearing the conductor announcing the next station.

"Winslow's next stop, folks," the conductor repeated as he hurried through the car.

She wet her lips. Her nerves were so frayed, she felt she might scream at the slightest provocation. It was so far out here. Why did that foolish boy want to come out to this God-forsaken land, anyway?

Tillie thought, *Thirty-two is hardly a boy, but Luther, I don't know about your choice.*

There were no trees at this place either. None for hundreds of miles. Maybe thousands, she had no way to know how long her butt had been on that hard bench as she stared out the dirty windows at nothing. She almost cheered at the sight of some cows grazing in the distance when they looked up at her or at the train's whistle. No mind. They looked at her.

In her only experiences with cows, she learned they gave milk and at the expense of a swishing tail of fresh manure or burrs or feet that kicked forward could spill all the hard-pressed effort. Mr. Rodiabaker had a cow named Gladdis like that when Tillie was a girl of nine and her family lived on his place. She hated Gladdis then for all the mean things she did to her, but in this land of nothing but rocks and brown grass, even that damn brown cow would be a welcome friend.

On the platform, she looked about. No sign of Luther. Perhaps he had not gotten her letter yet. She'd mailed it the day before she left Fort Smith. A knot formed in her throat. If he had gotten her letter, he surely would have been there. Then the worst imaginable thought struck her.

He had been killed. Her knees threatened to buckle, and she hurried to a bench on the platform. Seated there, she clasped her hands together, wrung them in her lap, and fought to recover her presence.

No. He couldn't be dead. She'd come all this horrible way to marry him. Not to be a sissy, nor have any more daydreams of all the bad things their union would bring to her life. In Arizona or wherever they lived, she would be happy. Why, when she left Fort Smith in that train car and waved her last good-byes to her "sisters" crowded on the platform, some were crying, others laughing and shouting rather obscene things for her to do with her new husband. Oh, well, they meant her well. Though no doubt, some onlookers within hearing distance didn't like them being there in public. She'd heard some grumble how they should never have allowed that lot of sluts out of their cribs.

She'd hung out of the window, waved her kerchief, and fought back tears until she could no longer see their faces. Oh, to hell with those snooty church sisters in the train car. The ones who sat there like cigar store Indians in their seats staring at her. Determined to make herself a life outside the whorehouse, she took her seat as ladylike as she knew how, sweeping her dress beneath her.

A tomboy for most her life and the rest of the time a woman of the night, she would have to mirror the ways of these fine ladies with their unsoiled reputations. Seated in the bright sunshine at Winslow, Arizona Territory, the cool wind sweeping her face, she realized she had more important things than pleasing fussy folks; she needed to find Luther.

With effort, she took her two bags inside the depot and left them with the train agent who agreed to keep them safe until she could come back for them. With her shoulders thrown back and the small box hat set and pinned on her head, she looked over the traffic. Then as deliberately as she could, she took her skirt in hand and went down the stairs to the street. She felt eyes on her as she prepared to cross the street, waiting for the passage of a freight wagon.

A teenage boy on top of the load shouted to the driver.

"See her! Wow, she's sure purty."

Mouth set, she dared not break into a warm smile for him, but stared ahead at the storefront across the way. Whores did such things as grin at foolish men's words to egg on their business. That was last week. This week, she belonged to a good man and he would expect her to be true. Her heartbeat drumming under her ribs, she hoped she had the willpower to do it all right.

The first man she asked in the store had not heard of Luther Haskell. She thanked him and with her shoulders back, went out on the boardwalk. After almost colliding with her, that same silly boy from the wagon jerked off his hat.

"Aw, ma'am, I'm sure sorry I got in your way."

"You're excused," she said, in a voice so cold, she hardly believed it came from her throat. Then with her chin up, she swept past the green-eyed youth with his mop of red hair.

A fear crept in her stomach as she went down the rough boardwalk. What if she couldn't find him in Winslow? No way she'd ever locate him out there on the treeless steppes. Perhaps she should check at the stables next? She went down the steps and the sour smell of horse manure swept her face as she entered the stables.

Skirt clutched in her hand, she peered around for anyone in attendance. It came to her that she had forgotten how strong horses really smelled. The aroma clung to men who visited her at Molly's, but it was so strong in the alleyway of the barn, it burned the linings of her nose.

"Ma'am?" A short man with three days' beard stubble stood before her holding his hat and a pitchfork.

"I am looking for Luther Haskell. Have you seen him?"

"Yes, ma'am. He—you all right, ma'am?"

Head in a swirl, she gulped in a deep breath. Her hand flew to her chest to contain the jolt to her heart. "Yes," she gasped. "Where is he?"

"Off buying cattle for Mr. Allen. I reckon he's over in the Christopher Basin, ma'am."

"What train goes there?" She tried hard to fathom how far away it could be to this basin he spoke about.

A worried expression spread over his gray whiskered face and with his lips peeled back, it exposed his yellow teeth. "There ain't none. There's a mail wagon goes there. You might hitch a ride on it."

"Where does it leave from?" she asked.

"Oh, here. But you better go find Jinxs, Jinxs Carter. He drives it."

"Where do I find Mr. Carter?"

He put the pitchfork against the wall. "I'll go get him for you. He's up in the Bucket Blood and they won't let the likes of you in there."

"Thanks. I will wait." She stepped back out of the barn's alleyway as the man hurried off to find Carter. Then she became aware she needed to act composed standing there and feeling everyone must be staring at her in the blue dress. Like it was not unusual for her to be before the open double doors of a livery and act unfazed by all this business about a mail wagon and a man called Jinx. She wanted to go squat on her heels and chew on a straw.

"Well, howdy, ma'am!" Before her stood a man as big as bear with a flowing beard that circled his face and the most prominent thing about him was a bright red bulb of a nose that stuck out of it. Dressed in a smoke-stained buckskin coat, he bowed clear over to sweep the ground with his great floppy brimed hat.

"Mr. Carter?"

"Yes. What can I do for you, darling?"

"I need to a ride to wherever you go."

"Fortune."

"Fortune?" She glanced for reassurance at the liveryman, who quickly nodded.

"Fortune," she repeated for him.

"You have any luggage?"

"Yes. I will go get it."

"No need in you wearing out your pretty shoes. Where is it at?"

"The depot."

"We'll swing by there and get it. You ready to go?"

"Now?" Strange, he wanted to leave in midday and wasn't ready to go a few minutes ago. She nodded. The quicker she reached this place, the sooner she could join Luther. Before she did another thing, she needed some immediate relief from the pressures inside her.

She held the back of her hand to her forehead. "Pardon me, but I need to . . ."

Both men looked at each other, and the lost look on their faces was enough to make her want to laugh aloud. Then Carter raised his index finger and pointed to the rear. "It is out there, ma'am."

"Thanks." With determination, she went past the switching tails of the many horses tied in the barn. The door to the outhouse hung on leather hinges and creaked in protest when she threw it open. Been a while since she had used such a crude place, complete with cobwebs and spiders.

Luther, I am coming if that big galoot out in front can drive a buckboard. A shiver ran up her spine standing behind the closed door. *Lord, please don't let a creepy crawly bug get under my dress.*

16

Miss Hmm tore open her purse and quickly handed him a short barrel small-caliber Colt. The major smiled in the darkness of the upturned coach. The feel of the revolver in his grasp gave him newfound confidence. He looked up at the stars. No way out but to climb through the door above their heads.

Nearby, a discussion began in Spanish, no doubt over their refusal to come out in the night.

". . . vamoose, Pablo!" Then came the sounds of someone running across the ground.

The major held his finger to her mouth for her to be silent. She nodded and remained frozen. The Colt cocked, he hunkered down, so the man had to get well up on top of the coach to see them.

Next there were sounds of a bandit climbing up, then the door opened to the sky, with the outline of his large sombrero against the starlit sky. The major sprung up, grasped him by the shirt, and jerked him down amongst them. A swift blow of the gun barrel silenced his shouting, and all was quiet. Miss Hmm made stifling sounds to suppress her terror.

"Pablo! Pablo?" Then there was the shuffle of horses being reined around and low talking from the others reached the major's ears. He crouched beside her and said to himself, "Don't shoot you fools, you might hit him!"

He drew the bandit's pistol out of his holster. Then he raised with the man's Navy in his fist. Once standing with his shoulders above the side, he fired the cap and ball at the shadowy outlines. One man pitched off his saddle. His horse shied sideways spoiling another's aim. The major sighted a silhouette in the starlight, took a snap shot. He thumbed the Colt into action again. Black powder smoke burned his nose. Must be homemade, he decided. At last the Navy hammer struck on empty and he fired her Colt at the elusive riders. The robbers clattered off into the night, shouting and beating their horses.

The outlaw moaned. The major looked back and could make out the small derringer that Miss Hmm held in his face.

"I didn't want him talking," she said.

"Good idea," he said, sticking the two revolvers in his waistband. "Come here," he said to her. "I'll hoist you up so you can get out."

"Yes," she said in a small voice.

He wasn't sure what she dreaded the most, him having to hold her or leaving the sanctuary of the coach. No time for concern. Under his feet, he felt his own pistol that he'd dropped earlier. Sweeping it up, he jammed it in his holster, then took her by the narrow waist and lifted her onto the side of the coach. He let her pull her legs out and scoot to the edge. Nothing the bandit could do, so he boosted himself from the coach and dropped off the side. Then he caught her again and set her down.

"We need to see if we can help the driver," he said, looking about in the dim light. As he started up the road to look for him, she crowded close by, clutching her dress in both hands.

They soon discovered the man's still body beside the road. In the darkness, the major knelt beside him and felt for his pulse. Nothing. He rose to his feet and shook his head.

"We can't help him," he said.

"What now?" she asked in a hushed voice.

"Catch a loose horse," he said. "If they haven't run off. There should be two of them, but one will get us out of here."

She hurried along beside him as he searched in the starlit night for the silhouette of an animal. Most western horses ground tied. Which meant they shouldn't go far dragging their reins.

"Over there," he pointed and headed across the road.

"Will they come back?" she asked, carrying her dress and purse. She twisted around to look back at the coach, as if she expected the outlaw to emerge.

"Whoa, whoa," he urged the pony, too busy to answer her questions. Acting anxious, it moved away, snorted and side-stepped from his grasp.

"Oh, horse, be still," she said with impatience, and the pony did. It drew a smile on the major's face. What he couldn't get done with coaxing, Miss Hmm did by command. He reached out and caught the rope reins on the bosal and contained the horse. A check of the cinch and he swung in the old Mexican saddle. Ready for her to get on, he bent over to offer her the crook of his arm.

"Astride?" she asked.

"We don't have time to find a side saddle," he said, impatient for her to swing aboard behind him.

"But I don't have a divided skirt."

He shook his head, checked the impatient horse, and lowered his arm for her. She might not have on any dress at all if those outlaws caught them. Without a doubt, he felt certain they would do some violent things to her.

"Come on. We don't have time for niceties. We need to get out of here right now."

"Oh, all right. But don't stare at my bare legs."

"The furthest thing from my mind," he said, and hoisted her up until she sat astride on the saddle behind him.

"Hang on," he said, feeling the mustang arch his back and fight the bosal, ready to go to bucking. Acting broncy, he danced around beneath them. Her arms rushed around the major's abdomen and she clasped herself tightly to his back. Satisfied she was in place, he dug his heels in the pony's ribs and they headed west in a half run, half buck. At least for the major's satisfaction, they were headed in the opposite direction from where the outlaws went, and also toward Yuma in the star-sparkled darkness.

Somewhere out across the silver-lit desert, a coyote moaned. He felt her shudder in revulsion at the sound and squeeze him tighter.

"My name is Gerald," he said.

"You told me."

"Well, then what is yours?"

"Anastacia Brown."

"I'll call you Ann."

"Fine," she said, easing her hold. "How far will we have to ride?"

"The next stage stop, I hope." He felt her twist in the saddle and decided she must be looking back.

"Will they return?"

"Chances are good they might."

"Make this horse go faster."

"He's only a small pony. I want him to make it there."

"How far is that next stage stop?"

"Ten to twenty miles, I figure."

"What if we lose the road in the darkness?"

"Ann, this horse will stay on it. He's desert smart and hates cactus spines worse than we do."

"I hope so, Gerald. I sure hope so." She scooted up to the back of the sorry saddle and against him. Another coyote warbled at the moon and she gasped. He shut his eyes. Some mess.

17

Luther squatted on his boot heels. His new crew stood around, mostly younger boys in their teens who could be spared from their own families' ranch operations. The buck a day and found that Luther promised made them grin. Each boy brought three horses to ride, and while some of their ponies were not the greatest-looking, it saved Luther renting a remuda. For ten bucks Hirk rented six ranch horses for extra mounts. So the four boys and Bones, the whiskered old man hired as the camp cook along with Hirk, made his crew.

Bones had hobbled across the street to the mercantile to get his order of food stuff they would load on the mules.

"You boys savvy? I don't put up with drinking or tomfoolery on the job. All I ask is that you try. We need to gather these cattle as quickly as possible, and with the least hollering, yelling, and foolishness. I'm sending word to the outfits. We intend to start day after tomorrow on the far end of the basin, bring as many B Bar branded cattle this way as we can find. I have a meadow rented we can put them in if we need to double back."

Their heads bobbed in agreement to the terms. Slick-faced boys who didn't even need to shave yet. Blondes, brunettes, and one redhead named Ute. Luther watched the cocky one, the smallest, Pyle, size up the deal.

"Suits me. I'm ready."

"Me too," the bucktoothed Jason said, with his hat off and scratching his tousle of straw-like hair.

"I'm ready, boss," the freckled-faced Ute said.

Tag merely nodded. A thin-faced boy who was the poorest dressed of the four, he'd brought the sorriest string of ponies.

"Hirk's the boss when I'm not here." He tossed his head toward the man beside the corral. "Now I need to go see the brand inspector."

He made Ben stay there, left his crew, and crossed the deserted street. In the Texas Saloon, he found Stran, the inspector, nursing a glass of beer. This made his second meeting with the big-gutted man.

"You got some good boys hired. They'll sure work," Strand said, and nodded in approval.

"Yeah, I think so. That Tag must come from poor folks." He signaled to the bartender to bring him a schooner of beer and took the chair that Stran indicated.

"Widow woman raised him. They've never had much. He caught them mustangs himself and broke them. Don't worry. He'll make you a hand."

"I wasn't worried. I'm starting east and driving this way."

"Sounds great. Less work for me. You coming to the pens with them, I'll check them here." Stran raised his mug and toasted him. "You must have ran cattle yourself?"

"I made a few trips up the trail to Abilene and Dodge. Most of the cattle I've seen here are tame compared to them brush-eating longhorns I went after."

"Crossing them on the British breeds has helped."

"Give me a double!" someone slurred, staggering inside and leaning on the bar.

"Mr. Reed. You all right?" the bartender, Earl, asked, sounding concerned as Luther and Stran turned to see who it was.

"Reed Porter," Stran said under his breath, with a scowl of disapproval in his hard-set eyes. "Boy's sure fell in the bottle these past few weeks. He never used to drink like that."

"I need to talk to him. His place is on this side of McKean's, isn't it?"

Stran shook his head in warning. "Better wait till he's sober."

"He won't recall much today anyway," Luther said as

the man at the bar downed a double and gave a great gasp.

"I better get home," Stran said, acting uncomfortable about Reed's presence. "See you at the pens in a week or so." Quickly, he finished his beer, and with a wary eye on Porter's back, he rose, then quickly slipped out the bat wing doors.

Left to his own devices, Luther wondered why the brand inspector wanted no part of the drunk at the bar. There had to be a reason. An inspector held as much authority as any lawman, though their primary task was checking brands, crediting the owners of lost and strayed stock that got mixed with others. For some reason, he didn't want to be around Porter. Had they had words? Or did the man's condition bother him? No answer.

Porter turned and with his elbows hooked on the bar to support him, blinked his eyes at Luther. Unsteady, he tried to straighten, weaving until at last he found his balance.

"Who the hell are you?" he demanded.

"A man minding his own business."

"You got that outfit out there?" Porter tossed his head toward the pens.

"That's my crew."

"We don't want no more crews in this basin." He made a wide swing of his arm. "You hear about them got hung?"

"I have. Why?" Luther turned his ear to listen. Did this man know who hung them? Was he drunk enough to talk about it?

"You ain't got no gawdamn—"

"Easy, Mr. Porter," Earl said to quiet him. Another man in a suit came through the green curtain from the back. In his forties with a thin mustache, he looked like an owner or someone in charge.

"I'll handle this. Reed, you've had too much to drink. Why don't you come in the back room and take a little nap?" He took Porter by the arm. "Sorry, mister. He never meant nothing. Just a little too much old barley corn. You know?"

"I understand," Luther said, and turned his attention

back to his beer. What was eating Porter? He needed to know, but how could he do it? Porter, steered by the man, went through the green cloth door and disappeared. The whole time, the drunken rancher mildly complained, but his host was not taking any of it for an answer.

After Luther finished his beer, he left the Texan and went by the mercantile to check on Bones' progress. He found him scratching his belly and looking in dismay at the goods stacked upon the counter.

"About got it, boss."

"Good." Then, with both hands on his hips, Luther looked in wonderment at the array of things. "How're we getting all that on two mules?"

"Need four, I guess."

"My boss ain't buying two more mules." Luther shook his head in disapproval. One more problem.

"We need a wagon."

"Hard enough to keep up with mules in this country."

"Naw, I can make camp every night with a wagon."

What next? Luther looked at the man for the longest while, considering his next course of action. Finally, he drew a deep breath. Allen said he couldn't use a chuck-wagon. Bones, who came recommended as a good camp cook and experienced about the basin, said they could use one. He better find one.

"You know of a wagon we can rent?" he asked.

Bones grinned big. "Yeah. It won't cost much."

"Rent it and get loaded. We haul out at daybreak. Them boys will need supper tonight and breakfast in the morning. You need help getting it shaped up, put them to work."

"Yes, sir, Mr. Haskell!" Bones said, with so much enthusiasm that Luther frowned at him.

"I'll be back to pay you when he gets done," Luther assured the storekeeper.

What really disturbed him the most was Porter and his veiled threat. Get out of the basin. Was it a threat or a drunk's warning? First time that notion had crossed his mind. Did Porter mean get out of the way? He went outside on the porch and studied the pines on the dark rock out-cropping across the hillside. Porter knew something; something more than he had said. Damn. Luther had cattle to gather, a crew, and getting a wagon to worry about. A quick check of the storefront, and he nodded to himself—different than being a U.S. deputy marshal. With a badge, he could have taken Porter in or at the least interrogated him. Up here, he had no excuse or real authority without exposing his identity. With a rueful shake of his head, he hoped those mules were broke enough to harness and pull a wagon.

"Where did you get that dog?" Ute asked him after supper.

Full of Bones's rich cooking, his crew lounged around the camp fire in the twilight. Luther felt better after the crew had snubbed each mule to one of their horses and brought them and the wagon out to the camp on the edge of town. The green wagon and harness looked reputable and only cost ten dollars to rent. Burtle's heirs could afford that.

"I got Ben in a trade," Luther said, recalling the first time he put him the fat pup in his coat pocket. He wasn't much bigger than two coffee cups. "Rode in my saddlebags for months."

"I never seen one like him," Tag said.

"Lots you ain't seen," one of them quipped.

"Hey, bulldogs ain't real common nowhere that I've been out west." Luther tousled Ben's ears. "But if he has his way, half-breed ones will soon be more popular."

The boys laughed and Ben sneezed for them. The conversation went on to how the deputies investigating the hanging had at last left for Prescott. His new crew was close-mouthed about the lawmen, and the conversation waned.

"They never learned a damn thing either," Pyle said, and looked away.

"Someone knew something about it," Luther said.

"Mr. Haskell, it's better for your health not to know a

damn thing about them lynchings," Jason said, and the other heads bobbed around the fire.

"You boys know them three?"

"Teddy Dikes?"

Luther turned to look at Pyle. "You reckon he was rustling?"

"Wouldn't matter what I thought, now, would it?"

Luther nodded in agreement. "No, but you have a notion."

"He learned how to rope, Mr. Haskell. He was a real hand with one, and he told me there were enough mavericks in the basin to make him a rich man."

"Mavericks?"

"Mavericks. But some folks think they own them, Mr. Haskell."

"Unbranded yearling past cattle?"

"Yeah. Unbranded."

"You boys chase mavericks?" Luther looked across at them in the growing darkness.

"Can't. Our families don't have any stock in this basin." Pyle shrugged and looked away. "They won't allow it."

"Who's *they*?" Luther used a stick to scratch in the dirt.

"Big outfits. They said the brand law won't let you maverick where you don't have cattle on the range."

"You boys get threatened?"

"Matt McKean made a circuit over a year ago and handed our folks a copy of that law. Says we could get five years in prison if we got caught."

"Pyle, you reckon he had words with Dikes over that?"

The boy looked around, then said in a low voice, "A couple of times."

"You reckon McKean was there?"

"I'd bet a month's pay he was."

"Hell, Pyle," Jason said. "Him and his wife were at the dance when word came. I saw them myself. He went out and helped cut them down."

"Damn it. They could've hung them—God knows what time they was hung. Afterwards they could've ridden a big circle and come back." Pyle's voice sounded angry and defensive. He glared at the other boy.

"You don't know that," Tag said, wagging his head with an edge of fear in his voice.

"Well, just who else would have rode in here and hung them?" Pyle asked, then clapped his hand over his mouth.

Luther tossed a handful of small sticks on the red-hot coals. Simple question. And a damn hard thing for him to prove.

"Anyone got a fiddle?" he asked. "This talking is getting too damn serious."

"Tag has."

"Good. Tag, entertain us."

The boy about blushed as he rose and went to the wagon for his instrument. Then, from the hands of youth came the waltzes that Luther recalled from his own boyhood. Made a knot rise in his throat when he recalled Tillie. Had she received his letter? He'd wasted his time and a two-cent stamp on his last-ditch attempt to get her to come join him. He might as well give up. She wanted no part of being his or anyone else's wife. What a waste.

And Porter, if he ever caught him drunk enough, he could find out if the rancher knew who lynched those men. A gut feeling said he did. Luther stared deep into the red glow on the underside of the alligator juniper log. Waves of heat distorted it and blue flames leaped up like figures, fading in and out of his vision. Someone knew more than they were telling about the hanging. But how was he ever to find out?

18

"**Why are we stopping?**" she asked in the major's ear. "**Aren't** those lights up there a stage stop?"

"I think so."

The weary horse bobbed his head and he finally blew exhaustedly into the dust. The major jerked it back up. Was the single lamp a sign of welcome or should they take caution in consideration?

"Why aren't we going down there?" she insisted with a sharp edge in her voice.

"What if those bandits are down there?"

No reply.

"I want to be certain it's not a trap."

"Yes," she said in defeat. "May I dismount?"

"Sure." He let her grasp his arm and set her down easy. But she collapsed. He bounded out of the saddle and swept her up in his arms.

"You all right?" he asked.

"A little light-headed is all. You can put me down. I'll be fine." She said it so dreamily, he knew she would never stand without help. In the starlight, he looked around. There was nothing but the sand of the road and silver looking low bushes. No place to set her down.

He decided he would set her on the dusty road rather than risk some cacti that might exist off the tracks. On his knee, he gently lowered her to the ground.

"You all right?"

"I'm sorry. I didn't intend to be so weak."

"No need for concern. I'm going ahead and see if the stage stop is safe."

She twisted her head around and quickly spoke. "Don't leave me here alone."

"Then you get in the saddle and I'll lead the horse."

"Do you think—"

"I have no idea, but to be careful."

"Major?"

"Yes?"

"Help me to my feet, I can ride now."

His hands under her armpits, he raised her. She felt light as a feather as he steadied her. Then with determination, she reached for the stirrup and put her foot in it. He gave her butt a good boast and she settled in the seat.

"All right?" he asked.

"Yes."

He took the rope reins and started toward the beacon, his eyes dry and gritty, as the yellow lamp shown like a lighthouse. Through his boot soles, he could still feel the day's heat in the dirt. The dread that they were walking into another trap preyed on his mind.

He paused in the road to reload and straighten out his handguns. They had gouged him in the gut long enough. He handed her back her pistol and she dropped it in her bag. Then he tied the Navy by the leather strings to the saddle, lacking any way to reload it.

The cylinders still loaded in his own Colt, he spun the cylinder around to the empty one and laid down the hammer. Holstered, he pushed on. The place still looked as far away as when they first noticed it. Obviously the clear desert air made it appear closer.

Trudging along, he thought about Mary and his wonderful bed at home. She would be sleeping at this hour, the soft murmur of her night breathing like a lullaby, while he walked this oven of hell, and wondered if there would be any safety when he finally reached the next port.

"Stay here. I'm going to scout the place," he said when he could make out the pens and mud hovels in the starlight.

"Be careful," she said, and reined in the horse.

He nodded and hurried to check the corrals first. Colt in hand, he made his way through the low brush. Inside the yards, horses snorted in their sleep and stomped. None looked like the Mexican mustang that the outlaws rode in on. He went to the side of the building where light shone from a window and looked in the small pane.

A man under a filthy sombrero sat drinking from a bottle wrapped in wet burlap. He looked harmless enough. A woman slept in a hammock. A wave of relief swept through his shoulders; they were safe.

He tracked around the building and entered the door.

"Hello," he said.

"Huh!" The old man started.

"The stage was robbed. The driver is dead. I have a woman passenger out here."

"Oh, come in, Señor," the man said, struggling to get to his feet. His woman, sleepy-eyed, came out of the swing and asked about her.

"I'll get her," he said, and went out to call to her.

She made the pony trot the last hundred yards. Bouncing like a sack and holding the saddle horn, she arrived and he helped her down.

"We're safe?" she gasped.

"Yes. We're safe."

She threw her arms around his neck and kissed him on the mouth. His eyes flew open and for a moment he felt unsure what to do.

"That's for being so damn brave," she said with a sharp nod, then she turned with a new spring in her walk and headed for the lighted doorway.

"Ah, the señora, she is muy grateful."

"I guess," the major said, and rubbed the back of his alkali-tasting hand on his mouth. No figuring out women.

"How many robbers were there?" the man asked.

"I don't know. Several. I shot one."

"Good. You should have killed all of them. They killed Billy, huh?"

"The driver? Yes."

The man's next words were in Spanish and the major recognized most as swear words. It drew a small smile on his face at the anger the old man showed. This tough hombre would not have left the other robber alive.

"When's the next stage west bound?"

"Be tomorrow night."

The major nodded. Perhaps they could sleep some. He could use a lot of it. Nothing out there but the distant, saw-edged mountains and another coyote talking to the quarter moon.

"Can we tell the law?" he asked the man.

"Sí, when you get to Yuma."

The major closed his eyes. By then those rascals would have ridden back into Mexico. No wonder Arizona needed his marshals.

"You have a couple of saddle horses?"

"What for, señor?"

"I'll track those robbers down."

"But, señor, you don't know the desert."

"The stage line could loan me some driving horses to ride and to catch them?"

"I guess."

"You have a saddle?"

"It is an old one."

"That'll work. Need some jerky, some water, and a rifle. You have one I can borrow?"

"Why don't you wait for the sheriff?" The man's face looked vexed by the major's demands.

"To come in a few days? No, they'll be in Mexico by then."

"I can't believe this," she said from the doorway. "You can't—"

"You're safe here."

"But—"

"I'm going after those killers." His next course of action set deep in his mind as he looked to the east. With two fresh saddled horses to use in relay, he could catch them. Another coyote howled and he nodded.

You better find a hole, you border riffraff. A territorial marshal is coming after you.

*   *   *

Jinx Carter's big frame took three fourths of the spring seat and that left Tillie one fourth, but she wasn't about to complain. Her head tied in a scarf, she wondered how sunburned her face would be by the time they reached Fortune. Her fingers gripped the small iron rail beside her while she feverishly hoped she didn't fly out. His high-pitched yell sounded like a charge of banshees, then the long-maned team shot out of Winslow. Their wild run through the streets sent cur dogs and half-naked brown children running for their lives as he headed for Fortune.

The initial fear inside her began to ease and her upset stomach settled some. Carter handled the team with an expertise that impressed her. He might be wild, but he controlled the fiery animals in the harness. Nothing stretched for miles beside the dirt road but the waist-high brown grass and an occasional light blue sage brush. No matter. She was going to find her man. The only concern that needled her was whether he was safe. Plenty of lawmen were shot in the line of duty. Many deputies for Parker came home in a wooden box in the back of some wagon, and she could recall the loud report of those twenty-gun salutes. One of the sisters would say, "Another brave man is being planted."

"You have kin down here?" Carter shouted over the clatter of hooves, huff of the horses, and ring of the wheels.

"My husband-to-be."

"Ah, bless you, girl. Can I dance at your wedding?"

"I guess," she shouted back. The buckskin fringe on his sleeves waved in her face as he swung the team around a turn and set out on the straightaway again. It would be all right to invite folks, she guessed. Never getting married before, she couldn't think a decent girl wouldn't be generous enough to ask a man doing her such a big favor by taking her to her fiancée.

At times, her new role frustrated her. If Luther were there, he could tell her how to do things, but he wasn't. So she had to imagine how she needed to act and hope it didn't disappoint him.

The mountains drew closer. She could see the darkness on them that Carter said would be pines when they got closer. All day, she'd hoped to see trees again. She took them for granted all her life, but since she left St. Louis by train and reached Kansas, she found trees began to thin, there was only waving grass as far as she could see.

Carter was respectful enough for a frontiersman. She'd known others like him. Grizzly as any bear about fighting and carrying on, but downright dainty toward a woman. They made frequent stops and he showed her places where she could find some privacy for a moment.

"Watch for them rattlers," he warned her each time she went off. Many times, dress in hand on her way to some comfort station in a dry wash, she stopped and held her breath at the alarming buzzing sound. Stood there frozen, until she discovered a fat yellow grasshopper clacking its wings clinging to her outfit. Then with a deep sigh of relief, she would brush it away and go on.

The water from Jinx's canteens tasted tinny, but she knew she needed the moisture. He fed her spicy jerky and told her funny stories about his many trips as they rolled southward. Before the sun dropped to the western horizon, she started seeing the scattered cedars he called junipers.

"We can spend the night at the next place. Jules will bust his buttons to meet you," he said with a shake of his head, letting the sweaty horses walk.

"What's he like?" She frowned with suspicion at him.

"Old rancher, but you'll like him."

"Where will I sleep?" she asked, wondering about respectability again. Being a bride had turned into such a worrisome thing.

"Oh, don't worry your pretty mind none. You'll be safe at Jules's."

"Thanks," she said. In the past, the company of two robust men for the night would have thrilled her, but that was then, and she had new obligations now. These folks knew nothing about her past; maybe she could keep it concealed. She looked to the blue sky. God help her.

≈ 19 ≈

Bones made camp at the mouth of Bear Canyon. When Luther rode up in sight of the setup, he wondered how the man ever managed to get the wagon and mules in there, but he felt satisfied. The remuda was scattered down the flats and the canyon full of the echos of boys' axes busting wood.

His visit an hour or so before with the McKean woman weighed on his mind. Attractive enough woman with a mist of freckles. He couldn't forget Stearn's painting when she came on the porch to speak to him. Hirk had been right—the artist knew his subject too well.

"Mr. McKean is in the Valley. But Jakes, our foreman, will be there to meet you or send someone," she said with a certain aloofness. A distinct kind of importance in her tone, so he didn't forget that her outfit was one of the biggest in that basin. Some women used this attitude as a disguise to appear indifferent toward a lesser visitor.

A teenage boy about the same age as his crew came out on crutches. He smiled friendly at Luther. "Wish I could ride with you and the guys, mister."

"You can't," she said coldly. "Not until that leg heals."

Settled on his crutches, he gave a disappointed head shake. "Tell Pyle and them others that I said howdy."

"I will," Luther promised, and prepared to mount. She'd made no offer to give him a drink of water or any hospitality. Perhaps she worried about her reputation. It wasn't respectable to ask a strange man inside. But her son was there.

Luther tipped his hat and started to rein the horse around.

"Mr. Haskell, I realize you are working for Mr. Allen,

but be certain those cattle you round up have the proper brands on them."

"I'll watch, and then allow Mr. Stran to do his job, ma'am. That's why they have brand inspectors. You've had some cattle stolen?"

"We've had several head taken."

"Strange, ma'am," Luther said, checking his horse, then slapping him on the poll with the flat of his hand to settle his fidgeting. "But I seem to recall hearing that your husband told the deputies, a few days ago, that he had no proof of any rustling."

"They've been stealing them."

"They?"

She blinked at him.

"Those three men that were hung?"

"Are you insinuating—"

It was the boy's face that Luther noticed go pale as a ghost. He choked, coughed. His hands went to cover his face. Then he fell off his crutches to his knees and began to vomit. She dropped beside him, her arm protectively over his shoulder.

"Oh, Randy, are you all right?"

"I'll—be—" He retched more sourness up in a milky flood from the depths of his stomach onto the porch steps.

"He's been like this since a bronc threw him," she quickly explained, as if she felt Luther needed to know the reason for his sickness. "Something must be hurt inside him. I can handle this." She waved him away as she hovered over her coughing son. "Jakes will send you help."

Time to ride on. Luther turned the roan and headed for the road. Why did he feel that boy's sudden sickness had something to do with the lynching? Maybe Pyle could answer some of his questions. But as he recalled the boys talking in camp, neither McKean nor Charboneau had anything to say to the deputies about rustling, nor the three suspected rustlers. Yet, Taneal McKean had a lot to say about all the rustling going on in the basin. The year before, Matt McKean had warned all the small outfits around the

basin's edges under the law that they couldn't legally maverick in the basin. The boys told him that, too, but the big
ranchers said they had no proof on the three dead men. Or
did they have the goods and wouldn't discuss it with the
law? In the next weeks, he would see all the cattle that
Burtle claimed. He'd seen enough blotched brands in his
life to know one when he saw one. If they were there, he'd
soon find 'em.

He short-loped Cochise for the first night's camp. When
he found the wagon tracks going into the mouth of Bear
Canyon, he smiled and set the roan into an easy gait
through the pines toward the sharp smell of wood smoke
coming on the afternoon wind.

Ute took his horse for the herd after Luther stripped off
his saddle and gear. Bones ambled over about to bust his
buttons wagging a cup of steaming fresh coffee.

"How's things going?" he asked, holding his suspenders.

"Fine. What's for supper?"

"Beef."

"Hope it was Burtle's." Luther said, and blew on the
coffee.

"We ain't rustlers—yet." Then Bones wiped his hands
on his apron and smiled sly like. "Next time we'll eat one
of theirs."

Luther shook his head after his cook's retreat to the
cooking fire. Range land practice was not to choke eating
your own beef at a neighbor's cow camp.

"Well, we made it," Hirk said, and jammed his hands in
his pockets.

"You did good. I went by McKean's today and he's
gone to the Valley."

"Salt River Valley, Hayden's Mill, and Phoenix down
there?"

"I guess that's where he went. Anyway, Mrs. McKean
ain't real hospitable, but that's beside the point. Sending
Jakes or someone up here."

Hirk looked around to be certain they were alone. "See
any resemblance?"

"Yeah, right off. She spoke about rustling and how I needed to be certain I wasn't taking her cattle."

"Things been touchy up here." Hirk shook his head.

"I'm going to ask you something private. Those boys said McKean spooked them out of mavericking in the basin. He did that, then the only others that could were Dikes, Burtle, and the artist."

Hirk nodded and looked off at the peaks. "You've got the answer, I figure."

"But there's a helluva lot of difference between rustling and mavericking."

"Not to some folks' way of thinking."

"Right," he quietly agreed. All he had to do was prove it. Whew. This job got rougher and rougher. But if you ran into a brick wall you needed to chink the mortar away to ever take it down. That McKean boy and Reed Porter looked like his best chance so far. Things sure went slow at this job, no riding up and serving a warrant or tracking down some wanted man that the grand jury had indicted.

"Supper!" Bones shouted, banging on a washtub with a wooden spoon.

Luther nodded for Hirk to go on, and remained to sip his coffee, still engrossed in his own notions about the lynching. In the absence of any other evidence, he needed solid witnesses. How many had been there that day? It took more than two men to pull it off. Had Randy McKean been there? One thing he knew, that boy didn't get sick over a bronc wreck. The talk about that lynching sent him into a tailspin. He saw him pale at the very words. That boy needed to be questioned. Maybe a grand jury could find out from Porter and Randy who did it. Still engrossed in his figuring, Luther finished his coffee and walked toward the camp.

Bones brought him a heaping plate of food, topped with perfectly browned dutch oven biscuits. "Stop your worrying. This crew's going to get them cow brutes out of the breaks, boss."

He smiled in surrender. "I believe they will."

"Stop worrying about it, boss. They'll get it done."

Luther considered the plate of food he handed him and nodded.

If that was all I had to worry about, Bones, I'd dance a jig tonight to that boy's fiddle. What was the major thinking about this matter?

20

The drum of the horses' hooves counted cadence for the ma-
jor as he galloped through the starlit night. Ride one and
lead one gave him double horse power by him switching
from one to the other. Earlier, he had found the coach,
without any sign of the outlaw they'd left. He considered
that Pablo might have found himself a wagon horse to ride
off on.

Ahead, the seam of the sky in the east turned purple. A
distant jagged peak to the left began to show in the first
light as the sun raced across the saguaro-studded country
side. He urged the horses on. They were too big to be
comfortable to ride, but the animals had run hard all night
for him. The two old Mexican saddles were little more than
wooden horns and tapaderos to put his feet in, but he felt
good when the green fields of the Indian corn and squash
began to appear. He'd soon be at the Papago Wells station,
and hoped to learn more about the outlaws there.

At the hitch rack, when the major drew up, he saw several skinny broomtail mustangs. He eyed the adobe station
and saw nothing but some cur dogs heralding his welcome.
The robbers wouldn't know him on sight, but they might
suspect a man riding one saddled horse and leading another
sweaty one. Both animals were too hot to be allowed to
drink. That would come later. Wary of someone coming
out shooting, he reined the horses to the back. A sleepy
Mexican came out of the shed, obviously taking a siesta in
a hay pile, for he looked like a mattress with the stuffing
coming out of it. His weather-beaten straw sombrero had
been bitten by a horse or a mule, and had three chunks
missing out of the floppy brim.

"*Buenos días,* señor." Then the man blinked and his jaw

sagged. "You are riding the stage line's horses?" Shock swept over his face and he looked ready to run.

"Shut up. I am a lawman. The men who robbed the Yuma stage last night are inside." He handed the man the reins to both horses. "How many men are in there?"

"Four, I think."

"Can we put that cart against the back door so they can't get out?"

"I guess so." He shrugged at the notion of wheeling the wooden cart against the back door.

"Tie these horses up and come help me."

The major already had the shafts picked up when the man came shuffling over in his sandals to assist him. The sun was higher and the temperature was already way over a hundred and ten.

At first their straining did nothing, then the axles began to squeal like a stuck pig, only more in a moan, as they could barely make the cart roll. At last, the right wheel rested against the door, he dropped the shafts and nodded for the man to get some sticks of firewood for a block. The man hurried to complete the job.

Satisfied he had the outlaws locked inside, save for the front door because the windows were too small for anything but a snake to crawl out of them. He strode across the burning hot ground, jerked the rifle out of the scabbard, and told the man to tell the help and the old man to come outside and see the new kittens.

"But the banditos?"

"They won't know what you are doing."

"Oh, I hope you are right, señor?"

"Tell them one of the new kittens in the barn has two heads."

"But what if the bandits they come?"

"Quit worrying. I'll handle them."

The man's brown complexion paled, but he did as he was asked and went around front ahead of him. He hesitated at the door, then he went inside. There was much

Spanish thrown about, and soon a man in an apron and a woman came out with the horse hustler.

The stage workers blinked in disbelief at the major, who stood on the porch with the rifle ready. He shook his head to silence them and motioned for them to get out of the way. It would be darker inside. He hoped the shade of the palm frond cover on the porch adjusted his eyes enough for him to see when he stormed in. Quickly, he ducked through the doorway, firing a shot in the ceiling that brought down a cloud of dust. The gunpowder smoke made seeing impossible.

"Hands up or die!" he shouted, making a motion with his gun barrel for them to go outside. The coughing outlaws came stumbling by him with their hands high. They grumbled, but he used his free hand to jerk loose their sidearms and dropped their hardware on the ground. Satisfied they were disarmed, he waved the bandits into the sunshine, forcing them to look east and have the brightness in their faces. Eyeing his prisoners carefully for any tricks, he edged behind and swept off their sombreros to further expose them. He removed a remaining visible knife or two, tossing the cutlery aside.

"What is wrong, señor?" the best dressed one asked.

"You are under arrest for armed robbery of a stage and murder." He stepped back satisfied he had the matter under control. "Someone go get some rope."

"Sí," the horse hustler agreed, and took off.

"These men robbed the stage and killed the driver, Billy?" the Mexican man in charge of the station asked.

"Yes. Last night," he said, then looked to the west at the sound of approaching riders. More robbers? he wondered, watching their dust. He could only make out their Chihuahua-style sombreros. "Who is that?" he asked the station man.

"Don Robles's men from Sonora. The man who leads them is Delgado."

"What do they want?"

"These men you have arrested."

He recalled talking to the same man before he left there on the stage. Some sort of Mexican lawman or bounty hunter. The leader pulled up the high-stepping black stallion before him.

"Ah, señor, we meet again, and you have captured these miserable wretches who were spawned by cur bitches with mangy coyotes for fathers." The confident-acting man leaned on the saddle horn and smiled.

"They're under arrest," the major said.

"Ah, for what, señor?"

"Robbery and murder." Sweat lubricated his hands on the stock of the rifle. He wanted to dry them, but did not dare.

"You are the sheriff here?" Delgado looked around as if searching for some post of authority.

"I am the chief marshal of the territorial marshals."

"Oh," the man said, acting impressed. "You have many more men?"

"Yes," the major said with force, but knew his bluff would soon wear thin.

"Let me have these bastards. I will save Arizona the trouble of feeding them and do it as a favor because you captured them for me. All, but one . . ." Delgado searched around.

"He's dead. I shot him last night."

The man turned back and nodded in approval. "Shame you didn't kill the rest."

"These men are my prisoners."

"You know, amigo, you and I could improve the relations between Mexico and Arizona today."

"By giving you the prisoners? No, I don't think so."

"Ah, mi amigo, think how the good man who runs this place and his wife and his hired man could be killed in the shooting. They are innocent. These worthless ones no one would cry for, but you and these others are good people. My men," he said, gesturing to the three armed riders, "they have wives and many children. They are always busy. They keep their wives pregnant. If your bullets kill some of them, those little ones would go hungry."

"You'd be the first to die."

"Ah, yes, but my men would kill you." Delgado pushed his sombrero to the back of his head. His rich curly hair shone in the sun.

"We have a standoff," the major finally said.

"Let me have the prisoners to take home. They will not come back to rob any more stages." Delgado crossed himself. "I swear on my holy mother's grave."

"But you have no authority here."

"My authority is four guns to your one and the innocent people at this place."

He heard the man's challenge. It didn't give him much time to consider his options. The three stage line employees were the pawns in this game of standoff. Despite his own convictions that the prisoners were his, he couldn't risk three civilian lives over four worthless felons. One more thing he wanted from this man.

"Sign a paper for me that you took them." At least he would have some evidence of the incident to explain to the stage people and the Arizona law.

"I will do that."

"Fine, go get paper and pen," he said to the woman, and she hurried off.

When she returned, the major handed her the rifle and used the saddle of the first pony to write on.

"What are their names?"

"Pablo Martinez, Regino Salleras, Gordo Valdez, and Nero Rico."

The major finished the list, walked over, held out the paper, and Delgado dismounted. He read the letter or he scanned it anyway, then signed his name at the bottom in flowery penmanship, Juan Cortez Delgado.

He remounted his black and motioned for his men to take the prisoners. Delgado's men began to talk to one another, but still looked warily at the major as they tied the prisoners' hands. Soon the bandits were bound and mounted.

Delgado rode over on his black to where the major and

the three employees stood under the palm frond shade.

"I can ever help you in Mexico, call on me, señor. You are a tough old man, and a good man, too. Adios, amigos." He touched his sombrero and they left riding southward through the desert for the border.

No way to ever catch them. The major squinted against the heat waves as they fled. Sick to his stomach, he turned when the thick-set woman handed him the rifle.

"Gracias, señor. You saved our lives." Then she waddled back inside. He shook his head to clear it. That was why he didn't fight with Delgado, for her sake and the other two men. He'd had his chance to die and decided he better stay alive and fight another day.

"I am sending to Tucson for a buckboard to take you to Yuma. The woman?" the stage manager asked.

"She's fine. She's at the station west of Gila Bend."

"Good. My boss in Tucson would be very mad if they had killed her, too."

"She's fine." Then he laughed aloud and clapped the little man on the shoulder. His slap raised a cloud of alkali tasting dust from his shirt. "Sorry about the hole in the roof."

"It don't rain much here," the man said, and shrugged as if it was a fact of life for him.

"No, it don't," he said, and sighed. He still had a prison contractor scandal to resolve. He took the cup of coffee from the woman and nodded. More work left to do in Yuma before he could go home to his cool house in Prescott. Whew! He wiped his gritty forehead on his sleeve. This marshaling had turned into some job.

21

Jules's place looked like a goat ranch, and the rank smell of his animals made Tillie's nose burn. She saw every color of goat imaginable come running out of hiding at their arrival. Several raced out of the junipers and others bounded from around sheds and pens. Black ones, white woolly, brown and white ones. Some had beards as long as an old man's and horns that curled. Others were sharp and pointed.

"Jules does like his goats," Jinx said in an apologetic way as he helped her down.

"They in the house, too?"

"Naw, but I better get my mailbags and your baggage. They'll eat anything left outside."

"I'll help," she said, and raised her hands defensively as the curious bleating goats encircled her. For a moment, panic spread through her. She'd soon even smell like them. A shutter of revulsion ran up her spine.

"Howdy, ma'am," Jules said, and swept off his shapeless hat. "Get back," he ordered, and a black and white collie took command. The dog's barking and charges drove the ring of curious goats back and away from her. She wanted to hug him. That was a great dog, not a sneezing, leering bulldog like Ben. Somehow in the near future, she must make her peace with Luther's best friend. But she dreaded the reunion with the bulldog. Quickly she scooted inside the picket gate with huge iron implement parts tied on a rope for ballast to keep it closed.

She had heard how early settlers ran inside forts to escape Indians. She had narrowly escaped ten thousand goats as the two men brought her things and the canvas mail sacks inside the gate. With her luggage safely on the porch, she relaxed some. This being a righteous woman was hard work. Through the goat episode, she questioned herself. Had she acted composed and ladylike? If not, she'd sure tried.

"Ain't often I get a pretty young lady here," the congenial Jules said, showing her the door like some grand marquis would royal company.

The cabin was neat. So neat, she felt her jaw sag at the sight of the yellow table and chairs. A bachelor with a yellow table and chairs. And the cabinets had doors, not curtains. They were painted yellow and had scroll designs like the Danish drew on their houses. Was Jules Danish?

"Ain't it a nice place?" Jinx asked, coming in behind Jules with her bags.

She managed a nod in agreement.

"Put her things in the lean-to. There's a fresh bed in there. It's all ready," Jules assured her.

She thanked them, and skirt in her hand, went to the doorway. The room had lace curtains that swept in the cool breeze and the iron bedstead looked so inviting that she wanted to jump in it and sleep forever. How many days had it been since she slept in a real bed? Must have been months.

"That suit you, ma'am?" Jinx asked.

"I think a queen could stay here. Thanks." She smiled at him.

Then she heard him tell Jules, "She's getting married in Fortune and I'm going to dance at her wedding."

"With who?" Jules demanded in a stage whisper. "Ain't a fitting woman in that town that's going to dance with a dirty galoot like you. You'll have to be cleaned up and get a haircut and pound them buckskins in corn meal."

"All to dance at her wedding?"

"Lord, yes, man. Aw, you're so damn uncouth, even a bath, a shave, and clean clothes couldn't fix you up."

"Listen here, you old goat chaser!"

Tillie smiled. God was sure looking out for her. Oh, she'd never been to a fancy cathedral or even gone to church much. Once or twice, she went to a revival under a brush arbor, but she'd never been afraid to pray when she was in real trouble. But she also knew enough straitlaced folks in her lifetime who looked down at whores, and then their husbands would sneak up the back stairs for a little. Those folks she figured to be hypocrites. And if God listened to them, then he damn sure would listen to a sincere dove.

She fell on her knees beside the bed and clasped her hands. "Dear God, this is Tillie McQuire. You done brought me across the desert and I'm grateful. Grateful for them two out there, 'cause they're surely your children. Maybe they're your angels delivering me to Luther. You have him be all right, Lord."

She squeezed her eyes shut, thinking of what else she could promise him. Then she overheard the two men in the other room.

"Lord, have mercy, Jules, I can hear she's praying for us in there."

"Leave her alone. Riding with you up here would be a trying ride on the old devil hisself."

"I ain't prying. Just nice to know there's still good girls in this world. That cow buyer, Luther Haskell, is the luckiest guy in this world to get her, Jules. Hope he knows how lucky he is."

"He does . . . he does," she said to herself. "Amen."

Mid-morning the next day, Luther met with the ranch foreman from McKean's who'd ridden over with his rep. The wiry man, well into his sixties, introduced himself as Jakes nodded toward the hand he was sending along to help. Henry Davis had three horses with his gear piled on one. Davis lacked two front teeth, but he still smiled as if pleased to be there.

"Henry, put your bedroll and war bag in the wagon," Luther directed. "Pleased to have you."

Davis grinned, agreed, and rode on by. Obviously, the cowboy knew Bones, for Luther saw the cook pouring him some coffee and talking friendly.

"Light a spell. We've got a fresh pot," Luther said to Jakes.

"Kinda need to talk to you. You spoke pretty sharp to my boss's missus yesterday."

"You hear me do that?"

"No, but she was damn sure upset when I got in. Her husband wasn't there and she said—"

"Hold it," Luther said, and sidled Cochise in beside the man's big bay. "She told me straight out to be careful of what I drove out of the basin. And she accused those three dead men of rustling. Her husband told those deputies there was no evidence of rustling in this basin. I never started that conversation. Then that boy got sick listening to it, and I mean plumb sick."

He could see Jakes had a hump in his back. He wondered how far the man intended to buck this deal. It was Mrs. McKean who did the charging, not him. He just asked some questions that needed answers. This might be the place to do her a real favor. He held no grudges.

"You and her close?" he asked.

"What the hell do you mean by that?" Jakes raised his head back in affront.

Luther shook his head to dismiss the man's upset. "I mean you've worked for them a long time?"

"I have, and I respect her. She's a real lady, and a good one. That's why I'm so mad about you—"

"Hold it right there. You swing around by Stearn's tent and get the paintings out of the trunk. Take them to her or whatever. Hirk and I saw them. We won't tell a soul. But they don't need to be circulated."

"What are they?" Jakes frowned suspiciously.

"You'll know when you see them. Wasn't our place to do a thing about them, so we left them. It won't need an explanation when you find them in the trunk."

"What is it I'm suppose to find?" Jakes frowned, and his diamond eyes glared in distrust.

"You'll see. Now extend the lady my apology. Tell her next time I will be more polite. But there was rustling in this basin before that necktie party, or why have one?"

"You some kin of Burtle's?"

"Nope. Just gathering cattle for the estate. But I heard the Dikes family has got a big reward up for the arrest of the parties involved."

"Big rewards bring in trouble."

"No. That lynching started it."

"You after that money?"

"I'm making day wages buying and gathering cows for Allen. Tell me how I could get my hands on a couple thousand to buy a good ranch in a hundred years."

"Lots of money," Jakes agreed, and calmed down. He reined the nervous bay around. "I need to go see whatever is in the trunk, huh?"

"Yes, and you don't need to tell her I sent you."

Jakes saluted him with two fingers and rode off standing in the stirrups. Luther watched him. Tough old man. They could pull his yellow fingernails off one at a time with fencing pliers and he'd never tell a thing. But Luther felt certain he had made a good cover for his asking all the questions. The reward. Simple greed made a good alibi for his interest. How much money they'd offered to pay he wasn't certain, or if they would pay any at all, but in other cases, rich folks paid rewards.

He nodded, pleased. The foreman was out of sight up the mountain and into the timber. Enough marshaling for one afternoon. Better go get Ben, ride out, and meet the boys coming in with the cattle. He'd also have to take Hirk aside and tell him about sending Jakes after the nude picture. He felt confident that the cowboy would agree that it was the best way to handle it.

With Ben at Cochise's heels, he rode out of camp to meet his crew. He could hear the cattle bawling long before they came into sight. Dust boiled higher than the tallest pines. They had gathered several hundred head and it would take some cutting to get down to the B Bar stock. But the only way to get them out of the range was bring what you had to a sorting area. They'd done great. He was proud of them. Hirk came riding out of the dust to join him.

Their horses pulled aside, Luther told him about Jakes; the cowboy agreed with a nod. "Good idea. I'd sure hate if it had got out on her."

"Me, too, but she ate me out yesterday about rustling and watching whose stock we took out."

"She did?"

"Then Jakes got hot under the collar for me talking roughshod over her."

"You calm him down?"

"Hope so. He left wondering anyway. Brought Henry Davis to help us for their part." Something was wrong; he could see how puzzled Hirk looked.

"You know that weekend of the hanging? It was sure strange that McKean gave them three cowboys that Saturday off and they had money to buy whiskey. Lots of it."

"The Saturday of the hanging?"

"Yeah." Hirk pointed to some breaking cattle. "We better go help them boys hold them cattle. There's some real spooks in this bunch."

Luther agreed and pushed Cochise down the slope. In a long lope he hit the flat and turned back some rowdy yearling heifers. What had Hirk told him? At the sound of Ben's barking, he looked around, then put spurs to the roan. The bulldog was fleeing down the hillside pursued by an angry half-longhorn cow. Luther began driving Cochise hard to save his bulldog from a horning.

Ben, I'm coming!

The hard-running cow's right horn dipped down, then without missing a stride, she flipped it out and upward. Her toss sent Ben skyward. He hit the ground and rolled down the hill like a ball. The cow was closing in for the kill. Out of nowhere, Pyle and his horse closed in on her, the youth swinging a rope. He threw the loop down and around her hind legs, then made a wrap of his rope around the horn. The cow's heels caught, and he swept his horse to the side. His actions sent the cow tumbling over and over.

Luther waved his thanks to the proud-faced youth and

headed for the black and white ball. At Ben's side, Luther stepped down, scooped him up, and put him over the seat of the saddle. No time to see how badly he was hurt. He swung up and steadied the shaking dog in his lap. Not much blood showed on him besides a few scratches. He really looked fine. The horn hadn't gouged him. One thing that Luther knew for certain—Ben would have to ride in the wagon with Bones for the duration of this roundup.

When they returned to camp, he wanted to talk to Davis to learn why his skinflint boss gave them that Saturday off. He still needed someone to testify. Porter would be his best bet. Weakest link in the chain. But how? In the morning, he planned to ride over and talk to Charboneau about sending a rep. The Frenchman would not be easy to deal with. He riled easily. Then the last man, Crain, no one spoke much about him. Luther shook his head. He had lots to do. He needed some real meat about the lynching to sink his teeth into. Not bare bones.

Ben sneezed and acted ready to jump down.

"Quit, you damn fool," Luther scolded him. "You nearly were roasted dog on that she-devil's horns." He shook his head in disapproval at the dog. Thunder in the distance pealed over the rim and some dark clouds distracted him for a second. He'd better go see Charboneau in the morning. They'd be close enough to his range in a few days at this rate.

Matt stepped out of the buckboard into an afternoon downpour that had followed him all the way from Fortune. He paused to catch his breath on the porch, behind a sheet of water pouring off the roof eaves. Stamping his sodden boots, he slipped out of the clammy rubber slicker and hung it on the wall peg. Jakes and Taneal stood in front of the fireplace. Cool maybe, but not cold enough for a fire. He turned his nose to test the strange smell of the smoke. He frowned; they weren't burning wood.

"What's going on?" he demanded.

His wife blocked him from seeing in the fireplace. "Nothing."

She was lying. Roughly, he turned her aside to find out what she concealed. Impatience raged in him as he stepped closer to see a canvas painting being consumed by the flames.

"What the hell is going on?" he demanded, looking first at her, then at Jakes. "Someone answer me!"

"Tell him," she said, and stalked away.

"That rustler Stearn had been spying on your wife."

"What do you mean?"

"He painted her swimming in the creek."

"Naked?"

"Sorry, I found them paintings up at his tent. Don't know who else saw 'em." Jakes shook his head.

"Was it her?"

"Hell, yes. That little sneaky bastard." Taneal stood in the doorway to the kitchen. Anger blackened her face. She could do that to him, blame him for everything. How could he know the son of a bitch was a Peeping Tom, too? Of course, looking at his wife's bare body probably gave that horny cowboy some kind of thrills.

"Were there any others?" he asked.

Jakes shook his head. "Not of her."

"Damn, what else?"

Taneal had gone into the kitchen. Jakes tossed his head toward the front door. Matt followed him, wondering what the old man had on his mind.

With his steel-blue eyes on the mountain, Jakes spoke softly. "I took Henry up there as the rep to the camp. I met that buyer that Allen sent." He never looked at Matt. "He said something. Dikes's family's offering two thousand dollars reward for information."

"I heard that. I met him. What's he doing, trying to collect it?"

"Matt, I had me a gut feeling up there. He ain't no ordinary cow buyer."

"Figure he's law?"

"He said he was working for day wages—that reward could buy him a place. Sounds to me like a man got a big purpose."

Matt glanced back inside the front door to be sure they were alone. "So?"

"My daughter and her man have a place down at Tularosa. I could run some stock down there."

"You're leaving me because of that sumbitch?"

Jakes shook his head. "You need a younger, tougher man than me to run this outfit."

The last of the rain ran off the eaves and dripped on the wet ground. A pine smell filled the fresh air. Thunder rumbled in the distance. Matt forced back his rage. How could Jakes consider leaving him? Where was the old man's loyalty after all these years? Now, especially with all the troubles he faced with this new outfit moving in the basin. An image of that angry gun hand, Burns, in the Valley made him reconsider Jakes's words. Perhaps he did need a younger, tougher foreman.

"When you leaving?"

"I ain't much on words and show. I plan to go pack right now."

"How did you find those paintings?"

"Prowling, after I took Henry up to the cow camp."

Matt rubbed his chin. "I never checked his place. Good thing you did. I'm grateful for all you done for me and this ranch."

Jakes nodded without a word.

"I'll have your money ready."

"Thanks." Jakes started for his shack. Matt watched him go off in his two-inch heels, stiff-backed. He was an old man. Best he did ride on or he'd have an old invalid on his hands. Time for change, he kept convincing himself.

More thunder in the distance, He looked at the sky. The storm was over in the west for the afternoon. He turned slowly, realizing Taneal was standing in the doorway.

"Better figure up what we owe Jakes," he said. "He's going to his daughter's place at Tulerosa."

She nodded.

Matt raised his brows at her. "You aren't surprised?"

"No. He told me it was time."

"Figure it up. Guess we owe him a bonus."

"We owe him a lot."

"You seen this Haskell fellow works for Allen?" Matt asked.

"Yes. He was here."

"What the hell for? Asking questions?"

"I think he knows about that lynching."

"Oh. What the hell is that?"

She shook her head and pushed her hair back from her face. "You tell me."

"How the hell should I know?" He pushed past her, opening and closing his fists to control his anger. In another second, he would have beat her within an inch of her life. Between his sharp-talking wife and lame-brained son, he had no allies in that house.

"You learn anything in the valley?" she called out.

"Yes. They're coming with cattle." He reached the liquor cabinet, threw open the cupboard doors, and grabbed a bottle. Cork in his teeth, he splashed bourbon into a goblet, spit out the cork, and downed the liquor. The rush of the bourbon in his throat burned and set his ears afire. He needed some escape, and soon.

The load of all this on his shoulders had reached staggering proportions. Why couldn't that big outfit stay away? He soon would have this basin to himself without Dikes and those cowboys. Charboneau and Crain would never get bigger, and they'd eventually fade away. Porter would drink himself to death. Another niggling thing: Lincoln told him when he came through Fortune about Porter's drinking binges in town and how he had forced him in the back room to silence his tongue. Damn. Damn! He poured more bourbon into the goblet. The sharp fumes ran up his nose.

"You planning on getting drunk?" she asked.

He ignored her words and considered the glass in his hand.

"You know he never draws much money." She waited for his reply, and when he didn't speak she went on. "We owe him five hundred."

He nodded that he'd heard her. "Pay him." The old sumbitch was running out when he needed him the most. He had nothing to say to him. "Take it down there and pay him."

"You don't—"

"I don't care if I ever see him again!"

"Well, I owe him more than that," she said, and with a swish of her dress, headed for the front door.

Yeah, Jakes saved your shiny ass from being exposed to everyone. He wished he had those paintings to blackmail her with. Might have made her act civil. He turned at the sound of crutches clattering on the floor. His stupid crippled son had come inside. In disgust, he turned his back to him and downed the liquor. Lots to do.

The dust churned up and the sun bore down on him as they came over the last pass. The major sat beside the young Mexican driver on the spring seat. He could see in the distance the cluster of adobe buildings and few cottonwoods along the Colorado River that marked Yuma. He twisted around and looked at the prim Miss Hmm in the rear seat.

"That's Yuma, according to Jose."

"I will believe it when we arrive," she said haughtily.

He nodded that he heard her and turned back. She was right. It could be a mirage. Enroute there, they'd seen enough of those shimmering ghost lakes. In Yuma, he could wire Sterling and learn if any of his men needed anything. Maybe Haskell had found out something worth while, but it was early.

Whew. He decided the temperature must be way over 110. The blistering sun high overhead proved relentless. That place ahead reminded him of hell. Ideal place for a prison, and that brought him back to his mission: to find the thieves. How long would that take? He hoped to make his tour of duty in Hades as short as possible.

Outside the stage office, Miss Hmm stood straight-backed in the oven breath wind. The driver swung their bags from the spring wagon.

"Well, Gerald, I am in your debt. I would never have survived the trip, save for your bravery."

"Nothing," he said, removing his hat. "Is there anything you need?"

"No. I must go find the lawyer in charge of my inheritance and see about it."

"I'll be staying at the Alhambra Hotel a few days, if you need anything."

A whimsical smile crossed her face. She nodded, then looked hard at him. "I haven't kissed a man since I was in pigtails." Her eyes looked moist. "I did it because I meant it, sir."

"I believe you."

She started to say something else, but must have decided better. With her dusty skirt in hand, she went inside, giving the agent details about her luggage's care. The major tipped his hat to her when she came out.

"Take mine to the hotel," he said to the dark-skinned youth who was dressed in rags, standing ready for his word.

The youth staggered under the load, but refused his assistance. When they walked inside the lobby, the air was still hot, but out of the breath-taking wind and solar blast, it felt better.

After the major checked in, the boy carried the bags into his room. When he tipped him a dime, the grateful youth said, "Gracias," and hurried away.

Nothing to keep him in that stale room with its barred window open on the alley. He locked the door, pocketed the key, and set out to make the rounds of the bars. No place held more information than these fraternal-like bases for the male population from the top to bottom of the social order.

Darkness inside the first bar forced his eyes to dilate. Olive-skinned girls wearing low-cut blouses and full skirts that swished about them served drinks. Their open laughter filled the air and a few men pawed them in passing, which caused cries of shocked protests from the females. But they cried out only for effect, not innocence, and to tease their tormentors. Two musicians played trumpets and one a guitar making the striking music he had heard in Mexico. Soon, one of the girls began to clack castanets and dance, which added to the shouts and cheers of the drunks. Midday and the Grande Cantina was alive.

With a place at the uncrowded bar, the major ordered a beer and was surprised at the coolness of the foamy brew. The bartender, a short Hispanic, smiled.

"So, señor, you are new in town?" The man wiped imaginary spots with a cloth-wrapped finger from the deep polished surface.

"Yes."

"You are here on business?"

"Yes, I have a sawmill at Prescott. I understand they're building a big prison here?"

"Oh, you need to see Señor Swopes."

"Oh, is he the contractor?"

"No, señor, but he is the one who sells all the lumber to the warden. You have to go though him to sell anything."

"I see." The major toasted the man and took another swallow of the beer. In town less than five minutes and he already had learned who sold the material to the warden. He quickly thought up a ploy that might work to trick the warden into admitting guilt. But did this Swopes know everyone who had a sawmill in Prescott? Chances were good he did. The territory was so sparsely populated, not much happened that could be kept a secret for long.

He left the man a dime tip and hurried to find the warden's office. His next move might be a confrontation with Hiram London. An ex-Indian agent, according to Sterling, the man was a political appointment forced on him by the party. Obviously if London knew how to steal from the Indian Bureau, this job was a plum. His low regard for the Indian agents he had dealt with during his military career made the major strongly suspicious of any former one.

On his way to the prison site, he heard the ring of hammers and several creaking carts pulled by dull oxen delivering adobe bricks.

He entered the new prison headquarters, and a young man in a blue wool uniform seated behind a desk addressed him. "Good day, sir."

"Good day. Is Warden Hiram London in today?"

"Do you have an appointment? The warden only sees people by an appointment."

"When is the next one?"

"Next week, I am afraid." The clerk looked over a schedule before him.

"I will have one right now. Tell him that John Sterling sent me." The major started past the protesting youth.

"You can't go in there—"

He tried the knob; locked. Then he used his shoulder to force the door open. The latch gave. The door swung back and a shocked man holding a young Latin girl on his lap looked up. She screamed at the sight of the major, forcing down her skirt hem and leaping to her feet.

"Who the hell are you?"

"The man who's firing you! Touch that desk drawer and you're dead." The major drew his Colt and scowled at the hysterical girl, who had backed to the window. "Shut up."

She obeyed. By this time, London was on his feet hollering for guards at the top of his lungs. With the gun barrel, the major directed him to sit down. The girl rushed out of the office.

"Now see here—" the red-faced warden began.

"No. You see here. You're under arrest until the books of this prison are examined."

"What are the charges?"

"Dereliction of duty, for one."

"There's no law—"

"London, there's lots of laws that I can and will charge you with. You better start talking." Two uniformed guards with rifles rushed in the room.

"Arrest this man," London shouted.

"Unless you want to spend time as an accomplice in jail with your boss, get the hell out of here and go get the sheriff, if there is one in this town."

"Don't leave!" London pleaded. "He's all wrong."

"I'll send someone after the sheriff, sir," the sergeant of the guard said. The two men left and a slow grin of satisfaction spread over the major's face.

"They must know about the corruption going on here. Now, London, start telling me all about it. First I want to hear about Swopes and his part in this deal."

"I swear this is a—"

With a wary head shake to cut off the man's plea of innocence, he holstered the Colt. "No, I want the whole story. I know about Swopes. Now you can tell me all about him."

Past dark, he left the telegraph office. The message he sent to Sterling simply said: *Your warden and four subcontractors are in the Yuma County jail on various charges. Please send a new warden, as the underwarden, T. Frailey, fled to Mexico earlier today.*

The heat still radiated from the adobe building walls. He could only imagine what the prison would be like. In full darkness with only an occasional light shining into the street, he headed for the music. Those same trumpets and guitar tunes carried on the night air. Another cool beer or two and he could perhaps sleep later on if some of the heat in his hotel room evaporated. He really missed the cool nights of the high country and Mary. Oh, Lord, it would be weeks before a replacement could arrive. He shook his head. One thing he felt certain about, hell itself couldn't be a worse place than Yuma in the summer.

22

Tillie thought she could see forever when they topped the rim in mid-morning. The peaks and mountains were covered in a carpet of tall pines. The thin, sharp-scented air was heady enough to make her feel dizzy. She didn't dare fall out of the seat because Jinx driving was a no-nonsense navigator, and he used the daylight hours to push hard. The horses acted rested and ready to run. Earlier, before she left Jules's place, she invited the goat man to her wedding.

With no family of their own out here, what could it hurt to have some nice people come to it? Everyone so far had treated her like a real lady, so perhaps she was making a good coverup of her past. She looked up at the azure sky through the needles and boughs over her head. Thanks, Lord. Whew, she'd have to become a real church-goer if all this worked out. Whether another person would screw things up for her was all she worried about. It would have to be someone else's fault if that happened.

Mid-morning, Jinx reined up on a grassy flat to rest his sweaty, hard-breathing team.

"We'll take fifteen minutes," he said, and pointed to the cover. "Take your time. There should be some fresh water a little ways up that draw where you can wash your face, if you like."

"Thanks." She put her slipper on the footstep and jumped down, well accustomed to boarding and unboarding the rig by herself. Skirt in hand, she hustled around to the back. After taking a Turkish towel from her bag and slinging it around her neck, she undid the scarf and freed her hair. With her fingers she tried to fluff it. Must look a sight. She had brushed it hard earlier, but the tight scarf was not good for it. Busy thinking how fine the cool water would feel on her dry face and lips, she skirted around some brush to push her way up the draw. Soon she saw a thin stream of liquid in between the worn round rocks. Must be a bigger hole of it around the bend. She glanced at the tall sides of sedentary gravel and dirt cut through by previous floods.

She could appreciate the force of heavy rains in the past, and was grateful the sky was clear. Then she saw the large pool. Heavenly, though not deep enough to bathe in. She gathered her dress up and dropped to her bare knees on the edge. The first application of water on her face felt so good. If she could only wallow in it. A close report of a shot broke her train of thought.

Her heart stopped. She listened. Jinx had never fired his pistol before at anything on a stopover. Was something wrong? The cutting edge of her front teeth bit into her lower lip. What should she do? No weapon. She studied the steep walls and saw no way to escape. Dropping the towel, she quickly rose to her feet. If it was a holdup man, she needed to sneak back and see if she could help poor Jinx.

He would have shouted to her by this time, had it been a wild shot. No. He treated her too nice not to have yelled. She ran over the round rocks until she spotted a crevice she thought she could climb through to reach the top of the bank.

The way proved hard. Her soles slid on the steep incline and she had to grasp a bush to save herself from falling. Her heart's heavy pounding under her breastbone sounded like a sledgehammer. It made her ears ring. She felt faint. The things she grasped to pull herself up with hurt her palms and fingers. At last, with her breath whistling through her nose, she reached the top.

On her hands and knees, she fought to recover her short breath. Still no call from Jinx. Had he shot himself? Oh, God, how could she ever drive those wild horses?

"Give me strength," she said, and got to her feet. With a handful of skirt, she walked her way carefully through the junipers toward the wagon. Then, realizing how loud her footsteps sounded, she began taking softer steps.

At last she could see a man's back. It wasn't Jinx. Too thin a build and the wrong hat. This hat was black and Jinx's was dirty brown. He turned, as if listening, and she could see his left eye was blind. She stepped back, hoping he had not seen her. Where was Jinx? She closed her eyes. Was he dead?

She bellied down on the needles and sharp burrs. Finally through the boughs, she could see Jinx's buckskins. Poor man. He lay on the ground holding his side. She grimaced. His hand looked bloody. Oh, no, he was shot.

"Where did she go?" the robber asked in halting English.

"Run off. How should I know?"

"Kill you soon if you don't call her back."

Kill him? No. She began to wiggle backward to escape. That rotten devil wasn't killing Jinx for him not calling her. Out from under the boughs, she picked up a two-foot-long stick and worked her way around the juniper.

Using the screen of the boughs, she made her way closer. At last, she rose to her feet and charged with her weapon held high. The robber reached behind and drew a gleaming blade from his belt. It flashed in the sun and he stepped past the sprawled Jinx.

A scream left her throat and she ran at him with all her force and strength. She could see his snowy eye. The blank one glared at her. He crouched down, the huge knife ready.

"Ah," he cried. "Kill you now!"

She never stopped her charge, raising the stick higher and higher. The cry came from deep inside her. She drew closer. Then one of Jinx's boots swung out and swept the robber's legs from under him. An instant later, she crashed the club on his head. Then again and again. Blow after blow, she battered him with both hands, grasping the stick until lightning pain ran into her shoulders and the club slipped away.

Her throat on fire, she fell to her knees and crawled to Jinx side. "You all r-right?"

"One little bullet ain't going to kill me, darling." He

made a pained face that hurt her, but he was alive. "We better get to Fortune, though."

"What about him?"

"Hell, he's looks bad enough off that they can send some of the men back to get him."

"Who is he?" she asked, getting under his shoulder and helping him toward the wagon.

"I never seen that one-eyed renegade before." He tried to pull himself up on the buckboard. She put her shoulder under his butt and drove him upward.

"Obilged," he grunted, sprawled across the wagon's floorboards. "I better ride here."

"But," she protested. No time for that, she ran back picked up the outlaw's handgun and knife, and tossed them in the wagon box. Then she quickly tied his horse to the back of it. Without a ride, if he did come to, he wouldn't go far. She raced around, climbed on, finding a place for her feet beside Jinx's bulky form.

"You surely ain't going to die on me?" she asked, undoing the reins with shaky hands.

"Not me."

"Good. Hee-yah!" She threw the lines at them and the horses spooked away.

"How far is it?"

"An hour or two."

"Good. We'll make it in one," she promised, looking down at him and wondering what else she should have done for the big man's comfort and health. Nothing to do but drive.

Too late, she missed reining the flying team around a corner. The wagon lurched over the rut and the horses tore through some junipers. Prickly pear cactus pads went flying in the air. Tossed all over the seat, she finally regained her place. Grateful the cutoff proved flat, she soon reined them between two junipers and back onto the road.

"Took a shortcut," she said to him and quickly looked up to see the way. Things could happen fast, and she had to be aware of them. Those crazy running horses would go anywhere unless she guided them. She planted her feet on the dash and drew them around the next bend in a flurry of dust.

"Good girl," he managed.

"I'm learning," she said, grateful for the straight stretch ahead.

An hour later, with her whole body shaking, she finally reined the lathered team up in front of the mercantile.

"Got a man shot here," she said, looking around for someone to help her. "Get a doc." She searched about feeling desperate. Then she spied a boy coming out of the store, wiping his hands on his apron.

"Don't stand there with your thumb in your ass. This man's hurt. Go get him some help!"

The red-faced boy blinked in disbelief.

"You heard me!" she said, filled with sinking embarrassment. Oh, excuse me, Lord. I've been so good and I had to blurt that out. Maybe she should have stayed in Fort Smith. How could she ever . . .

In minutes, storekeepers in aprons and others came running to help her. She chewed on her lip. The crimson blood on the floor of the buckboard worried her. Thank goodness, at last people were there to help him.

"Be careful with Jinx. He's been shot," she reprimanded the men trying to get his bulk out of the wagon.

"We will, miss," one said to reassure her, but Jinx's big form was wedged between the dash and seat.

"Well, he's been hurt bad enough." She shook her head in disbelief, but six men soon had his burly form free and were carrying him off. Anxious and worried about Jinx, she looked all around for Luther as she hurried beside them.

"Who did it?"

"Some one-eyed breed. I left him lying in the road and I took his horse. Well, dang—" she said, hands on her hips. She stared at the back of the wagon. Only the broken reins remained. "His horse must have torn loose."

"Get some horses, men," the man in charge directed. "How far back?"

"Ain't sure, but we were stopped at a small trickle of water, I know that." She pointed north.

"My name's Lincoln."

"Mine's Tillie McQuire. Anyone seen my betrothed, Luther Haskell?"

"Yeah, he's out on a roundup."

"He's all right?"

"Yes, ma'am."

Her head began to swirl. Luther was all right. A weakness raced through her frame. Her vision blurred. Her knees buckled and the whole world began to darken. She felt faint, and started to fall forward. Someone caught her. She heard him scream.

"Someone help me!"

Then silence swallowed her.

Three young Indian cowboys squatted in the dust by the corral. One flipped a lope back and forth as they eyed Luther. He stepped down off his horse.

"Charboneau here?" he asked. The place looked lacking. Side of the barn needed several boards replaced. Poles were broken in the pen fencing. The cabin sat too close to the pens. A shanghai rooster strode proudly across the barnyard obviously out to get on one of the small brown hens dusting themselves under a bunker. He crowed nosily. Luther decided that was what those three boys were waiting to watch for their entertainment. Ole Shanghai on his way over to show off and top a hen or two.

Bare-headed, Charboneau came to the doorway, a cigar in his hand and the same contempt look that Luther expected in his eyes.

"What do you want?"

"Send a rep, if you want. We're moving this way."

"Where you going to camp tonight?"

"Alma Creek."

Charboneau frowned. "Why there?"

"Ask my cook, Bones, he chooses the places." With that said, he swung up on the bay horse he had ridden out that morning. Actually, he lied to the man. He'd chosen Alma Creek and aimed to invite all of them there, Charboneau, Porter, and Crain. If it made them edgy, so much the better.

"I'll be there," Charboneau said to Luther's back. "You boys, go saddle up!"

The three Indians rose, looking hard at the strutting rooster who was dancing around a fluffy hen. Then the cockerel reached out with his beak and caught her by the nape of the neck, taking two tries to mount her. He climbed on her back, tucked his tail down, and made contact.

The boys elbowed each other, grinned at the feat, and laughed. The rooster jumped off her, shook himself, and crowed loudly. Luther rode on by, between the birds and on-lookers. To each his own. He heard Charboneau over his shoulder telling them again to get ready. Some folks could spoil all the fun you had in life. Why, there were three more females left for that red-tailed rooster to take on. He set the bay into a lope. Daylight was burning. He had others to see about joining him at the ford.

An attractive brunette of eighteen came out on the porch at Porter's ranch headquarters when he rode up. She must be Margie. Dressed in a divided skirt and a blouse to match that hugged her figure, she looked him over with care. Hirk was right. She was attractive, not as good-looking as Tillie, but nice to look at. He removed his hat for her and checked the anxious bay. A very neat place. All the logs had been squared for their erection and the rambling two-story house was fronted with a wide porch where she remained. Their pens were built with peeled poles. Sheds were constructed from sawmill lumber and all white-washed. Sharp-looking headquarters.

"Good afternoon, ma'am. Name's Haskell. I work for Mr. Allen and I am gathering the B Bar cattle to settle that estate."

"I've heard of you," she said.

"If your outfit wants to send a rep, we're moving this way. We'll camp at the Alma Creek crossing tonight."

"Why there?" She frowned at him.

Luther shrugged. "My cook, Bones, picks the camping spots, ma'am."

"I'll tell Reed," she said, acting withdrawn, either about the notion of the site or them sending a rep.

He touched his hat. "Sure appreciate it. Good day."

"Good day, Mr. Haskell."

He wished he could have bottled the coldness in her tone when she wished him adios. Would have lasted him all summer long. Oh, well, they weren't supposed to be nice to him. But he wasn't used to attractive young ladies being that glad to see him leave. Maybe he looked too trail dirty or perhaps she, too, knew something about the hanging and feared he knew the same.

One more left to invite. That would be Crain. Bones said his place would be easy to find. Take the wagon tracks west from Porter's and turn up Turkey Creek. He jobbed the bay with his spurs and short-loped him westward.

At the creek, he let the horse drink, bellied down himself, and sucked up some of the cool clear water. Shame that Porter gal was so cold. Hirk told him she and Dikes were seeing each other. He might have considered—oh well, Tillie sure wasn't ever going to do anything. He put his foot in the stirrup and on the second bounce, swept his chap-clad leg over the horse's butt and rode on.

Dead grass sod roofed Crain's cabin. No one was around, so he wrote the rancher a note in pencil and stuck it in the door, leaving without going inside. They'd all been warned. He ducked his head going off the porch and started for the hitch rack and the bay. This place wasn't much; a bachelor outfit. He doubted that Crain even had any regular hands. No bunkhouse. The corrals were poles piled between double posts, half rotted. A blue roan stud horse in the far one screamed good-bye after him.

He glanced at the sun time. Mid-morning. He still had time to swing by Fortune and check the mail. Maybe there would be some word from the major. Had Tillie ever even bothered answering his letter? Did he put a return address on it? No telling; he should have stormed that damn cathouse, taken her out by the nape of the neck, and had some JP marry them. Then he laughed out loud; she'd probably left him anyway and gone back. Why did he have to love such a hardheaded woman?

What was it Bones needed at camp? He reined up in front of the mercantile two hours later. Deep in his own thoughts, he looked up as the young clerk came out in his apron. The look on his fresh face told him something was up. He dropped heavily from the saddle and undid the girth.

"You all right today?" Luther asked

"Yes, sir, and do I have news for you."

"What's that?"

"Your fiancée is here."

Luther blinked at him. "Here?"

"Up at Doc's office. But they say she's doing fine."

"What happened? You mean Tillie's here?" He pointed at the dirt under his boots.

"Sure is, and quite a hero. They got the robber she beat half to death with a club when he held up Jinx's mail wagon. A guy calls himself Curly Meantoe."

"He's here, too?" How did that no account get to Arizona so fast? He'd gotten away from him and Choc down in the Kiamish at Windgate's revival. No telling.

"Yeah. He was still addled when the posse rode up on him. Doc said he'd lose his ear, though. It was hanging on by a thread. She must have been real mad. Why, he's got knots all over him."

That one-eyed breed didn't need to know he was even there. He better go see how she was. Why was she at Doc's? No telling anything except that she came. He could hardly suppress his excitement. Dang! The girl got serious and came clear out there on her own. Filled with the notion of seeing her, he raced to Doc's yard gate, jumped the low fence, and bounded up on the porch.

At long last, she'd surrendered. Oh, hell. The only thing better was if she hadn't told anyone about his marshal role. Never mind. He could work around that. The drunk Porter and the McKean boy should tell a grand jury all they needed to know. Still, he hoped to get more evidence. He pushed in the door and, there on the couch looking extra pale and holding a wet towel to her face, sat his woman.

"Tillie!"

"Luther!"

They rushed to each other and hugged. He swung her off her feet, then around and around, their eager, hungry mouths kissing in a fury.

"Easy there, son. She's been through a heckuva lot today."

Luther heard the older man and set her down. "You all right?"

"Fine. Doc says this high altitude must have got me a little."

He held her at arm's length. "Tell me all about it."

"Take that boy and you two sit down on the couch," the doctor said, herding them over there.

Luther listened to her story of the robbery and all about her coming west. He shook his head, amazed, filled with pride at her bravery.

"I need to get back to camp," he said with concern about leaving her. "You be all right here?"

"She'll be perfectly fine here," Doc assured him. "Besides, she's helping me care for old Jinx."

"I'll be all right until you can come for me."

"Fine, I get this roundup over . . ." He shook his head in disbelief. This was really finally happening. "We're going to have a heckuva wedding."

"We will, but I promised Jinx he could dance at our wedding and that will be a few days anyway before he can get up."

"I can hardly wait."

"Me either," she said

If he were ever going to leave her, he better do it now. He swept up his hat, kissed her on the mouth, and hurried out the door. Dazzled by the turn of events, he rumbled down the boardwalk to the bay, mounted up, and raced for camp. He had to solve a lynching and do it right. Soon he'd have a new wife to feed and care for, so he needed to keep this good job the major gave him.

23

"What did that Injun boy bring you?" Taneal asked, trying to look over his shoulder as Matt stood on the porch reading the note.

"It's from Charboneau. That's one of them Apache cowboys rides for him."

"Figured it was one of his killers."

"Killers?" What the hell did she mean by that? Them Apache boys rode for the old man, worked for half wages. Saved him lots of money.

"They ain't no better than them filthy Comanches in Texas. Same thing. They'd rape a white woman first chance they got. Steal their babies and raise them as their own. Damn heathens. But he ain't much better. Well? What did he say?"

"I need to meet him this evening."

"Something else wrong?"

"I'm not certain. That cattle buyer is camping at Alma Creek Ford tonight and wants the other reps there."

"Why at that bloody place?" She made a displeased face.

"I'm not certain," he mumbled, deep in his own thoughts. Before Jakes rode out, the last thing he did was warn him about that guy Haskell being so hell-bent on collecting that reward. What if Porter got loose-tongued up there?

It was time. He needed to do something about Porter. But how? Who knew about Jakes leaving? Maybe he could get rid of Porter and point the finger at Jakes. Why, the old man was long gone to Tularosa. They'd never find him. A smile creased Matt's face. One troublemaker dead, another disappeared.

Could he leave some evidence to point at Jakes? He

would have to check his foreman's shack and see what he left behind for him to use, but the idea had merit.

"What're you thinking?" she asked.

"Nothing. Where's the boy?"

"What do you need him for? Doc said—"

"He can oil harness. That won't hurt his damn leg! Get his ass down there to the tack room and have him oil every piece of leather in that shed! Let him earn his keep around here."

"All right, Lord High Ass. I'll go up and tell him. But if you so much as raise a hand again to him, you and I are going to have a fight."

"Come on. Let's go." He took a prize-fighter's stance, raised his fists, and shook them at her.

"It won't be no fair fight, Matt McKean. I'll make you wish you were dead."

"I'd like to see it."

"What happened that day you brought him home so sick?"

"What do you mean?" A cold chill ran up his cheek. Had the boy told her something about the lynching? No, or she'd not be asking, she'd be accusing him. If that boy had whispered one word to her—one word.

"When that cattle buyer mentioned the lynching—"

"He was here talking to you about it?" Matt looked at her in disbelief.

"Yes. A couple of days or so ago."

"What did he ask?" He needed to know. Jakes must have known he'd been there. Maybe the old man knew more than he had told him about Haskell. How did Jakes know to go check Stearn's tent for the paintings? Things didn't add up.

"When Haskell mentioned the hangings, Randy got violently sick again. Fell down. I worried he had rebroken his leg."

"What did Haskell say?"

"I'm not certain. Oh, yes, how you told him that there was no evidence of rustling in the basin to him."

"I never—what did you say then?"

"Don't holler at me," she snarled.

Her angry look of indignation blinded him. He whipped out his hand hard across her face and sent her reeling backward. Then in a flash, he had her by the upper arms, shaking her. "What did you tell that sumbitch Haskell?"

"That there had been rustling. Lots of it!"

He shook her with such fury that she paled. "You stupid bitch, that's why he's here! He's after that reward. He got you to tell him . . ." So shaken by his newfound knowledge, he released her and stared at the wall.

"Tell him what?" she asked, sprawled on the floor and rubbing the side of her face with her palm. "Damn you, Matt McKean."

But he had no time for her. Two steps at a time, he rushed upstairs and burst into the boy's room. He wasn't there. Where was that lazy ass? He came back down. Still dazed, she leaned on the table and avoided looking at him.

"Where did he go?" he demanded

"Who?"

"The boy! That stupid boy of ours!"

"He's not upstairs?" She stared in disbelief at him.

"No. He's gone. Listen, if this family doesn't close ranks, and quickly, we stand to lose it all. Everything. Do you understand?"

"What for?" Then she slapped her hands over her mouth. Her green eyes widened in disbelief. "You hung them? Oh, Jesus, you hung them."

"Get yourself together." He scowled at her in disgust.

"Oh, my God, you took him—you took Randy along with you for that." She staggered around in a circle like a drunk. "How could you have done that?"

He stepped in, grasped her arms in a vice-like hold and shook her hard. "You better listen good. Yes. We hung them. Your precious son was there. In the eyes of the law, he's an accomplice, and if you don't want him hung, you better quiet this down. It won't only be the end of this ranch, but your life and your son's as well."

She fell to the floor when he released her and raised up to a sitting position, with one arm bracing herself. The other hand swept the hair back from her face. "You dirty rotten bastard."

"You heard me?"

She waved him away. "I don't care. Don't give a damn about you, this ranch—nothing."

"You will if you don't want that boy hung."

"That's why Jakes left you, isn't it?" she screamed after him.

He turned in the doorway and glared back at her. "Yeah. That old sumbitch lost his guts, too."

"I hate you, Matt McKean!" she screeched.

He could hear her still ranting and cussing him, dishes breaking, while he saddled his horse at the corral. Must have gone mad. He might have to have her institutionalized, she kept that up. Regular stark-raving crazy woman. He grinned to himself over the notion of her in the crazy farm, while he and Lana shared the bed upstairs.

With a look around to be certain no one saw him, he headed the hump backed buckskin for Jakes's shack. He sawed hard on the bits and tried to spur the buck out of the gelding. The cowpony danced in a circle, made a short run, two or three hard pitches, before Matt got his head up. He really needed a stupid horse at this moment. One simple piece of evidence to plant was all he wanted. He gave the buckskin a hard jerking from side to side to make him settle down and behave

Better hurry. It looked like rain again. Clouds were gathering in the south. At last, he dismounted and tied the reins to the hitch rack. Angry with the horse, he scowled at him, then hurried for the plank door of Jakes's small shack.

Inside, he searched the room. The stained feather tick was rolled up on the end of the cot. Couple of old riatas on the antlers. Broken, short, or too old and rotten was why Jakes left them. The room smelled sour and moldy. Dog-eared calendars decorated the walls. A couple of cracked nude girlie pictures were concealed underneath the framed racehorse ones. But he knew where they were. Then, on the floor under the table, he found the old spur strap with the initials S. J. carved on it.

That would do. Where would he find Porter at this time of day? He better ride that way. Watch out to be sure no one could pin the man's death on him, and get it over with.

That left Randy, and he'd impressed Taneal enough to have her keep his mouth shut. Where had that worthless boy gone? Made no sense where he would go on crutches, but for the moment he had other things to worry about. He should have known from the start Porter was too weak for such an undertaking. That old man Yancy Porter, he'd hung his share. But Reed had no guts, none whatsoever. He'd have even less before sundown.

Matt stepped in the stirrup and before his right foot found the other one, the buckskin exploded.

"All I needed. All I needed," he kept repeating, fighting the horse's bogged head upward with little success. Half a mile from the ranch, he finally got him into a lope. The worthless cull. He lashed him from side to side with the reins to run faster.

WILL SEND A NEW WARDEN A.S.A.P. PLEASE STAY IN CHARGE AND GET IT ALL STRAIGHT DOWN THERE. STER-LING.

The major put the telegram on his desk. Here he sat in the inescapable heat of the fiery furnace, and all Sterling could say was stay there. When was he sending the new warden? As soon as—oh, it would not be quick enough. He looked up, and with a new white parasol came Miss Hmm through the door. She wore a rather colorful peach dress. A new one, he suspected. He blinked, for her black hair was done in long spiral curls and she wore a very fashionable wide-brimmed straw hat.

"I need some advice," she said.

"Well, you look very nice," he said, and gave his head a bob to the side in approval.

"My thanks. I have my rig outside. If you wouldn't mind going for a ride with me?"

"Of course." He drew down the flat-crowned panama straw that replaced his felt one from the hat rack. Too hot for his usual felt in this place. "I'll be back," he said to his secretary.

Outside, he blinked at the fancy two-seat rig with matching black horses and a uniformed driver.

"I see you have found your inheritance," he said, and helped her up as the driver made certain the top shaded the rear seat for them.

"Yes. My uncle was a great adventurer. A scallywag and, I am told, a whoremonger. He died here two years ago, leaving his estate to me. I had three years to claim it. The will said I must come in person or the estate would go to a monastery.

"None of my family was ever Catholic." She made a displeased face at him. "Why my crazy uncle threatened me with that I don't know. Besides the fact he had been in the desert too long, we will never know. His lawyer kept the estate together. But he was never to divulge the amount until I personally came to Yuma to claim it.

"Needless to say, I suspected to inherit a black box full of rotten eggs."

"And he left you . . . ?" The major hung on for her words as the carriage rumbled down the caliche street.

"Three hundred thousand. A ranch in New Mexico and a mine near Prescott. A gold mine."

"Quite a sum. But what can I do for you?"

"I know you work for the governor, but would you oversee my gold mine, too?"

"Well." He dabbed his forehead with his kerchief. "What if the mine's worthless?"

"Then close it. I shall leave that to you. I know you won't spend good money after bad. You are too damned honest, Gerald Bowen. That's why I am offering you five hundred a month to oversee the mine manager up there and the operation."

"That's lots of money. Why, you could hire—"

She placed a hand on his arm. "I don't want anyone else."

He shrugged, trapped. How could he turn down such a lucrative proposition? No way.

"So you will do it?"

"I reckon."

She grabbed him, kissed him on the mouth, and then shouted, "Hot damn!"

"Ann, you can't kiss me like that. I have a wife."

She settled back down and adjusted her hat. "I surely won't ever embarrass you again. I simply couldn't help myself either time I did it."

He twisted and frowned at her.

"I know." She held out her hands defensively. "I am only hiring your services as an overseer." Eyes closed, she lay back on the patent leather. Then she shook her head in disbelief. "Your wife is a very lucky woman. Hope she knows that."

"Oh, she does." And she's very lucky, 'cause she's in Prescott. Where it is a helluva lot cooler than this buggy ride. He took off his panama and wiped his forehead again. Whew.

24

The sound of the cattle bawling carried a long way. Luther could hear them over the drum of his horse's hooves pounding the hard-packed road. He had informed everyone about the meeting at Alma Crossing. That completed, he hoped that his crew was safe and had no bad wrecks during his absence. He had a lot to be pleased about. Tillie came to Arizona to marry him. He also stood a good chance to get someone to talking about the lynching if he had to pry it out of them.

When he drew near, he could see the herd size. His boys had made a large gathering early that morning and also moved the B Bar herd westward. As far as he could see stretched a sea of cattle. Be lots of cutting to do from this herd. Perhaps they should push the B Bar cattle they had already gathered to the rented pasture, then make another drive. Burtle had branded several head. He put the current count at over three hundred, but so far the brands on them looked real enough, none of them were worked over. The man had been busy to brush out that many head. Of course, he might have bought or traded for some, too. They didn't all come from mavericking.

Hirk came trotting toward him. The man reined up and let reins drop on his horn. His horse looked worn down enough to snort in the dust and stand hip-shot.

"You did real good this morning."

"Good enough. Funny thing. Once or twice earlier I've seen that Randy McKean and some girl riding with him. Following or spying on us. They had two pack horses with them."

"Who's she?" Luther asked, recalling the boy on

crutches. He wanted to ask Randy some more questions without his mother present.

"Don't know, but they sure acted plumb interested in our business."

"Never rode down to the herd or anything?"

"Not that I saw."

"Maybe Pyle talked to them. He knows Randy, don't he?"

Hirk agreed. The two rode into camp. Luther saw Pyle taking a fresh horse and changing saddles. He hurried over to him.

"Oh, it's you, boss man," Pyle said, as if startled by his presence.

"I heard Randy McKean was tracking you boys this morning?"

Pyle nodded and quit cinching his mouse colored horse. He shook his head, buried his face in his arms on the seat, and began to cry. "It was them! It was them, boss. Randy came down and told me all about it. He couldn't stay here any longer. Him and that girl, Lana, they're leaving the country. Says his paw headed the whole thing. Jake's left, too." Pyle's shoulders shook and tears streamed down his tan checks.

"That's who lynched them?"

"Yeah."

"Who else?"

"Charboneau, Crain, Porter, Jakes, Randy's dad. They was all in on it." Pyle whipped off his kerchief and wiped his wet eyes. "Gawd, we all loved that Teddy. He made a hand, boss. He could have bought this whole gawdamn country. His folks have lots of money." Pyle blew his nose. "He wanted to build it himself. Son of a bitch, I ain't never cried in my life about nothing. Nothing. Why did they do that?"

"So Teddy couldn't build that ranch." He clapped a hand on the boy's shoulder. "Pyle, get hold of yourself. Do the others know?"

"Not yet."

"You've got to keep it quiet till I get back. I need to be certain Porter stays alive. With Randy gone, I'm going to need a witness, and Porter is my best bet."

"You knew?"

"I suspected. I'll tell you the truth when I get back. Right now I'll tell you I'm not a real cattle buyer, I'm a territorial marshal working undercover."

"My gawd. You fooled me."

"But I may have overplayed my hand. That's why I figure Randy ran off."

"Randy said that Jakes left the country this morning, too."

"You couldn't fool that old man. Let me have that horse," Luther said. "I need to ride." He turned around as the anxious Ben jumped on his leg. He patted the dog on the head. "And keep Ben here."

"You'll need your saddle. My stirrups are way too short." Pyle took off at a run for the bay.

Hirk rode over frowning, then watched the boy carrying the saddle to him. "What's Pyle so upset about? He's been crying?"

"Long story, pard. Can't say yet. We may have company soon, so act like everything is all right. I need to go get a man." Luther stripped the boy's rig off the gelding.

"Who's coming?" Hirk asked.

"Charboneau, Crain. Hold them here as long as you can. I'll be back."

Then Pyle arrived with his saddle, set the pad, and tossed it on. Working on each side, they adjusted the cinches and Luther drew them up tight. The whole time the bulldog climbed up on him to get his attention.

"Ben, you can't go. But you will never guess who's in Fortune. No, sir, you'll never guess. Tillie's there, pard." He scratched the dog's ears and then with both hands tossed him across Hirk's saddle. "Take care of him. Pyle, you tell Hirk what we know and keep the rest a secret until I get back."

"Yes, sir."

"Whatever you do, be careful!" Hirk shouted after him

"I will." In a bound, he was in the saddle and charging across the flats before he even had his other foot in the far stirrup. Pyle's gray horse could sure run.

Where would Porter be? In town drinking, at his ranch, or coming to the camp on the Alma Creek Ford. Luther charged the horse on. Before this afternoon was over, he might regret how hard he had to run the pony. Nothing small about his heart, anyway.

No one on the road but some farm families. When he stopped them and asked, none had seen Porter in Fortune during the day. Luther decided to check his ranch first. Since his sister never said where he was, he might even have been doing ranch work. He whipped the horse to go faster.

It was before noontime when Matt left his ranch. He was still in a fury over his wife and stupid son, but his thoughts were on his biggest problem and how to solve it. Reed Porter would be drinking in that line shack all afternoon. Since the last trouble in town and his warning, Porter promised to not get drunk again in Fortune. So the drunk ordered copious quantities of liquor and hauled them by pack horse to his hideout near the rim. The best way, Matt felt, to do this job was to coax him out of the cabin and kill him where the body and the spur strap could easily be found.

Matt spotted Luther coming in time to get off the road. When the troublemaking cattle buyer rode by him, he had stayed hidden in the brush and watched Haskell go on his way to the Alma Creek Ford and the meeting he had planned. He had some bad news for that sumbitch—Porter wouldn't be at his party tonight.

Matt wiped his sweaty hands on his leggings. What a temptation to have shot that worthless ranny, but Haskell soon was gone east to his cow camp. Should have killed him. Might have to before this was over anyway. No matter. He'd do what he had to do to preserve his ranch.

Ready to move on again, Matt booted the buckskin out

of the brush and on toward the Porter place. He needed to stop close by the house and check to be certain Porter wasn't at home, to save the ride up to the cabin. And not let that girl see him either. Good-looking heifer, too. That Teddy Dikes was probably dipping in her. Matt's memory came back of how she squalled like a pig under a gate when the word came in he was hung. She could do a lot better than that rustler. Her old pappy would have never let Dikes put his boots under their table. Porter had no guts.

He came up the back way to Porter's headquarters, tied his horse in the pasture, and used the brush along the small branch for cover. No sign of anyone. He dropped to his knee behind the barn and caught his breath. In a minute, he'd slip inside to see if Porter's saddle was there.

At the back walk-through-door of the barn, where they turned horses loose into the pasture, he raised the bar with a string hanging on the outside. Then like a cat he slipped inside the shadowy interior. It smelled of sour horse piss. Slow and steady, he moved past the empty tie stalls until he reached the tack room and swung the door open.

Porter's saddle was nowhere in sight. He drew a deep breath and leaned against the frame. This would make it so easy. He'd find Porter at the line shack, probably facedown on the table passed out. Filled with newfound confidence, he eased out of the structure and made his way to the cover. In a few minutes, with his shirt soaked in sweat despite the cool breeze feeding off some afternoon shower, he was aboard his buckskin again and headed up the trail for the shack.

An hour later, he reached the wood-framed building. When he burst in the door, he found Porter sprawled on his back on the cot. Good, Matt decided, and lifted the open bottle on the table to his mouth. He studied the snoring Porter and swallowed a deep swig. The sharp liquor cut off his breath and he coughed up a spray of it that hurt his throat. Tears ran down his face and he set the bottle down. Damn.

Next thing he needed was to find Porter's horse and

throw his carcass over it. Tie him on so he didn't fall off. No rush. He heard the thunder coming over the rim high above the shack. Better wait to go for the horse until the shower passed, then he'd load him and go down to the main road.

His mouth crawling for another swallow, he lifted the bottle and this time took a smaller drink. It went down, but hurt his throat where the big one had exploded. Rain began to drum on the shingles and a leak in the roof forced him to move his chair back. It would be over soon.

Luther made the trip back in record time, riding into the yard at the Porter ranch on his lathered horse. He slid Mouse to a stop, looking for someone. Clouds up on the rim had begun to build into storms. He shrugged, dismounted, and headed for the front door. Porter's welfare filled his every thought.

"Hold it right there," Margie ordered. Armed with a shotgun, she blocked the front door.

"I don't have time to argue, ma'am. Is your brother here?"

She shook her head, then reiterated the threat with the muzzle of the shotgun aimed at him.

"We may not have much time. Your brother's life is at stake." He tried to see past her.

"What are you talking about?"

"I think someone's going to try to kill him."

"What for?" She frowned hard.

"Over what he knows about the hangings."

"He . . ." Her face paled. "He knows nothing—"

"I'm sorry, ma'am, but all this hard drinking he's been doing—it's because he was there."

"You lie!" she screamed, and threw down the shotgun.

He shuddered when it hit the floor, but it didn't go off. "Where is he?"

"At the line shack," she said in defeat. Thunder rolled across the sky and Luther looked around to see the first drops fall.

"Ma'am, I hate to ask you, but could you tell me the way?"

She stood there, a look of indecision set deep on her worried face.

"I'm a lawman. Territorial marshal, sent up here by the governor to solve this hanging business. I don't want your brother hurt. But the sooner he's in my custody, the safer he will be."

"I'll show you the way."

"It's started raining."

"No matter. I can take you there. You'd probably get lost."

From the wall pegs, she took down a rubber slicker and hat and quickly donned them. Then she ran out of the house for the barn. He followed her, leading Mouse. Inside the alleyway, he offered her assistance. She refused. He took down his own slicker as she saddle her own horse.

Mounted, she lashed her bay out of the barn into the rain. "Let's go!" Luther followed on his, ducking his head at the nearby grave digger that went zigzagging off through the sky. Damn. He sure hated lightning.

Despite the rain and mud, she flew to the back of the pasture. He dismounted to open the Texas gate, let her and Mouse through, closed it, and remounted. She had already disappeared into the timber.

He ducked the wet boughs, pushed his horse, and soon caught sight of her. Their horses scrambled on the wet rocky pathways. Leather creaked and cinches strained. The way proved straight up the mountain, and Luther kept checking over his shoulder in the torrential downpour to see if they were being followed. Blasts of blinding lightning made him edgy and thunder unsettled him more. This timber was not where he wanted to be in such a storm.

The trail broke out into a flat meadow and he was forced to whip Mouse to keep Margie in sight. The rain let up for an instant when he finally caught up with her and reached out for the reins to stop her.

"Let go of them!" She struck at him with her fist.

"We can't simply ride in there. Someone may be with him. It could be dangerous."

"Who? Who are you talking about?" She finally stopped her mount

"I ain't sure, but I know that things have gone from bad to worse today for some reason. Two of the men involved in the hanging have ridden out of the country." He swung his horse in closer to talk to her. They turned them away from the driving rain that beat on his canvas coat.

"Who was there?" she asked pointedly. "You keep saying they. Who are they?"

"McKean, father and son, Dan Charboneau, Crain, Jakes, and your brother."

"Not Reed. I can believe all the rest, but they had to have him at the point of a gun to have had him there."

"Believe what you wish. How much farther?" He motioned toward the mountain.

"Half mile," she said in defeat. "Don't kill him. He's all I've got."

"You stay here. I don't intend to kill anyone." He reined Mouse around and pushed him up the path under the dripping ponderosas. After a hard lope, the steepness soon forced him to back off to a long trot. The way grew more like a cow's face and the pony was forced to cat hop up the rivulets of brown water rushing down the trail. Hooves slipped and the horse hunched up to regain his footing. Finding the solid parts, he recovered and went on.

At the edge of a meadow, Luther could make out a big bay horse at the rack before the small cabin. Someone in a slicker came around the side of the shack leading a horse with something strapped over it. Too late.

He reached back and jerked the Winchester out of the scabbard. The familiar hat worn by the man on the ground was unmistakable. Matt McKean did a double take, then whipped back his slicker, went for his pistol, and fired at him. The range was too long. Nevertheless, Luther stepped off the horse and rested his rifle across the seat.

"Give up, McKean, I'm the law! You're under arrest."

"Go to hell!" The man punctuated it with two more shots.

"Whoa," Luther said sharply to the upset Mouse. The rifle stock jammed in his shoulder, he cocked the hammer and took aim down the rain-splattered barrel. His rifle roared. Shocked by the report, Mouse hunkered down. Matt McKean threw his arms up and fell back on to the porch, hit hard in the chest.

Talking softly to the pony to settle him, Luther levered a fresh shell in the chamber. When McKean did not move from where he lay, Luther swung up and advanced on the cabin. Was he too late to save poor Reed? He almost knew the answer as he eased his way up, convinced McKean was either dead or near dead. The dark hole was in the center of his chest and red blood issued forth on his white shirt. The man's eyes were closed. Luther shook his head with disgust. McKean had made his own decision about that.

He walked over and took the blanket-wrapped form off the horse. Then he carried the body inside and laid it on the cot. When he peeled the wool blanket back, he saw the blackened bullet hole in Porter's forehead. Thirty minutes too late.

He closed Porter's eyes. Then turned at the sounds of his sister on the porch, her sharp gasp as she discovered McKean's body. He rushed to block the door and prepare her for the loss.

"Reed! Reed? Did you kill him?" She tried to push past him.

"No. We were too late. McKean had already done that."

"You mean he's dead?"

Luther nodded and let her pounding fists ricochete off his arms and chest until she collapsed in a heap in the doorway.

"Can't be—can't be . . ." she sobbed.

He looked out across the basin. A rainbow had formed. Somewhere off east where it struck the earth must be the pot of gold. Maybe right on Doc's house there in Fortune, where Tillie was staying. No telling who that girl had invited to their wedding by this time.

He helped Margie Porter to her feet and led her inside the shack. Then he sat her down in a chair with her back to her dead brother.

"It's going to take me some time to get everything together. Will you sit here while I do that?" Luther asked.

"Yes," she said, sounding numb.

"Won't make it any easier, but I'll send you my foreman to help you with the ranch until you can decide what you want to do."

"That's very generous. But will he work for a woman?" She peered up at him through wet lashes.

"Oh, yes, I'm sure he will."

"I can help you now, Mr. Haskell. I'm better," she said with a newfound resolve.

He listened. The rain on the roof no longer drummed. The storm must be over. Thunder sounded distant again. "You gather the horses. I'll tend to the rest of this."

He watched her get up, pause to look at Reed, then go outside. Tough girl, but she'd have a good foreman. He could hardly wait to tell Hirk.

Everyone in Fortune turned out for the wedding. Margie Porter took charge of the event. The Texan Saloon was washed down and polished for the reception. Two fat steers were butchered and Bones barbecued them for twenty four hours over a spit. Luther's cowhands grew weary of hauling and splitting wood for the old man's fires, and peeling potatoes. Every Dutch oven in the community was borrowed for the biscuits.

Bones complained about all the females bringing pies and cakes. He'd wanted to do that, too. Tillie and Margie made a quick trip to Winslow and found a wedding dress. No one recognized Margie's spruced-up new foreman, Hirk Silver. Haircut, shaved, polished boots, in a new hat and outfit, he looked ready to bust his buttons. So by the afternoon of the ceremony, every cowboy, woman, youngun, drifter, farmer, rancher, storekeeper, and logger was in town dressed in their Sunday finest.

Standing near the cooking, taking it all in, Jules said, "It looks like civilization has struck Fortune in the face,"

"All we lack is the governor," Jinx said, seated in a chair where he could see everything going on.

"No," Pyle, Luther's new trail boss, said, going by with his arms full of split wood. "He came in an hour ago."

"For the wedding?" Jinx asked in awed disbelief.

"Yeah. Something about Luther's boss, the major, having to run a jail and he couldn't be here."

"Luther," Sterling began. "The major wants you to finish the rest of the roundup. Since Mr. Allen was so gracious to hire you and all. Will that interrupt your honeymoon?"

They walked beyond the corrals, through the thinly wooded pasture. Luther shook his head. "No, Tillie won't mind. We've discussed it"

"Good. Also, I have some serious news to share with you. Gerald and I spoke about this via telegram before I came up here. Not good news, I'm afraid. Before I left Preskitt, I also visited with the county prosecutor. He doubts that a grand jury will ever charge those ranchers with the crime. Strong sentiment in this territory about that kind of vigilante action. I know you've worked hard."

"Maybe it won't happen again, sir."

"I hope you're right. Perhaps your efforts here will stop it from ever happening again."

"I hope so, too. I guess we better get back or they'll think that I've run out on the bride."

"Oh, yes. Isn't it such a shame that her own family couldn't be here for this?" Sterling asked.

"Yes, it is," Luther said, and almost laughed aloud about her being so tickled that even Winston, the livery man from Winslow had come down for the festivities.

Thunder rolled in the distance. Let it rain. Nothing

would spoil this day. He glanced back at Ben, who was trailing along with them. Guess, old boy, we've got us a housekeeper.

Ben sneezed and licked his face like he approved.